DOWNTIME

DOCTOR WHO – THE MISSING ADVENTURES

Also available:

GOTH OPERA by Paul Cornell

EVOLUTION by John Peel

VENUSIAN LULLABY by Paul Leonard

THE CRYSTAL BUCEPHALUS by Craig Hinton

STATE OF CHANGE by Christopher Bulis

THE ROMANCE OF CRIME by Gareth Roberts

THE GHOSTS OF N-SPACE by Barry Letts

TIME OF YOUR LIFE by Steve Lyons

DANCING THE CODE by Paul Leonard

THE MENAGERIE by Martin Day

SYSTEM SHOCK by Justin Richards

THE SORCERER'S APPRENTICE by Christopher Bulis

INVASION OF THE CAT-PEOPLE by Gary Russell

MANAGRA by Stephen Marley

MILLENNIAL RITES by Craig Hinton

THE EMPIRE OF GLASS by Andy Lane

LORDS OF THE STORM by David A. McIntee

DOWNTIME

Marc Platt

First published in Great Britain in 1996 by
Doctor Who Books
an imprint of Virgin Publishing Ltd
332 Ladbroke Grove
London W10 5AH

ISBN 0 426 20462 X

Cover illustration by Paul Campbell

Internal photographs by Robin Prichard

Typeset by Galleon Typesetting, Ipswich
Printed and bound in Great Britain by
Mackays of Chatham PLC

For Daniel

With alphabetical multi-thanks and love to:

Ben Aaronovitch, Keith Barnfather,
Christopher and Venice Barry, Andrew Beech,
Roy Bell, Nicholas Courtney, Terrance Dicks,
Leoš Janáček, Emilia Marty, Simon Rooks,
Lis Sladen, Mike Tucker,
Debbie Watling, James White
and all the tremendous cast and crew of
Downtime

Which was more abominable?
Me or the Yeti?

Foreword

The novelization you are about to read is based on an independent drama production which I originally approached Marc Platt to write over four years ago.

Television being what it is, it took nearly three years to finally get the cameras rolling, but the end results have more than justified the producers' faith in the project and Marc's ability as a writer.

Downtime continues and concludes what might now be called the 'Yeti trilogy' begun with the two Patrick Troughton *Doctor Who* stories *The Abominable Snowmen* and *The Web of Fear* – so if you haven't read them I suggest you do so immediately!

In truth this is more than a novelization, as Marc has expanded upon the original script to include scenes and locations we couldn't possibly afford. A comparison between the two might prove rewarding and details of *Downtime* the drama are printed at the rear of this book.

With, at this time, no certainty *Doctor Who* will reappear on our television screens, it is commendable that Virgin Publishing have taken over the mantle of producing original stories based on the series. I am extremely grateful to them for publishing *Downtime* and hope you enjoy reading the story as much as the cast and crew enjoyed making it.

Keith Barnfather
Producer
August, 1995

Prologue

Oxford, 1857
A Golden Afternoon

It seemed an awfully long time since dinner. Victoria was sure it would soon be time for tea and Mr Do-do-dodgson still had not taken any photographs.

She clutched her doll tightly and tried very hard not to move, but she was very, very bored. The sun was in her eyes and the little stone bench seemed to be getting harder the longer she sat there. And just when Mr Do-do-dodgson said, 'All r-ready then,' and disappeared under the black cloth behind the camera, the sun would go behind a cloud, or the breeze would catch her petticoats and they would have to stop again.

Victoria puffed out her breath and kicked her legs in frustration. A fat woodpigeon, waddling across the grass, took off in lazy alarm. 'Victoria, you must stay still for Mr Dodgson,' insisted her father, who had been hovering beside their visitor all this time.

'I'm trying,' she protested.

'Yes, very,' he agreed.

While they waited for the sun to come back, he talked and talked to Mr Do-do-dodgson about the scientific principles of silvered plates and photo-zincography, and Mr Dodgson smiled patiently and smoothed out his long ruffled hair.

'So the lens entraps the image in time like a frozen looking-glass,' her father said yet again.

'Exactly, Waterfield,' declared Mr Dodgson. 'Imagine that, Victoria. A frozen teatime, when the tea never gets cold. You must come to my rooms in Hall at Christ Church and see some of my other photographs.'

'I don't like tea much,' Victoria said.

'Lemonade then . . . and muffins.'

The sun peered round the side of the cloud. 'Let's t-t-try again,' Mr Dodgson added and ducked back under the cloth.

A bee, who had been exploring the tiger lilies behind her, decided to investigate Victoria as well and flew noisily in circles round her head. She gave a little scream.

'Please, Victoria. Sit still!'

The distant bell of Magdalen Tower chimed across the meadows from Oxford. From the lane came the steady clip-clop of the drayman's horse.

'Will you come in to tea?' called Mama from the french windows.

Her father pulled his gold watch from his waistcoat. 'Good heavens. Four o'clock. Where has the afternoon gone to?'

'Time has such a t-t-terrible appetite,' Mr Do-do-dodgson agreed. 'There's no pleasing him. Why, he eats minutes, hours, days, even whole weeks at a time. And just when you think he's finished, do you know what he comes back for?'

He fixed Victoria with a twinkling eye.

'More?' her father suggested.

'No,' she giggled. 'He comes back for seconds!'

London. The Sixties and beyond

'Tea. That's what we all need,' the Doctor cheerfully informed Jamie and Victoria. His young companions stood awkwardly, watching him chip the white residue away from the TARDIS doors. It was settling on his frock-coat and baggy trousers. 'Assam. That has a particularly agreeable flavour. Or Lapsang Souchong.'

The crystalline substance covered the outside of the police box and extended like a virulent frost along the tunnel of Covent Garden's southbound platform. Only a few hours ago, it had been a pulsing radiant web that infested most of London's underground system, fouling the nether regions of the deserted city. But with the dark thoughts that engendered it banished, it withered. It crackled as it dried and hardened.

'Och, just give them a good boot,' piped up Jamie, all set to administer the blow to the police box.

'Not to my TARDIS, you don't!' the Doctor protested. 'The very idea. You can't just kick in the doors. The lock is an extremely delicate and complex mechanism!'

'Jamie, come and wait over here.'

As the young Scot sidled sheepishly back to Victoria, the Doctor re-applied himself to the residue and listened to the muttered conversation behind him.

'Go on, Jamie.'

'Go on, what?'

'You ought to apologize.'

'No fear . . . What for?'

'For spoiling the Doctor's plan.'

'Listen, don't you start. We got rid of the Intelligence and that's that. It's well away.'

'Not permanently though.'

'How was I supposed to know what the Doctor was doing? He didn't let on he had a plan.'

'I still think you should apologize.'

'Och, why do you have to be so . . . so . . .'

'Reasonable?'

There was a long pause, and the Doctor knew that Jamie was sulking. Then . . .

'Maybe *he* should apologize to *me* first!'

'Jamie!' she scolded.

With a loud crunch, the Doctor booted in the TARDIS door. He waited a moment for maximum effect and then turned, arms flourishing, his face lit by a triumphant smile. 'Jamie, I think we both owe Victoria an apology . . .'

The Doctor had entirely forgotten about the tea by the time Victoria found him. He was sitting on the floor in a darkened corner of the TARDIS with the entire contents of his pockets strewn around him.

She picked her way through the debris and presented him with his cup. 'Have you lost something?' she asked.

He surveyed his work and took a sip of tea. 'Actually, Victoria, I think I've just found any number of things I thought I'd lost.' He sighed. 'Only they weren't what I was looking for.'

'And?'

'Ah. I expect you want to know what's missing. I certainly do. The trouble is I can't remember. Where's Jamie got to?'

'He ate enough porridge for three people and fell asleep in an armchair. This thing you lost? When did you last have it?'

'I'm not sure that I did. It might have been somebody else. All I know is that something's not right. Something's not complete.'

'You're still upset about the Great Intelligence,' she said. 'And there was no need to apologize.'

He smiled gently at her. 'Dear Victoria, you're always so thoughtful. But I thought it might be you that was upset.'

She looked up in surprise, but he continued anyway.

'You see, I haven't forgotten that when we first met the Intelligence in Tibet, it took over your mind and used you as its pawn. I know what it's like to have the control of your own thoughts stolen by something so callous and cruel.'

'At least it didn't happen again,' she said. 'Not to me anyway.'

'I think you've been very brave when really you've been having a very frightening time.'

She was quiet for several moments, and he wondered if she was going to burst into tears. 'Sometimes,' she said at last, 'we arrive somewhere and I worry about what we'll find out there.'

He nodded, even though it was just that sort of mystery that made him so eager to experience it. 'I promise to try to get us to somewhere a little less harrowing.'

'And whatever it was you were looking for?'

'I expect it'll turn up where or whenever I least expect it.' So saying, he proceeded to return the impossibly vast range of obscure objects to his absurdly small coat pockets.

He suggested that Victoria take a much needed rest, and headed for the TARDIS console-room, where Jamie was snoring fit to wake a score of Sleeping Beauties.

Comforted that nothing unusual was occurring, he activated the scanner and gazed out at the vast prospect of space and time.

He had become parent by proxy to Victoria Waterfield, but he wondered how grateful her late father would be if he witnessed the changes in his daughter. Certainly Edward Waterfield, Victorian scientist, unjustly martyred by his cruel Dalek oppressors, would not approve of the 1960s miniskirt for which his child had abandoned her voluminous crinolines. Yet she remained gentle and kind, and a little prim, as Jamie knew to his cost. Yanked brutally from her own time and home, she was learning rapidly how to fend for herself. Good housekeeping, he supposed.

Jamie's snoring changed note. Brought out of his reverie, the Doctor stared at the scanner screen. Stars were there. And more stars beyond them. And clouds of gas in imperceptibly slowly billowing iridescence. And more stars. And clouds of imagination and possibility. And space curved slowly through the stars, turning oh-so-gradually round, above, below, so that beyond the infinite abundance of stars, he thought he eventually saw, far, far away, the back of his own head.

And somewhere in the darkness between the stars, lurking, waiting, an insubstantial mass of hateful thoughts, perhaps just behind him, was the Great Intelligence.

Again the thought nagged at him. He tried to remember what he had forgotten. Bother! It was obvious. He had slammed the door on the invader, but he had not plugged the keyhole.

Brigadier A.G. Lethbridge-Stewart
Bassingbourne Barracks
Royston
Herts

Ministry of Defence
Whitehall
London SW1

Ref: 176YT/309DA4013

Dear Brigadier

Thank you for your letter of 13th May, which the Chief of Defence Staff has passed to me. The Minister has studied your suggestions regarding the setting up of a watchdog unit to deal with extra-terrestrial incursions.

While acknowledging your key role in the offensive pertaining to the 'London Event', the Minister feels that such an event is unlikely to recur. Furthermore the formation of a new defence division would at this time be a prohibitive drain on the National Expenditure. He also points out that any incursion originating from outside this planet would constitute a global threat, thus any defensive action should not and could not be undertaken solely by the United Kingdom. Perhaps the NATO or even the Extra-Terrestrial Society are better placed to deal with your suggestions.

Yours sincerely

C. A. Fortescue
pp Chief of Defence Staff

'I'd say I'd been fobbed off as a crank,' the Brigadier complained.

'Usual whitewash,' agreed Air Vice-Marshal Gilmore and passed back the letter. 'This is from some Whitehall pen-pusher who's seen less action than the average housewife.' He drained his whisky and studied the cut-crystal tumbler.

The lounge of the Alexander Club on Great Portland

Street was a sanctum heavy with tradition. From the walls, a gallery of generals, entrapped in an amber of cracked varnish, viewed with disdain the sunlight that fought to angle in through the high windows. The long velvet drapes were stiff with decades of cigar smoke that seemed to stain the very air. In such company, Brigadier Lethbridge-Stewart felt humble and untried, but also oddly comfortable, as if the rank recently settled on his shoulders was a right justly earned.

Gilmore briefly lifted a single finger into the air like a Russian Tsar proclaiming his divine right of regency. A waiter, steward, batman, whatever he was, summoned by the Air Vice-Marshal's divine proclamation, recharged their glasses.

'Just leave the bottle,' said Gilmore. His sandy hair, greying at the temples, was brilliantined and his moustache clipped in RAF regulation style. 'Your letter caused quite a stir. There are still copies circulating – you know what government departments are like. And you may be surprised to know that more people took it seriously than this absurd response would have you believe.'

'Then why . . . ?'

'Expenditure. It's too complicated for them. Defence is a nightmare to the government mandarins. Ministers with bees in their bonnets over expensive military developments which they know next to nothing about? Heaven forbid! It won't do, will it? Especially suggestions from some newly promoted brigadier that would cost half next year's defence budget to set up.'

'So they just knock it on the head.'

'Absolutely.'

Lethbridge-Stewart leant forward, his anger barely contained. He couldn't tell if Gilmore's tight smile was mockery or just bored complacency. 'I saw this city invaded by an alien intelligence,' he said. 'I lost a lot of men. Battles in the streets against squads of robot machines. The population evacuated. Yet six months later, it's hardly mentioned.'

'Good Lord, old chap, even *you* whisper about it. And

the government invent a nuclear accident that didn't quite happen. Very clever, isn't it? The public are so relieved, they seize the official line without a second thought. And now there's the Ulster situation and the hippies to occupy them. And Whitehall must thank God for the Vietnam demos.'

'All right, the invasion was restricted to London. But who says it didn't constitute a global danger?'

Gilmore's indolent smile suddenly filtered up into his eyes and became something more knowing. 'Absolutely. It's happened before, after all.'

'What?'

'Shoreditch. The winter of Sixty-three. Different circumstances and not quite so disruptive as your "London Event", but still an incursion by aggressive alien lifeforms. And all hushed up of course.'

'Yeti?'

'No, no. More technological than that.'

'Then I'm not wrong. They must know that.'

'Of course they do. I've been lobbying the government for five years now on the same principles.' Gilmore leant in and topped up the Brigadier's tumbler. 'I soon realized that to get anywhere I'd have to spread my net considerably wider.'

'NATO?'

Gilmore shook his head grimly. 'No. I went underground.'

The Brigadier raised an eyebrow.

'I set to gathering as much top-secret information on extra-terrestrial encounters as I could lay my hands on. In the States, I was able to pull rank often enough to see files that would make Harold Wilson choke on his prime ministerial pipe.'

'UFOs? But have you actually seen any?'

'Oh, yes,' said Gilmore, and the smile flickered on his lips again. 'Shoreditch. Sixty-three.'

'You were there?'

'All documented. My own report.' He patted the briefcase beside his chair. 'And the Yanks have at least two classified craft stashed away on secret airfields in Arizona.' He waited for the statement to sink in. 'Over the past few years, we've been sending probes further and further out into space. Hardly surprising that we've been noticed.'

He dug into the briefcase and tossed a packed ringfile onto the table. Lethbridge-Stewart opened it and flicked through the copious notes and cuttings held in clear plastic sleeves.

Gilmore was now into his well-tried routine. 'There are archive files here on world-wide alien encounters and activity. The States, Australia, Peru.' He pointed to the photograph of a crumbling parchment. 'This one dates back to twelfth-century Romania. But there are stories going back to the Pharaohs.'

The Brigadier squinted at the document. 'Sorry, my Latin's not up to much,' he admitted. 'But surely most of these only amount to fairy tales and myths?'

'Good,' said Gilmore. 'I don't deny most of these stories are nonsense. But how do we know? Healthy scepticism is just what we need. Don't want any of these psychedelic namby-pamby chaps. "God is a Spaceman . . ." Damn silly occultists and flower children.'

'We?' Lethbridge-Stewart intoned.

'Hmm. Once I'd got a substantial amount of this material together, I took it to Geneva.'

'The UN. That's ambitious. And what did they have to say?'

'The Security Council were interested from the start. Especially the Australians and the Soviets. Any chance to outgun the Yanks.'

The Brigadier nodded. 'And once the Soviets are in, the Yanks will have to follow suit, with the UK trotting obediently along behind.'

'Oh no, old chap.' Gilmore sat back, suddenly weary. 'I allowed myself the luxury of imagining that once our government found out where the initial idea came from, they'd try to take all the credit for themselves. In fact, they've gone into an almighty sulk. Hence the response to your letter.'

He drummed his fingers on the ancient leather of his armchair. 'If we get any sort of squad set up here, it'll be a miracle.'

'But you said that my letter stirred up a degree of interest.'

'In the lower echelons maybe. But the top brass are immovable.' He glanced across the room at a *Daily Telegraph* that had remained propped over its reader for the entire length of their conversation. 'That's why I got in touch. We need more people with like minds.'

'Ah,' grunted the Brigadier. 'All this way up and I'm back with the recruiting officer.' Perhaps it was the drink, but he suddenly remembered that he had left the house this morning without saying goodbye to Fiona. And that meant the usual box-of-chocolates counter-offensive or no peace treaty again tonight.

Gilmore trickled another whisky into each of their glasses. 'The plan is to set up a coordinated global taskforce to deal with anything unexplained or extra-ordinary. Areas no one else covers. That includes the scientific and, I suppose, the paranormal. *And* we'll be engaging civilian specialists as advisers. Running it will be a hell of a commitment. So what do you think?'

The Brigadier studied a particularly bellicose general on the wall opposite. It reminded him of an aunt of Fiona's. He thought about the duties that kept him away from home too much; of Fiona's reproachful looks when he was off on manoeuvres while she had morning sickness. These days she could hardly walk and had constant backache. He wasn't even sure if he could get time off for the birth. He heard a cough and felt Gilmore's stare as the Air Vice-Marshal waited for an answer.

'I'm not sure,' he said.

'Good Lord, man! Isn't this just the sort of thing you were suggesting?'

'I was thinking in terms of specially trained paratroops with specialized weaponry to deal with any invaders.'

Gilmore shook his head. 'It won't all be *War of the Worlds.*'

Lethbridge-Stewart downed the last of his whisky. It had sounded lame even as he said it. He knew he was searching for excuses. 'Frankly, I'm not convinced that the armed forces are the right people to deal with what you have in mind.'

'Well,' snapped Gilmore, 'perhaps you can tell me who *is* going to do it?'

1

Victoria's Journey

Thalassa
Billows Drive
Thorpesea
Yorkshire

13th May 1984

Dear Victoria

Well, what a lot of news you have for us. Frank and I are so proud of you over the job. You see, all that work on the OU courses was worth it.

The British Museum must be a very exciting place to work. Thank you for the postcards. Are you allowed to handle the antiquities? There must be lots of famous archaeologists working there. Let us know if you meet anybody famous! Perhaps one day you'll go on expeditions too. Frank says he wouldn't recognize an archaeologist if he dug one up in the garden! Well done from both of us.

I've put in a couple of letters that have come for you. They look very important and official. We've been having a bit of excitement too. Frank's been 'headhunted' from the Gas Refinery to work on a scheme for restocking the North Sea with fish. All very hush, hush. But maybe he'll bring home the occasional free mackerel. Between the two of you I need never be short of fish or antiques again!

Your flat looks lovely from the photos. How lucky you were to find it so easily. Mrs Sivinski (How do you spell it?) sounds rather eccentric (Frank says 'batty'), but I'm sure you'll cope. As long as you can keep the cats out of your flat. Did you really say thirteen of them? (Frank says 'coven'!)

It seems very quiet up here without you, Victoria, dear. The garden is full of candytuft, but it's very windswept as usual. The cliffwalk is all over with sea pinks. Can you believe they've cut the local bus service back again? Of course Frank won't have a word said against Mrs Thatcher.

I think you were very brave to strike out on your own like that. Ever since you first came to stay with us, I always thought you were a bit of a loner, but I'm sure you'll soon make lots of new friends.

Don't forget us, will you? Your room's always ready. Write soon and take care.

All our love

Maggie.

Victoria folded the dog-eared letter and slipped it back into her bag beside the two official envelopes – only one of them opened. It was four weeks since she had last written or even spoken to the Harrises. After ten years, that was hardly a clean break. She wouldn't consign them to the past – not exactly. But there was another past, older and more forbidding, that had to be dealt with.

She checked her watch. Five to two. Time for the tour of the West Cemetery again. This was the seventh time in six weeks. She had started to get looks from the guides.

She had already blocked off areas of the East Cemetery on a rough map, covering them systematically, checking the weather-worn inscriptions and devotions on the headstones, but there was no sign of the grave.

The first time she had come, dawdling down the hill from Highgate Village, half eager, very afraid, she had turned in through the gates and thought she was in the wrong place.

And it wasn't the first time. How could she forget the *real* first time? In her memories, she saw spacious parklands and a broad cedar of Lebanon that rose like a giant out of the cold misty morning. She had been frightened of the huge horses, tossing their black plumes, as they stamped their hooves and snorted steam. There had been a shiny-handled casket, piled with flowers, which bore no relation to the warm and loving, sometimes sad person who, whatever *they* all imagined, was still her mother. It was just an object carried on the shoulders of men in black with long, sunken faces. At any moment now, Mama would appear, radiant in her summer visiting-dress, shaded by her parasol, smiling graciously as she apologized to the gloomy guests for arriving late at the burial.

It was a game wasn't it? But the game was going all wrong.

Her father looked pale and clung to her hand as if he was afraid of getting lost in the throng. The other mourners stared: the gentlemen holding their top hats to their chests; the ladies dabbing at their eyes, whispering loud enough for her to hear that the poor child was the very image of her so-beautiful mother. And she had walked slowly, unable to cry, her wide black dress rustling across the dew-laden grass.

But now, nowadays, the funerary park was overgrown with a century of gravestones and statues, and the neglected lawns had run to seed under a jungle tide of undergrowth.

She had been just eleven when her mother had died of pneumonia – forced so suddenly to grow up in an age when children were already perceived as little adults. No longer in the charge of her governess, she'd been a dutiful daughter and housekeeper, while her father had buried himself in his scientific research.

That was all gone.

One hundred and twenty-five years had passed, time careering ever faster as the modern world shrank, and Victoria was still only twenty-eight. She had slipped by the century in between. There were graves here of people who had been born and grown old, and danced the charleston, and fought in terrible wars and died – all in the hundred years that she had leapfrogged.

She had cheated time, or time had cruelly cheated her. And now she was ignoring what she had missed, spending time searching for what she had lost. She took the tour into the closed side of the cemetery and listened to the guide's commentary on this grave and that memorial, as he led his group of tourists on a pre-ordained route.

But she'd heard all this before – the notable graves of lion-tamers and equerries to Queen Victoria. There were paths here that were ignored, that she must explore. She lingered, examining a crypt door in the mock Egyptian necropolis, until the group vanished round the next corner. Then she slipped through the sunlight into forbidden regions.

Shoulder deep in a sea of white cow-parsley, she saw butterflies that she had seen nowhere else. The very air seemed to hold its breath. She was certain that Mother's grave was somewhere here and began to cast about, the matted grass tearing at her ankles. The afternoon heat was stifling her. She caught her shoe on a bramble and pitched headlong.

When she looked up, she saw a white pyramid rising above the long grass. It was smooth, untouched by the weather, and it threw back the light as if a cold sun burned inside it.

Victoria shuddered in the heat. Her throat dried. The pyramid pulsed with energy, humming a malevolent chord into her head. After a moment the barrage of sound relented, and in the sudden calm, she thought she heard the tinkling of tiny distant bells. It seemed to lift her as if she was weightless, spiralling up on a thermal above the grass and the flowers, and below her a figure lay sprawled at the foot of the pyramid.

Then something tugged at her. A wrench in her stomach that jerked her back down to the ground, back into cumbersome bones and her earthly body.

Gasping for air, she scrambled to her feet and ran.

* * *

Mrs Cywynski, elderly doyenne of number 36 Aubert Avenue, Hampstead, crouched at the window, appearing to study the clusters of white star-flowers studding her precious money-plant. It was a large specimen, rather dusty and much prized, because it was one of the few plants she had found that the cats would not eat. In fact, Mrs Cywynski was spying. She peered between the fleshy leaves, scrutinizing the avenue outside.

That man had gone. No, there he was again. Sitting opposite, on the bench by the park entrance.

He had come to the door asking for Victoria Waterfield. Mrs Cywynski did not like his expensive coat, sunglasses and slicked hair – all at odds with his barrow-boy accent. Three of the cats came to look at him and were not impressed. The others, perceptive creatures, could not be bothered. Mrs Cywynski thickened her own Polish accent to make him uncomfortable. Reaction to an accent, she always said, was a sure sign of character. He looked irritated and spoke loudly and slowly to her. He needed to contact Ms Waterfield as a matter of urgency. But he would not say why.

She said, 'No, no, no. I do not know this person. My *piernicki* will be burnt.' And she shut the door.

She had heard Victoria's phone ringing in the flat upstairs several times during the day. Nothing unusual in that, and of course no one was in to answer. Nevertheless, she had an intimation that something was wrong. All day she had been conscious of something. Some intangible disturbance in the ether, but nothing that had been foretold by her cards. Even so, she had an instinct for this sort of thing.

It was past seven-thirty and Victoria was always back from the museum by now. Mrs Cywynski, ever protective of her tenants, but never interfering, determined to waylay Victoria before she reached the house.

She put on her coat. No, that was no good. How could she leave the house with that man outside? *Still* outside. She went back to the window.

The dark shape sat motionless on the bench in the

lengthening shadows. Mrs Cywynski thought about phoning the police, but they would never understand her *instincts.* Ignoring the cats' demands for their dinner, she went into the kitchen.

Ten minutes later, she descended the front steps carrying a tray with a solitary cup of tea. 'Such a waste of time for you,' she said as the mirrored sunglasses looked up. 'I thought you might like this.'

'When you see her, tell Ms Waterfield I called, all right, love?' He planted a card on the tray and walked off up the avenue into the dusk.

The card was marked 'Byle and Leviticcus – Solicitors and Commissioners for Oaths'. Mrs Cywynski put it into her cardigan pocket and went back indoors. She poured the tea down the sink in case any of the cats drank it and were sick. Then she fed her complaining rabble and toasted herself some cheese. She put on Sinatra and sat down on the window seat to wait for her prodigal tenant.

The sound of the key in Victoria's front door woke her. A hard orange light cut into the room from the streetlamps outside. Thanking Heaven, Mrs Cywynski groped for the table-lamp. It was a quarter past two. She heard laboured footsteps on Victoria's stairs, followed by familiar movements overhead.

Her worst fears unrealized, the landlady felt for the card in her cardigan pocket. She decided to wait until the morning before speaking to Victoria.

Something must have disturbed the air, for the prisms that hung around the edge of the lampshade began to tinkle like tiny distant bells. Looking round the room, she realized that she was being scrutinized by thirteen pairs of eyes. The cats, who could never normally endure to be seen all together in one room, were arranged all over the furniture, all staring.

'Stupids,' she said. 'You had your dinner hours ago.'

She left them to it, filled her hot-water bottle and went to bed.

It was all quiet until about a quarter to four. Then Mrs

Cywynski was startled out of a restless sleep by what sounded like a yell. She lay in bed, certain that she could hear someone upstairs crying.

Muttering, she pushed four cats off the counterpane and slid out her feet. Wrapped in her candlewick dressing-gown and an ancient hand-woven shawl, she mounted the back stairs that connected to Victoria's flat.

She knocked gently on the door and waited. After a second, she stooped creakily and called through the keyhole. There was an ominous silence.

'Victoria, dear,' she called again. 'I wanted to be sure you were all right. It's very late.'

After a pause she heard, 'Yes. Yes. I'm all right. I promise.' The voice was half choked.

'Would you like to reassure me of that?'

A very long pause. Suddenly a bolt on the other side was drawn. Then the second bolt, followed by the jangle of the security chain. The door opened a crack and Victoria peered out, her hair tangled and her eyes very heavy.

'Oh, *kochano*!' exclaimed her landlady. 'My God, what has happened?'

Victoria tried to suppress a sob and failed completely. Before she could be stopped, Mrs Cywynski was inside and hurrying her into the little sitting-room.

'What has happened? Victoria, have you been hurt? No, stay there while I make you some tea.'

Victoria sat on the ancient settee, wrapped in a blanket, trying to do something with her shaking hands. It was another ten minutes before she could begin to talk.

'I don't know where I've been. I can't remember. I mean, to start off with I was at the cemetery.'

'At Highgate?'

'Mmm.'

'Why? Has somebody died? Your tea's getting cold.'

'No. It's not like that.' Victoria sipped at the herbal concoction. 'It's my mother. I took the afternoon off to try and find her grave. It's been a long time, you see.'

'I see. And did you find it?'

'I don't . . . I can't remember.'

'There, there, *kochano.* It's well past getting late. It's already getting on for early. Tell me after you've had a good sleep.'

'No. Please, I must tell you now.'

'So you do remember.'

Victoria had been staring at the floor, but now she lifted her eyes to look straight into Mrs Cywynski's face. 'Something happened in the cemetery. Something' – she searched for a word – 'overwhelmed me, but I can't remember what. A dizziness. It wasn't any person,' she added. 'Not just then.'

'Not then?'

'Perhaps I just fainted. But afterwards I was wandering about.'

'Until two in the morning?'

'Was it that time? I know I was walking for hours. Miles and miles through the city, until I finally recognized where I was. But there weren't any buses or taxis, so I had to keep on walking.'

'*Kochano*, sweetheart, you know it isn't safe for a young lady to be out on her own at that time of night.'

'I know,' Victoria snapped. 'That's what I meant.'

Mrs Cywynski gently squeezed her hand. 'You *have* been attacked, haven't you? Where was this? Oh! I shall . . . My dear, this man, I shall damage him personally. Are *you* hurt? He didn't touch you, did he?'

Victoria shook her head. 'I was walking up the hill and I heard footsteps running behind me – that always frightens me. The man ran straight on past me and so I thought I was all right.

'But then he turned round and he had a knife. And he was pointing it at me. A kitchen knife. And he said he wanted my money, so I opened out my bag and purse, but I wouldn't let go of them. I just opened the bag wide to show him. And he pulled out the notes and started flicking through the other papers and things with the point of the knife. And all the bits were falling out onto the pavement. And he kept apologizing, saying he was sorry for this, but he had a wife and children to look after and he couldn't afford to keep them.

'I said to him, "Let me keep the cards please, because you can't use them, you know." And he still kept apologizing. So I told him it was all right. I felt *so* sorry for him.'

The landlady hugged her tightly. A smell of eau de cologne and cats. 'What did he look like? Was he well dressed?'

'How could he be well dressed? He had no money.'

'But was he wearing sunglasses?'

'At night?'

'You poor child. You mustn't feel sorry for a crook like that.'

'But I do. I had some loose change in my pocket and I offered him that too. But he said no, I would need that to get home. And I said I only lived round the corner.'

'Sweetheart!'

'But he ran off down the hill. And halfway he called back, "I wouldn't have used the knife. Honestly." And then the poor man was gone.'

'Poor man, indeed! How much did he take?'

'I don't know. About fifty pounds.'

'Fifty! You should have come in to me straight away. Now we must call the police.'

Victoria's already tense frame tightened. 'No. Please, no. I don't want to talk about it over and over.' The mask finally cracked in a welter of tears.

Mrs Cywynski rocked her gently back and forth in her arms. 'It's all done with now, Victoria. Nothing else to worry about. You drink this down and you'll get a good night's sleep.'

Through the sobs came a choked tirade. 'There's so much sadness in the world. People have so little, they're so lonely – no wonder they do such terrible things.'

'Yes, dear. I know.'

'Why don't the people who have power do something? *I'd* do something.'

'Once they have power they are reluctant to share it.'

At that remark, Victoria seemed to freeze again. Mrs Cywynski sighed and said, 'I think I must stay up here for a while. Yes? No?'

'But . . .'

'No, dear. No arguments, please. I often sleep all night in a chair. The cats usually get to the bed before me.'

Victoria blew her nose and tried to sound composed. 'Thank you, Mrs Cywynski.'

'Roxana, dear. There's no point in having formality among my friends.'

'Thank you. I'm glad I came here.'

'I should hope so, too. Now off to bed with you.' And she pushed her charge gently back to her room. 'It'll all seem much better in the morning,' she said, but something in the ether told her that she was wrong.

Victoria considered her office. From up by the ceiling it took on a completely different aspect. She wondered why she spent so much time on the confining floor when there was so much wasted room higher up.

She watched herself seated at her desk down below, surrounded by schedules and inventories. She seemed to be dozing in the warm sunlight, and if she wasn't careful, she would knock that stone-cold cup of 'hot' chocolate over. There seemed to be some sort of cord like a silvery umbilical that connected the two of them above and below. It tugged slightly at her, but was not uncomfortable. Strangely, as she floated she thought she could hear her dusty little pot-plant humming to itself.

She slid through the wall just by the cornice, and out into one of the main halls. For a while she floated gently over the cosmopolitan heads of the tourists as they milled around the antiquities below. They didn't seem to notice her at all.

At this height she could examine the details on the strange deities painted around the upper walls of the Egyptian rooms. The gods shared Upper Egypt with her. The mortal masses were confined below to the lands of the Lower Nile.

She was about to slip out through a window, when she felt a sharp tug at her stomach. With a snap, she was back in her office, startled and dabbing at the chocolate that had spilled across her desk from the overturned plastic cup.

Messrs St J. R. Byle
Thom. K. Leviticcus

192d King's Road
Chelsea
London W3

SOLICITORS
COMMISSIONERS FOR OATHS

8th May 1984

Reference: StJRB/TKL/EJWaterfield

Ms Victoria Waterfield
Thalassa
Billows Drive
Thorpesea
Yorkshire

Dear Ms Waterfield

ESTATE OF THE LATE EDWARD JOSEPH WATERFIELD

As executors of Mr Waterfield's estate, we have been trying for some time to trace any relatives of the deceased. We have been led to believe that you may be able to help us and would be grateful if you would contact us as soon as conveniently possible.

Yours sincerely

St John Byle

'I'm sorry,' Victoria kept saying. 'I know I should have answered the letters, but . . . well, it's rather complicated.'

St John Byle, consciously handsome, studied her across his mahogany desk with a detached curiosity. His ice-blue eyes made her feel like an exhibit in the museum. She wished she had asked Roxana to come with her, but she might have to discuss things that her landlady would never understand.

The solicitor took a rolled document from his drawer and undid the dark-blue ribbon that bound it. The paper was yellowed and the script written in a sloping, elegant hand.

Victoria took it from him and put on her spectacles.

'*I, Edward Joseph Waterfield . . .*'

She felt a pit open in her stomach. Her skin went cold. She tried to concentrate on the rest of the document, but the words danced before her eyes without registering in her mind. She pulled her spectacles off again and sat fiddling awkwardly with the rims.

'Where did you find this?' she asked.

'We've held it here for many years. The will was drawn up by the original Mr Byle in July 1865. In it, Edward Waterfield left all his property and goods in perpetuity to his only daughter, Victoria Maud.'

'I see,' Victoria said. 'And I suppose you think that because my name is Victoria Maud as well, you might be able to trace some family connection.'

'Unfortunately I don't think that's very likely.' He gave a little smirk as he sat back in his seat. 'Edward Waterfield was presumed killed in an explosion at a house near Canterbury in 1866. No one could trace Victoria Maud.'

'Perhaps she died in the explosion too,' said Victoria.

'She was thought to be residing in Paris at the time.'

Of course, thought Victoria, that's the story Maxtible put round. That's why no one came to rescue me. No one in the household knew I was being held prisoner by the Daleks in the same house.

'If she had later married and had children,' Byle continued, 'then she would have adopted her husband's name and that would have been the end of the Waterfield line.'

'Not necessarily,' Victoria retorted.

'And with three, maybe four generations in between . . . ?' He shrugged and smirked again, staring as if he expected or knew of some information she might be hiding. 'It's always been our firm's most mysterious case. Of course, if you feel you have a claim to the inheritance, we would need some sort of evidence of your own family. Say a birth certificate at least?'

'How many generations of Byles have there been?' asked Victoria. She was making a weak show of disinterest, but her eyes kept wandering back to the will, even if it was too late to take it back from him. 'Anyway, what makes you think I might have a claim?'

St John Byle reached into his drawer for a second time, producing another scrolled document, this one less battered than the first. He balanced it between two fingers as he stared at her. 'This is a revised version of the original will.'

'Then doesn't it supersede the first one?'

'Oh, yes.' She noticed a sudden quaver in his voice. 'If we could prove its veracity.'

She sighed. 'I don't see how I can help you.'

'Normally we would contest this as a forgery.' He unrolled the document. 'It alters very little of the original, except that now the property is left to the descendants of Victoria Maud. And you see here, the same signature.'

Victoria forced herself to stare at the writing. She remembered the hand from the regularly maintained notebooks stacked on his secretaire. Next to her father's signature, a witness had carelessly scrawled the name 'Keith Perry'. She reached for the document. 'Please may I see? What makes you think it's not real?'

Mr Byle kept firm hold of the scroll. 'I don't. But there's some new text added at the end: "There are dark forces beyond both time and understanding that prey on my mind. God keep you all from such horrors." '

She tried to retain her composure, but he read those words, her beloved father's words, with an ignorant flippancy. 'I'm sorry. I think I'd like to go now,' she stammered.

'I think you should see the date first.'

'Why?'

'Because the document, which is unquestionably in the

same hand as the original, was written in May 1966, over a century after the original.'

'It's a mistake,' she said.

'No.'

'He died.' Her voice was cracking. 'He died. He couldn't still be alive.'

Byle never flinched from his stare. His eyes were like ice. 'How can you be so sure?'

She was fumbling miserably with her bag. 'I have to go.' She stood and headed towards the door.

'Ms Waterfield, I apologize,' he called. 'But in view of the total capital invested in the trust . . .'

She had stopped, facing away from him. 'It doesn't matter.'

'As trustees we have to follow up all possibilities. And you did say it was very complicated. Victoria Maud Waterfield is an unusual name after all . . . these days.'

'I'm sorry I can't help you.'

She walked out of the dingy office into the sunshine. The date on the will was impossible – a slip of the pen. Her father had died – been murdered on Skaro. The Doctor had told her. It was impossible.

On the bus back home, she dozed gently, letting her thoughts spiral up above the grey-brown city, skirting the towering office blocks and rising towards a mountainous range of stormclouds that loomed on the horizon.

A voice seemed to be whispering into her ear. She thought she caught her name, but the wind at this height drowned out the sense of it.

Below, the city dwindled into a dark stain on the landscape, a spider crouching on a web of tangled roads.

The cloud-mountains loomed closer.

With a start, Victoria realized she had almost missed her stop. The old man in the next seat hissed and muttered through his teeth as she pushed her way off.

When she reached the house, she nearly fell down a hole in the pavement right outside the gate.

'They're laying cables, dear,' said Mrs Cywynski, looking up from her biscuit-making. 'Phones or computers or something. The cats haven't been out the front all day.'

Three paving stones had been lifted and the hole underneath was quite deep. To Victoria, it looked like a grave.

The mountainous landscape rolled far below Victoria, like the sliding painted panorama in a theatrical transformation scene. Snow touched the peaks, blowing streamers of white across the air like flames on monumental candles.

In the sky around her, she could see other distant figures: grey phantoms in the misty air, travelling on voyages of their own.

Again, she heard the voice. It was the wind whispering her name. '*Victoria. I'm here. I've waited so long.*'

'I'm coming,' she called. 'Where are you?'

'*I'm waiting,*' the wind answered.

She was stooping lower now, moving along a great ravine and skirting a huge mountain with a broken top. It seemed oddly familiar. The land was barren and strewn with boulders. In the next valley, she saw a cluster of grey buildings that crouched for shelter against the rocky slopes.

'*Victoria. Release me.*'

She began to spiral down. She remembered this place, but it seemed even wilder now than she recalled. The ornate roof was dilapidated. There was no sign of the monks who lived there. The voice came again, mingled with the distant tinkling of tiny bells.

'*At last you're here.*'

She knew the voice now. They must have been wrong when they said he was dead. *She* had never seen his body, so how did she know they were not mistaken? She passed directly through the solid walls, flying across the courtyard with its massive overturned statue of Buddha, and down, down, towards the dark Inner Sanctum of the monastery of Det-sen.

'What you need, dear, is a holiday.'

'A holiday? Oh no, really . . .'

'Yes, really!' insisted Mrs Cywynski. 'Mr Cywynski

never took a holiday either. Heaven knows, I tried often enough to get him to go away. Anything for a bit of peace.'

'You mean you would have stayed behind?' asked Victoria.

'Of course, dear. What a treat. He was always under my feet.' The fierce heat from the Aga made her mottled forehead shine with perspiration. It was a burning July afternoon and the kitchen was a sauna rich with the smell of bubbling chutney.

'You must miss him very much,' said Victoria.

Mrs Cywynski stirred the chutney vigorously. 'Sometimes. Even when it's so familiar that you want to scream, it's difficult to let go. Still, I have poor Andrzej where I want him now. And for the first time in his life, he's tidy! So that leaves the rest of the place to me and the cats.'

There was a key hanging above the dresser – the only key Victoria had seen, and by default it must go with the only inner door in the house that was always locked. 'Just Mr Cywynski's odds and ends,' Mrs Cywynski had said. And Victoria knew that it was a sanctum, a shrine, where she would never presume to intrude.

She suddenly realized that Mrs Cywynski was watching her with a look of surprising affection. 'Poor *kochano*, just look at the shadows under your eyes. How gloomy! They work you like a Trojan at that museum.'

Victoria stopped searching through the bottled fruit in the cool pantry. 'I like it there.'

'Surrounded by all those fossils.'

'That's at the Natural History. Not the British Museum.'

'I meant the professors.'

Victoria giggled. 'They're not so bad. Or so ancient.'

'Harrumph.' Mrs Cywynski heaved herself onto the kitchen stool and wiped her hands on her apron. She clearly meant business, so Victoria said, 'I wish I could remember the ingredients for that lemon flummery.'

Mrs Cywynski wagged a finger, the same gesture she reserved for an errant cat. 'You don't look after yourself. What am I to say to Mrs Harris the next time she rings?

For a start-off I can give you something to help you sleep.'

'Sleeping isn't the problem.'

'But you don't sleep well. I hear you calling out in the night.'

'Do I?' That flustered her. 'Are you sure that's not the cats? Or the ether?'

Mrs Cywynski nodded. 'That's possible. The ether *is* very turbulent at the moment. Gives me no peace.' She sniffed. 'Come. If you like, I will read you the cards.'

Victoria flinched. 'Oh, no. That's very kind, Roxana, but not now. The future can be complicated enough without knowing it in advance.' Besides which her father, and the Doctor too, had always insisted on a scientific approach to everything. 'Fiddle-faddle' father had called it once, when he had caught the maid consulting the tea-leaves.

'How unadventurous. Still, if you don't have expectations, you can't have disappointments,' retorted the landlady. 'How are you getting on with the book on astral projection I lent you?'

'Well, it's *quite* interesting,' floundered Victoria. 'But I don't think I really believe in out-of-body experiences.'

'Not scientifically proven?'

'Not yet, anyway.'

'Of course, dear. Nothing exists until it's discovered.' Mrs Cywynski shrugged. 'So you must find other means of travel. It must be a holiday then.'

'I don't need a holiday. Who would I go with anyway?'

'Oh, for heaven's sake, there must be someone. Some nice young man . . . or professor.'

'I don't think so.'

'No excuses. I can't think why you've never travelled.'

'Well, actually . . .'

'A holiday for you must be something cultural. Italy or Greece?'

'Oh no, not the Grand Tour. Everybody goes on that.'

'Then where would you really like to go?'

Victoria lifted one of the saucepan lids and stirred the rich brown chutney. 'Tibet,' she smiled. 'That's where I want to go.'

When she had glided up to Lukla, the village had looked no more than a few houses bunched on the green mountain slopes around the airstrip. A high cluster of white buildings with blue and green windows. But today was the day of the bazaar and the place was suddenly alive with Sherpa in coloured hats and dealers with bamboo baskets selling rice and fruit.

It had taken a night to recover from the bumpy flight from Kathmandu. The little Twin Otter craft had been tossed about in the air as if the clouds were playing tennis with it. Victoria felt as if her stomach was still somewhere over the middle of Nepal.

She sat outside the local teahouse content to drink tea and watch the comings and goings of the market. There was no sign of the Sherpa guide she had arranged to meet, but Eric, who ran the teahouse, said that there were delays on the road north and he would arrive soon. Eric was wiry with long grey hair tied in a ponytail and had a vaguely American accent. On the walls, he had dog-eared posters of John Lennon and a man with a moustache and a beret, who was called Che. When she told Eric where she was going, he seemed startled. 'Bad karma, man,' he said and went back to his kitchen. Still, the mountain air outside was so sharp and clean, and the sun so warm, that she began to doze.

'*Dzu-teh, dzu-teh!*'

The voice startled her awake. She saw the squinting brown eyes of an old man only inches from her face.

'*Dzu-teh,*' he insisted through broken teeth. He was waving a brown object in his hand. It was desiccated and covered in matted grey hair.

'No. Sorry, I'm not interested,' she said, pulling back as far as she could, but he only persisted, chattering in Nepali and waving the object in her face. Around the street, other villagers turned and stared without intervening.

'*Dzu-teh, dzu-teh!*'

'No. I said I don't want it. Leave me alone!'

'*Pa gyu!*' Another voice cut across the street. 'Go on, you heard me. *Pa gyu*. The young lady doesn't want to buy it.'

The old man faltered and turned. He fell back as the newcomer approached.

'That's right. No sale. *Bidaa chha*. Thank you.'

She swallowed hard and turned to look up at her rescuer. His hand was reaching out to take her arm. 'Sorry about that,' he said. 'That was a phrasebook mixture of Nepali and Tibetan. It did the job anyway.'

For a moment she thought she knew him. His sandy hair was brushed over his high forehead and his eyes were fiercely penetrating. He wore khaki shorts and looked like an overgrown school prefect. 'Are you trekking on your own?' he asked.

'Yes,' she said, taken aback.

'That's brave.' He glanced after the old man. 'You'll have to put up a better fight than that, though.'

'I think he wanted me to buy that thing he had.'

'It was a yeti scalp.'

'A yeti?'

'You look startled.'

'Well, yes. I thought yeti were terribly rare.'

'Very nearly extinct in the wild. And only a few in captivity.' He plunged his hands into his pockets and grinned enthusiastically. 'Don't worry, the scalp was almost certainly a fake. Goat hair, I expect. He's probably got dozens.'

'Thank goodness,' Victoria said.

'That's right,' he nodded and sat down next to her. 'You see, Yeti are a bit of a hobbyhorse as far as I'm concerned.'

She smiled and said cautiously, 'I only know what I've read about them in books.'

His eyes lit up. 'Ah well, the three different types are protected species, of course. Which is why our friend there scarpered pretty sharp-ish. The *mih-teh* and the

Dzu-teh, they're both closer to apes as species, while the *Ye-teh*, aka *Yeti Traversii*, is more bear-like and particularly timid. London Zoo's trying to breed from a couple at the moment. They've flown the male over from Peking.' He paused. 'I'm babbling on, aren't I?' He grasped her hand and shook it firmly. 'Charles Bryce. Pleased to meet you.'

'Victoria Waterfield,' she said. 'You're the travel writer, aren't you? I thought I recognized you.'

He grunted. 'That means I look like my dust-jacket photo. How appalling.'

'Thank you for rescuing me, Mr Bryce. I'd been sitting here trying not to look too English.'

'Always a dead giveaway. And call me Charles, please.' He stood and yelled at the teahouse door. 'Eric? Two more teas when you're ready.' He sat down again and added confidentially, 'Stay off the yakburgers. It's the thin end of the greasy slope that leads to the Big Mac. Nothing is sacred.'

'Are you writing a book now . . . Charles?'

'Maybe. I dabble in zoology and botany too. At the moment I'm looking for rare plants. *Gentiana* and *Meconopsis*. The *Khumbu Himal* is full of unknown species. I've been here several times now. But what about you? Where are you headed?'

'I'm travelling up into Tibet. I want to visit one of the monasteries not far across the border. Det-sen. Do you know it?'

Eric clumped their mugs of tea down next to them. Globules of yak-butter floated on the surface.

'It's bad news, that place,' he muttered.

'Why do you say that?' Victoria asked.

'There's only bad vibes about it.'

'But it is still open?'

'Oh, yeah. Open for business.' Eric scowled and disappeared back inside leaving the bead curtain clattering to and fro.

Charles smiled sheepishly. 'Take no notice. Eric's a leftover from the hippy trail. He came here in Sixty-seven and didn't have the money to get back.'

'Ah,' said Victoria, suddenly sympathetic.

'Never really got over the Beatles splitting up.'

'Oh yes, I've read about them.' She would normally have reprimanded herself for such an awkward remark, but here, so far from what passed for civilization, she found she didn't really care.

Charles studied her for a moment with raised eyebrows over the edge of his mug, plainly trying to fathom her out. Then he scrutinized his tea carefully. 'Eric knows a fair bit about plants though, judging from some of the stranger substances growing in his garden.'

Victoria watched him, finding that she had started to like his excitable manner and boyish grin. In her head, she heard the words 'nice young man, nice young professor' repeating in an all-too-familiar Polish accent.

The voice, her father's voice, had been growing in impatience.

'*Why don't you come? You have deserted me!*'

'You know that's not true.' Victoria passed down through the roof of the deserted monastery, and back along the now familiar halls deep in shadow. The solid oak doors that guarded the entrance to the Inner Sanctum were barred across with massive planks.

'Where are you?' she heard herself ask. For the first time, she was aware of the dress she was wearing. The rich purple satin fabric was hooped out wide on a stiff crinoline. Over it and covering her head, she wore a black cloak with a voluminous hood. The dress rustled gently as she floated. She was sure her mother had worn it.

'*Here! I'm here!*'

She had never heard him so angry. She was searching, yet the voice was always close at her ear.

'*Here in the darkness.*'

'I *shall* reach you, dear father.' She had pushed at the doors before, but unlike other walls, through which she passed like light through glass, they resisted. Where everything else was intangible, the doors had substance. They had a force that repelled her as if they contained a heart of darkness that must not be disturbed. She wanted to turn away, but the certainty of what she sought drove her. Steeling herself, she set her hands to them again and, this time slowly, she began to push through.

It was like forcing herself inch by inch into a wall of molten toffee. Then suddenly her arms were free in the cold air on the other side of the door. She had never felt the chill before in this dream state and she longed to return to her sleeping body far away in a lodge in the mountains of Nepal. But even in waking, she was being drawn closer.

'*Victoria.*'

How could she turn back now? His voice was close to despair. Her face pressed into the treacly substance of the door. She was being crushed against it. With a lurch, she was finally through into the baleful light of the Inner Sanctum of Det-sen. The moon was shining through a hole in the ceiling. There was rubble on the floor and a broken chair beyond a torn curtain.

But the chamber was empty.

'Good morning.'

She had opened her rickety window, hoping that there might be a sign of him. The sunlight made her blink, it was so fierce, but there was Charles in the street below, infuriatingly enthusiastic for the time of morning and grinning up at her.

She groaned. 'Is it?'

'Bad night?'

'Queasy.'

'You've drunk too much yak-butter tea. It takes getting used to.'

'Probably. I'll be down in a minute.'

She took her time, trying to wash her face awake before she was forced to cope with anyone else. She was glad that Mrs Cywynski was not there. The landlady would only disapprove.

She had sat up late, listening to Charles relate stories of his trips to Russia, Australia, New Guinea and South

America. He seemed to relish juxtaposing the beauty and grotesquerie of each culture; to him it was all the ravishing cruelty of nature against artifice. He had only to point to the tiny houses nestling on the roots of the mountains for her to see how arrogant and puny humans were.

When he asked about her, she steered the conversation away from travel. A famous explorer like Charles would never believe some of the bizarre places she had visited.

She had gone to bed unable to sleep, her head racing with thoughts of the dashing adventurer Charles Bryce. Somehow he seemed as unworldly and out of time as she felt. A fellow outcast forced, as she was, to wander the ways of the world. Finally, exhausted by her fantasies, she had slipped into oblivion and out of her body.

When she emerged from the lodge, Charles was a little way up the street, joking with a young Sherpa in a green hat and pointing away to the road that led north. A couple of other Sherpa sat nearby on a pile of logs. One of them, a girl in a red gingham scarf, was spinning a prayer wheel.

Charles turned to meet Victoria and his face immediately clouded with concern. 'Your guides haven't arrived yet,' he said.

She faltered. 'Oh, no. Now what do I do? The travel firm told me that everything would be organized.'

He fixed her with a very serious frown. 'You could always set off on your own. I'm sure they'd catch you up.'

She heard herself say, 'Do you think so?'

'Oh, yes. I'm sure Eric'll find you a map.'

She glanced across the street to the teahouse and saw Eric leaning against the door. He shook his head glumly and ambled unsteadily off up the street.

Charles burst into a fit of laughter.

'Oh, you,' she said and tried to feign amusement.

He grinned and squeezed her arm again. 'Don't worry. You really mustn't take everything so very seriously.' He pointed to the Sherpa in the green hat. 'This is Tundu.

He's been my guide on several expeditions and I'd trust him anywhere. I know it's a lot to ask, but if you trust him, then he'll trust you too. And that's important round here. He already knows the way to Det-sen – if that's really where you insist on going, although I can think of a dozen more interesting, more *touristy* monasteries with decent roads and souvenir shops.'

She sighed. 'No, Charles. It must be Det-sen. I'm sorry, I can't explain.'

'All right,' he shrugged and exchanged a glance with the young Sherpa. 'Tundu's ready and waiting.'

She was starting to feel trapped and now she was going to offend him too. 'No. No really, Charles. I just can't afford this. It's very kind of you, but I've already paid for the other guide.'

His tone changed, almost became angry. 'I insist, Victoria. This other group's let you down. And *I'm* dealing with the payments. No arguments, all right? You can trust Tundu with your life. I have – more than once. But don't dare think for one minute that a silly little girl like you can go backpacking round the Himalayas on your own.' He was squeezing her arm tighter and tighter. 'You must be crazy doing all this. You know I'm right.'

For a moment, she thought she was going to hit him. Then he let go of her arm and smiled again, but not at her. He smiled at the Sherpa Tundu, who was grinning back from under his green hat. She could see that there was a deep bond between them, more than just a reliance.

'When you like to leave, miss?' Tundu said. 'Soon, I think. My sister will carry your packs.' He indicated the Sherpani with the prayer wheel.

'It'll take you a good seven days' trek to reach Det-sen,' said Charles.

'I don't know,' Victoria said. 'I need to think.'

Tundu pulled off his hat and scratched his head. 'You trust Mr Bryce, miss. I saved his life twice. Only do that for people I like.'

'Twice?' she said.

'Three times, actually,' muttered Charles.

'When we go shooting for *dzu-teh*,' added the sherpa.

'You mean Yeti?' Victoria exclaimed. 'You didn't tell me that you were a hunter.'

Charles scuffed Tundu's head. 'Shooting as in cameras, you dolt.' They both laughed together.

'Besides,' added Tundu, 'you will have fellow traveller.' He pointed up the street to a little figure seated outside the Trekking Supply Shop. A wizened old man apparently gazing out across the mountains, dressed in a weathered saffron robe and holding a long staff.

'A monk?' asked Victoria. 'You could have told me. Is he going to Det-sen too?'

Tundu nodded. 'But he doesn't talk – not allowed. And he doesn't see either. So I am double important as guide and eyes.'

Victoria stared uneasily at the ancient monk. 'All right, I'll go with you. I have to get there somehow.'

She tried a weak smile as Charles pulled in close and said gently, 'And get back again. Do you think I'd really let you wander off on your own?' He leant closer and kissed her on the cheek.

Blushing vividly, she headed into the lodge to change and fetch her luggage. She had been wrong and had found someone who really cared for her.

Eric was inside, sitting on a chair by the desk. She thought of asking his advice, but as she approached him, he looked up and, staring straight through her, said, 'There's a big green space inside my head, man. No flowers, just green big space. You got any decent stuff, man? Ain't seen no decent stuff for years.'

'Sorry,' Victoria said and hurried to fetch her bags.

She pulled on her walking gear and boots, planted the khaki hat that Mrs Cywynski had given her on her head and settled her bill. At least she could pay for that.

When she came back out into the street, the ancient monk had gone and she couldn't see Charles. She stared up and down, half panicked. There was another burst of his laughter, mingled with Tundu's giggle, and she followed it eagerly around the side of the lodge. She faltered as she saw Charles, his arm around the Sherpa's shoulder, smiling deep into the young man's brown eyes.

Charles turned and smiled at her too. 'Good. Here you are. The sooner you get off the better. Tundu will get you to Phakding tonight, Namche tomorrow. Maybe three more days to Det-sen.'

Tundu shouted something and his sister appeared leading a big brown yak. On it sat the ancient monk. The girl, whose name was Sonam, took Victoria's bags from her. As they loaded up, Charles proffered Victoria a small packet.

'Dairy Milk,' he said. 'Not yak milk. Chocolate'll make your diet a bit more interesting. It's got my address on the back. Stay in touch. I don't know if I'll be here when you get back.'

'Thank you, Charles,' she said. 'Good luck with the gentians.'

He laughed and slapped the yak on its rump. He waved for a long time until the street disappeared out of view and only the mountains were rising around them. Victoria was not sure if he was waving at her. She wasn't sure what she thought any more.

The road to Namche Bazar and beyond twisted its way through the wild country between the mountains. The lower slopes were dark with pine forest, which stretched up to the snowline from where the peaks tore against the blue air. They crossed a wooden bridge over a rushing meltwater torrent and followed the course of the *Dhud Kosi*, travelling north. Tundu insisted on stopping at the *chorten*, little way-temples that stood at the roadside like huge chesspieces abandoned by the mountain giants. They were intricately carved and hung with ropes of fluttering prayer flags. And along the route there were prayer walls, spotted with lichen and engraved in huge letters with the lotus prayer – *Om mani padme hum*.

Victoria, travelling in foreign territory, equipped with an entourage of porters, imagined herself as a *sahiba* from the days of the Empire. This track was the main highway. They passed other trekkers and merchants, women carrying bamboo baskets bigger than themselves and groups of travelling monks in robes of startling orange.

The old monk, perched on the lumbering yak, seemed oblivious of this. His lips, although silent, mouthed endless mantras as they trudged northward.

Tundu chattered to Victoria in extraordinarily idiomatic English. He said he had picked it up as a child from friends who knew Tensing, the Sherpa who accompanied Sir Edmund Hillary at *Lachi-Kang*, which they called Everest. And Bonington said this and Mallory said that, but Victoria couldn't tell if Tundu was telling stories second-hand. She avoided asking what Charles Bryce said.

Tundu pointed out to her the wild goats and flowers. There were fields of *meconopsis*, Charles's blue poppies, their petals like fallen fragments of the azure Himalayan sky.

Among the plants by the road they saw evidence of the opening up of the region to the outside world. Clusters of drinks cans discarded among the flowers. It was Charles's 'thin end of the greasy slope . . .'

By late on the second day, Victoria was starting to wonder if they would ever reach Namche Bazar. They had crossed and recrossed the river by means of precarious wooden bridges and were scaling yet another interminable slope. The air was thin and she was starting to feel light-headed. She topped a ridge with what might have been her last breath and gasped. In the distance, maybe twenty miles away, rising beyond the closer peaks, was the majestic colossus of Everest, rose-coloured by the sunset on a throne of blue-grey clouds. Victoria felt suddenly insignificant, dwarfed by the enormity of what she had set out to do.

'It is a god,' said Tundu. He took Victoria's arm. 'But we travel the opposite way. Come, the town is not far now. Then you can sleep well tonight.'

* * *

On the third day out, beyond Namche Bazar on the road to Thame, they encountered a traffic jam of yaks. Two groups travelling in opposite directions had met with room for only single-file progress. There was already a tailback in both directions, compounded by the bored yaks, which sat down and refused to move despite the shouting of their drivers. It took an hour and a half to clear and reminded Victoria of the rush hour at home.

To Victoria's surprise she had not dreamed since they left Lukla. Perhaps it was the crystal mountain air that made her feel easier, although the lure of her destination, ripe with memories and threats, was still darkly compelling.

When they reached Thame, the old monk insisted on visiting the local *gompa*. The walls in the little lamasery were covered with gaudily coloured paintings of holy figures.

'The whole world is full of them,' said Tundu's sister, Sonam. She was turning one of the painted prayer wheels that were set in the wall. Her English was even better than her brother's. 'All of us are on the wheel of life, tormented by gods and demons and hungry ghosts.'

The prayer wheel turned, its coloured letters dancing on its drum, and Victoria began to feel drowsy.

There was a mountain flying towards her. It surged through the air, filling half the sky, as if the mountain giants, weary of their chess games, had plucked Everest from its throne to see what monsters might be trapped underneath.

Distant thunder rumbled as the huge displaced peak continued its remorseless approach, blotting out the sun. Lightning flickered across its upper slopes. She could see a rain of rocks and dust falling from its dark underside. She was in its path. A tiny ant about to be crushed. Then its snowy crags billowed and seemed to shift form. The rocky cumulus slowly altered in shape, its lines softening and rippling like a colossal amoeba. Its progress did not falter as it engulfed the sky, but its shape was uncertain, the massive bulk suddenly as insubstantial as a fluttering prayer flag.

The formless phenomenon shuddered and was webbed with a skein of electric blue. As the wind began to tear at its edges, shredding its dark pall, there came the distant roar of some lost denizen from an outer existence. A demon or a hungry ghost. Victoria knew that cry. That voice was in her, too. It embodied the despair and loneliness of a being cast out from its old and native haunts.

She opened her eyes and saw the old monk standing over her. His staff slowly raised itself and levelled at her. It moved of its own accord, the hand jerking to follow. His wizened face crinkled with pain. His unseeing blank eyes were piercing. He knew what she had seen, she was certain of that.

Suddenly she blurted out, 'My father, Edward Waterfield. Is he at Det-sen? Do you know? If he is, please tell me!'

The old monk returned her stare. Slowly he raised one finger to his lips in a gesture of silence. Then the staff swung away and his body followed. It tapped its way across the floor and he moved after it, clinging to the upper end for fear of being left behind. She was certain that the staff was leading him.

Sonam was still turning the prayer wheel as she watched her employer. Victoria took a deep breath. 'Can we go now please?'

'Food first,' replied the Sherpani. 'I've made special potato bread.'

'All right. But then please can we go?' From outside the *gompa*, Victoria could hear the tap-tap-tap of the old monk's stick as it led him clockwise around the walls of the lamasery as was the custom.

Once they had crossed Nang La Pass into Tibet, it was another day's walk to their destination. Victoria had hardly spoken and the others seemed to catch her mood.

At last, she began to recognize the terrain over which she had repeatedly flown: a long valley strewn with scree and at its head, a mountain with its peak cracked like a dead volcano.

Fifty years before, when she had been only ten years younger, she had stood at the broken gates of the monastery and watched that mountain throbbing with unearthly energy. A livid mixture of plasma and lava had belched from the shattered summit, pouring down the slopes as if the wounded earth was casting the suppurating filth of the invader out of its system. The Doctor and Jamie had stood beside her and she had wept because the Great Intelligence, whose death was causing so much violence on the mountain, had been inside her body too. But she had been raised not to talk of that. A lady always maintained her self-composure in company – no matter how great the violation.

The party rounded the mountain and looked down into the next valley. The monastery of Det-sen lay on the lower slopes of the next mountain, a cluster of tiny grey buildings, more like a fortress than the coloured *gompas* she had visited along the route.

The track leading down was in poor repair. Twice it vanished completely under landslides that had not been cleared away. Tundu and Sonam exchanged worried glances as they struggled to guide the yak over the loose rock. The old monk sat tight on his steed, clinging to its curved horns as it lurched back and forth.

As they approached the monastery, they could see that the ornate roof was in a bad state too. There was no sign of life apart from the tattered prayer flags that fluttered from the broken walls. Victoria struggled to calm her nerves. She could not believe that all this had been in vain.

Suddenly there was a cacophony of drums and cymbals and deep horns. The massive gates of Det-sen swung wide and a group of monks robed in red issued forth. They stood at either side of the entrance, waiting as the raucous din continued.

Victoria's little group stopped opposite the gates and stared as a single line of ancient lamas with crested yellow hats moved forward out of the inner courtyard towards them. Each lama carried a stick which tap-tap-tapped ahead of him. Like the monk who had travelled from Lukla, all of the lamas of Det-sen were blind.

Two of the monks came forward, and with great veneration helped the old man from his place on the yak. It was obvious that all this ceremony was in his honour. He allowed them to lead him towards the monastery and the line of blind lamas parted for him to pass.

When he reached the gates, he signalled and one of the young monks inclined his head as he received instruction. As the old monk passed on into the courtyard, the young man approached Victoria and bowed.

'The Abbot Thonmi asks that you be brought into the monastery as his honoured guests.'

The room that they gave Victoria was austere, but comfortable enough; certainly better than the cell she had spent time in during her previous visit. Although the Sherpa were housed in a separate dormitory, Sonam had brought her a meal of dumplings and sweet tea. Victoria sat on the bed, picking at her food. Now she had reached her goal, she had no idea what to do. Worse, she was convinced that the ancient abbot, the old, old man with whom she had travelled, must be the same Thonmi she had known as a handsome young monk some fifty years before. To journey through Time could be so abrupt and cruel.

She decided to press every available monk for an opportunity to speak to the abbot. Plainly his vow of silence existed only outside his monastery, so surely he would now reveal to her what was happening. He might even explain the dreams that had drawn her back to this forsaken place.

There was a light knock at the door. When it opened, the abbot himself was standing there dressed in his full robes and crested saffron hat. His voice was frail. 'Miss

Waterfield, please may I speak with you?' Without waiting for a response, he started to edge his way into the room and she saw that he was without his staff.

She took his hand and guided him to a chair.

'I think that perhaps we already know one another,' he whispered as if he was afraid of being overheard.

'Yes,' she said. 'I think so too.'

He reached forward with his gnarled fingers and she let him run them gently over the contours of her face. 'Are you really the same Victoria who came to Det-sen so long ago?'

'Yes. I was here fifty years ago, when the monastery was attacked by the Yeti and the Great Intelligence.'

The old man groaned. 'And I was little more than a novice.'

'You were very kind and brave,' said Victoria and she started to feel tears welling in her eyes. On a sudden impulse, she reached into her bag and produced the chocolate that Charles had given her. She broke off a piece and put it into his hand. 'It's all I have to give you. I hope it's not against your vows.'

He sniffed at the chocolate and then popped it into his mouth. As he chewed a smile crept across his wizened face. 'The books tell that your companion the Doctor returned to us after a gap of three hundred years. And now you return and time has not touched you either.'

'Well, not much anyway,' she murmured. 'But what's happened here? Why is the monastery so neglected? And the other lamas. What's happened to their sight?'

He was silent for several seconds. In the distance, Victoria could hear the tinkling of tiny bells.

'You are still too inquisitive,' he muttered. 'Some things are better left unseen. We follow our disciplines.'

'You can't mean you've willingly gone blind? That's horrible!'

His voice was grave and quiet. 'Victoria Waterfield, what do you seek?'

'I'm looking for my father. Is he here?' It was the first time she had admitted as much to anyone. It had frightened her for years. Now that she spoke the words, they seemed flat and hopeless.

'What makes you think he is at Det-sen?'

'Please, you must tell me.'

The Abbot Thonmi sighed deeply. His every action seemed part of a weary task. 'You should not have come. Det-sen is no longer a welcoming place. We do not deal with outsiders. Our disciplines must be maintained.'

'Why?' she said. 'You've cut yourselves off. What do you have to hide?'

'Much,' he replied.

'And my father. Is he really here?'

Thonmi slowly shook his head. 'If *you* still appear so youthful, how old must your father be?'

'Please. Just tell me.'

'You must leave here in the morning.'

She studied him for a moment, unsure of what to believe. 'You could have stopped me coming here days ago. And if you don't speak to outsiders, what were you doing in Lukla?' She suddenly thought he might have come to meet her.

He smiled grimly. 'Life is a journey, my child. The Thonmi you once knew lived in the light, but his path led into darkness. It is an eternal battle. The Great Wheel turns. The flame gutters. Sometimes the light is only seen when we stand in the shadows. That is our journey. Not yours. Yours goes on from this place and time.'

'I don't know,' Victoria said. 'I was certain . . .'

'Do not seek him here in this sad place. You are remembered with grace at Det-sen. But this time you cannot help us. You are a welcome guest tonight, but do not stray into the holy shrines. They are sacred and must not be disturbed.'

She nodded sullenly. 'I understand.'

He rose and started to grope for the door.

'Shall I fetch you your staff?' she asked.

'No! Not that!' he snapped. For a moment he glowered and then his courtesy returned. 'You are kind. When we have moments of lucidity, we must seek to find our own way . . . without guidance.' He bowed his head in her direction. 'Sleep soundly,' he said and disappeared into the darkness outside.

She lay in the dark still fully dressed, unable to sleep, expecting at any moment to rise weightless out of her body and begin her nightly journey.

Somewhere the monks were chanting a mantra, a deep pulsing chant that seemed to well up from subterranean depths like shadows echoing endlessly in the black throat of the night.

The Abbot Thonmi was nurturing forbidden secrets. The sad old man had admitted as much. But what did he mean by his 'moments of lucidity'? Or, by implication, his moments of darkness too? As a blind man he must know all about that. Det-sen seemed to be in the grip of some new terror. She was determined to help rid the monastery of its curse. Surely that was what the Doctor would have done.

'*Victoria! Where are you?*'

The voice again. It filled her with relief and fear. Yet this time it was distant, not close by her ear and she was still wide awake.

'*Are you listening, Victoria? I know you can hear me.*'

It was real. It was calling from somewhere in the very depths of the monastery. So much for the abbot's sermon. She slid off the bed and opened the door slowly. The chanting had stopped. The hall was deserted.

She moved silently out and darted through the shadows. The flagstones were cold on her bare feet. In the courtyard, a huge statue of Buddha lay where it had been thrown down by the rampaging Yeti robots over half a century ago. Another smaller Buddha had been set up in the place where it had stood. The past was accepted here and could not be changed.

'*Why do you neglect me when you are so near?*'

His voice was raging on and it occurred to Victoria, not for the first time, that he must be much changed from the kind and gentle father she had known and loved so much as a child.

She moved along the torchlit corridors, past the halls and kitchens, trying to remember the way, constantly frustrated by the walls and doors that she could pass directly through in her dreamstate.

Finally, at the end of a passage, she saw the great doors that she knew led to the Inner Sanctum. These were barred by a heavy bolt of wood the size of a plank and she could not simply push through.

'*Well? How much longer must I wait?*'

'Where are you?' she called aloud.

'*Here. Alone in the darkness.*'

The voice came from beyond the doors. She set her hands to the wooden bolt and started to push it laboriously away. Her hands were soon full of splinters, but slowly the barrier was yielding. With a final effort, she yanked the bolt free and started to push the doors inwards.

Inside, the chamber was exactly as she had seen it, with an overturned chair, a torn veil and moonlight that cut in through the broken ceiling like a blade.

She leant against the door in despair. 'Now what do I do?' she complained aloud.

'*I am here in the darkness. Find me!*'

'Where?' She walked slowly into the Sanctum.

'*Here!*'

A gentle voice at her shoulder startled her.

'Turn back now, Victoria.'

The Abbot Thonmi had been waiting in the shadows inside the door. His crested hat caught the moonlight like the beak of a huge bird of prey. He carried an ornately carved ceremonial staff. Either there was another way into the Sanctum, or the monks had locked him in for his vigil.

'*Victoria . . .*' echoed the voice.

'I have to find out,' she protested. 'My father died far away. On another world.'

The old lama's head turned towards her voice. He edged slowly towards her using the staff as a guide.

'There are many other worlds, other planes.'

She reached out to touch his hand. 'But I can hear his voice in my thoughts. He called me and I travelled all this way.'

'No,' insisted the abbot. 'Demons and hungry ghosts steal many shapes. Please turn away, Victoria.'

'*Why do you delay? Release me!*'

Her father's voice seemed to be coming from somewhere below. She noticed a shadowed alcove set into the side wall of the Sanctum. There was another arch inside the alcove from which a green glow had started to filter.

'I know he's here.' She started to move towards the alcove, but the abbot's staff swung up to block her way.

'A second time I ask, what do you seek?'

'What have you done to him?' she demanded. She pushed against the staff, but he held her firmly, forcing her back.

'*I am alone in the darkness,*' the voice groaned despairingly.

'Do not disturb it,' warned the lama. 'It is *not* your father. It is delusion!'

The staff pinned her to the wall.

'*Victoria!*'

'Let me through!' she shouted.

'I cannot!'

It was more than she could bear. 'What are you hiding here? Who is it then?'

'For the third time I ask, what do you seek?

'I want the truth!' she cried in despair.

There were long moments as her plaint echoed away through the cold arches of Det-sen.

At last, the Abbot Thonmi turned wearily away from her. His will and spirit were finally broken.

'You were expected,' he said quietly. 'My task is ended. I cannot prevent your journey into the dark.' He ceremonially raised his ornate staff towards her. 'Perhaps Truth may light your way.'

Victoria stared in disbelief at the frail and blind old man.

'Take it!' he insisted.

Bewildered, she took the staff from his outstretched hands and watched as he started to grope his way out of the open Sanctum door.

There was a low moan from the depths.

'Are you there?' she called and approached the alcove.

Cold air was welling up from below carrying a dank reek of decay. The walls glimmered with a putrid green.

'*I've been alone so long. Like you, Victoria. But together . . .*'

'I'm coming,' she whispered and started down the crumbling steps.

She went down step by step, clinging to the damp wall, using the staff for support. She called out again but there was no reply. The cold air devoured sound, sense and hope. She reached the foot of the stairs and the glimmering light revealed some sort of private chapel. There were faded paintings on the walls, dancing monsters in once-gaudy robes. She shivered with the cold. There was a groan from the far end of the dark chamber.

'*Victoria? Are you there?*'

'Yes. I'm here.' She could just make out an archway with something strung across its portal like a cobweb.

'*Release me.*' The pitiful voice came from beyond the arch.

'I heard you. I've come all this way.' She went closer and saw that the web was composed of coloured threads, all intermeshed and stretched across the opening. It was a Tibetan spirit trap, built to contain evil and malevolent demons. Filaments of waving gossamer had caught on the strings. Inside the trap, something shuffled in the shadows.

'*I said, release me! I can endure the darkness no longer!*'

She tried to see through the mesh, but could make out only a dark, hunched figure in the gloom. 'I don't know. How can I be sure? They said you were dead. But in the dreams . . .'

'*Victoria.*' His voice was suddenly calm with authority. It was familiar. Something she could not doubt.

'Father,' she said. The sense of relief and recognition

went beyond the circumstance. From her heart she said, 'Yes, of course I'll help you.'

Inside the trap, a bony hand was reaching out to her. She raised the abbot's ceremonial staff and thrust it into the web.

A roar of green flame.

Victoria stumbled back, shielding her face. Burning threads were falling all around her. She heard the tap-tap-tap of a stick and the rasping of breath. A figure was shuffling against the light, emerging from the archway. Victoria fell to the floor staring up in disbelief.

This wasn't her father at all. It was delusion. Its ancient features were wasted and slack. Its white hair and beard matted; its eyes sunken and blind. Blind like all the people in this God-forsaken place. Yet she knew the face. It was an uninvited memory resurrected. Lost in time like her.

'You!' she whispered.

His white stick touched her.

The figure faltered. Its voice, the voice that had been in her head for so long, was fierce and tortured. 'Find me the Locus!' it commanded.

She heard the tinkling of bells, the fluttering of prayer flags and a surge of demonic laughter.

The darkness forced itself into her head. It devoured her thoughts and senses. It swamped her consciousness. She sank under its weight.

'Well,' said Charles 'you've led us a fine dance, I must say.'

To her drowsy eyes, he looked like a hovering angel, his yellow hair shining. She closed them again and went back to sleep.

When she woke again, she saw that he was still sitting close at hand. Beyond him, the ceiling and walls were a sort of municipal conformist cream colour. There was a strong smell of something clinical. Very soothing.

* * *

This time, the third time she woke, he said, 'Well, are we going to have a conversation for a change?'

She groaned and felt a sharp pain in one of her arms. But at least it would keep her awake.

'Hello,' he said very gently.

She tried to talk, but her throat felt like a cheese-grater.

'Don't worry, sweetheart. You're in hospital in Kathmandu. Everything's fine now.'

She managed a vague smile and was content to lie and let him talk, although everything he said seemed to get jumbled up in her thoughts.

She had been flown back from Lukla. That was two days ago. Did she want a drink? Tundu and Sonam had brought her out, carried her back. She was managing a bit of solid food now. They had all been very worried. She was doing well. They thought it was altitude sickness. He had squared it with the British Embassy. She shouldn't move too much. Did she want a drink? The burns were healing quickly.

'That's good,' she murmured drowsily.

'Iodine,' she said and managed to sit up. 'That's what I can smell.'

Charles looked startled. 'Well, *you're* much better, aren't you?'

She slid back into the sheets. 'How long have I been asleep?'

'About ten days on and off. Mostly off. We were very worried.'

'Yes. I remember, you said.'

He sighed. 'They want to fly you home as soon as possible.'

'Good. I don't think I can manage that by myself . . . not at the moment.' The grin that spread across his face puzzled her. 'Don't you ever take things seriously?' she said.

'Not if I can help it. Too depressing.'

She smiled at him. 'Was I badly burned?'

'Yes.' He seemed cautious. 'On your hands and feet mainly.'

'Hmm. I can't think how that happened.' She saw him shrug.

Then a Nepali nurse appeared and said, 'Hello. Good to see you awake at last. The doctor's here to see you.'

'Really?' She started to sit up again. 'That's amazing. I'd been thinking so much about him lately.'

But the man who came through the door was tall and Asian with thinning hair and a white hospital coat.

The postcard arrived just as she finished packing her bags. It was battered and had been forwarded from Lukla. The picture showed Trafalgar Square. How typical of Mrs Cywynski to send a postcard from home to someone who was on holiday.

'Hope you are having a wonderful time,' it read. 'The cats say you should come home soon. I say so too. The ether is very strange. Regards, Roxana.'

She plainly knew nothing about the accident.

'I wish Tundu was here. He might tell me what happened,' said Victoria. She sat nervously in the passenger seat as Charles drove her to the airport. The Kathmandu traffic was a dusty nightmare. 'I've been so frightened, Charles. I keep thinking I should go back to Det-sen.'

She gasped as Charles slammed on the brakes to avoid an errant cyclist. 'You can't be serious?' he joked. 'Even *I* can't afford to pay for you again.'

'I'm sorry. I will pay you back, I promise.'

'No problem.'

'Will you see Tundu soon? When you do, give him my love.'

'Sometime. I'm flying to Paris tomorrow, once I've got you packed off safely. Jill will be waiting for me.'

'Jill?' asked Victoria.

'My wife. She helps catalogue my plant specimens.'

For the first time, Victoria noticed a wedding ring on his left hand. She was certain it hadn't been there before.

She sat silently watching the traffic until they reached the airport. Once they had booked in her luggage, she gave him a long hug.

He laughed and hugged her back. 'We'll be in London soon. I'll give you a call.'

All she could think to say was, 'Yes.'

2

Bug Alert

The mountainous terrain scrolled below like the graphics on a computer game. UNIT helicopter *Valkyrie* 74D dropped to one thousand feet so that the pilot could follow the track.

From the passenger seat, Second Lieutenant Douglas Cavendish watched the landscape from inside the perspex security cockpit. 'Pretty wild out there,' he opined suavely.

'Yeti country,' said the pilot.

'Right.' Cavendish scrutinized the ground below more carefully. 'Don't most sightings turn out to be lost backpackers or leftovers from the Hippy Trail?' He laughed out loud at his joke.

Pilot Per Londqvist, a hulking flight lieutenant drafted in from the Swedish Air Force, smiled politely. He had about as many flying hours as his passenger was old.

'What's that?' shouted Cavendish, pointing at two grey shapes scuttling across rocks below the snowline.

'Goats.'

'Ah.' Cavendish sat still for a while. On his lap was a file marked 'UNIT Operations – Gargarin Tracking Station' and dated 84/18/08. It consisted of enhanced satellite images of Section China 9G: Tingri Plains, Tibet, timed 23.08 hours GMT. There was also a monitored report from Reuters and two transcription reports from CNN and the BBC's Delhi office.

In fact, Cavendish decided, he was on a bit of a mercy mission. The file had sat on a desk at Geneva HQ for four days while the relevant duty officer was away on leave in St Moritz or somewhere equally *recherché*, and it wasn't until New York came down the blower breathing fire that anyone had noticed.

The enhanced satellite images showed the mountains north of Nangpa La. On the contours between the white snow peaks, there was a brilliant splash of gold and red.

The reports referred to a mystery explosion in the Himalayas. A remote Buddhist monastery had apparently been totally destroyed.

The *Valkyrie* was flying along the length of a valley that twisted sinuously between two white-capped mountains. Another peak rose ahead, its summit snapped off to reveal a dead crater, blackened and free from snow.

'It's an extinct volcano,' said Cavendish incredulously. 'I didn't think the Himalayas had any seismic activity.' From the far side, there was a veil of dark smoke rising against the clear sky.

They rounded the mountain and saw, in the pit of the next valley, a dark smoking lesion burned into the slope. Londqvist circled the helicopter while Cavendish took photographs. 'What in hell caused that?' he murmured.

Where the Det-sen monastery should have stood there was a huge black hole as if something had burst up through the mountainside catching the buildings in its path. The hole still smoked. Mounds of rubble lay scattered around it and right up the slopes.

Londqvist put the helicopter down and Cavendish clambered through the detritus wishing he had worn more practical shoes.

There was no sign of a living soul – or any sign of the emergency services for that matter. Lying among the broken stone and wood was the sheered-off head of a huge Buddha, its blank eyes staring at the sky. The head was still hot. Here and there, tatters of something like web clung to the rubble, rippling in the wind as if they were alive.

Cavendish set up a tripod and took the standard reading for radiation. The geiger-meter registered nothing. He bagged up a few samples from the soil round the crater – important evidence for establishing any trace of UFO landings.

'Lieutenant!' He was just going to relieve himself

behind a lump of tossed-aside masonry the size of a small bungalow, when he heard Londqvist shouting.

The pilot was leaning out of the *Valkyrie*'s cockpit. When he saw Cavendish, he gestured up at the ridge that overlooked the valley.

A row of motionless figures was ranged across the crest, staring down at the intruders. They were dressed in orange robes like monks and carried tall staffs.

Cavendish heard a deep sepulchral chanting and felt a tangible wave of anger hit him. He was thought a profanity in their sacred place. He started to walk up towards the ridge, but the stare from the orange line was implacable, so increasingly angry that he found it physically difficult to face. It forced against him like a current of energy. The chanting grew in strength. He began to get the shakes. He turned and ran for the helicopter. Its blades were already scything the air.

'Let's get out of here!'

The *Valkyrie* lifted, then baulked under a surge of turbulence. They veered sharply sideways. The rockface loomed. Loose stones rattled onto the fuselage. Londqvist fought with the juddering controls to stop the machine smashing into the mountain. The force beat against them like a tide of invisible fists. The helicopter, its engine screaming, tilted down towards the mouth of the black pit. Londqvist wrenched the control column back with a yell. The machine pulled up with metres to spare. It cut through the veil of smoke and rose away. The force of the guardians of Det-sen broke.

Behind them, Cavendish saw the line of figures begin to file slowly down into the valley. They were searching out their path with their long staffs, moving like a group of blind men.

'What was it?' he kept repeating.

'Put it in your report,' snapped the pilot. 'I am flying on to Lukla.' He was plainly concentrating on putting as much space between themselves and Det-sen as he could.

Cavendish was still shivering. His hand stung a little

where tiny fragments of the web had clung to it. He tried to brush them off.

'I said, I am flying to Lukla,' insisted Londqvist. 'What is the name of the contact there?'

Cavendish pulled the file out of his holdall. He flicked clumsily through the pages and eventually found the list of civilian auxiliaries. All the entry for Lukla said was 'Eric'.

By the time they reached Lukla, Cavendish had settled himself again. Londqvist flew over the settlement and then turned to drop down to the airfield. As they passed over one of the tin-roofed houses, they saw a man with wild grey hair staring up at them. Then he began running frantically about, tearing up a row of plants from a makeshift allotment at the back.

'Eric?' suggested the pilot.

'Right,' said Cavendish. 'I'll deal with him. You get yourself some tea or something.'

Cavendish found the teashop quickly enough and was soon joined by Londqvist, which was not what he had intended. 'Wait outside, old chap,' he advised using his inimitable Sandhurst charm. 'Don't want to intimidate him, do we? I'll bring you out a tea.'

There was an old man in the shop, but he ignored Cavendish's questions, seemingly content to stare ahead and turn his prayer wheel. The officer was just heading through to the back when he came face to face with Lukla's legacy from the Summer of Love. Eric was waving a half-empty bottle of cheap whisky.

'What's the hurry, man,' he slurred, blocking the way.

Cavendish flashed his UNIT pass. Eric peered at it, mystified. Then an expression of recognition dawned across his face. 'Hey, UNIT. That's cool. I thought you guys were checking me out as a drop point.'

'Sorry about your garden,' said Cavendish, curtly. 'I'll take two teas while I'm here.' He eyed the old man in the corner.

'That's Uncle,' Eric said. 'He's cool too. No talka the

Inglesi, eh Uncle? He has a neat line in Tibetan hats though. Only eight *yuan*.'

Uncle ignored this and concentrated on his prayer wheel.

'No thanks. Just the tea,' said Cavendish. 'Do you get much news down from Tibet?'

Eric swigged at his bottle. 'Bad news. This place is getting too busy. Backpackers and trekkers. Like, soon there'll be a Hilton. That's all the crap I came to get away from, man.'

'Have you heard about the monastery at Det-sen?'

Eric nearly choked. 'Oh no, man. Not that place again. That's bad news. No one goes there. No trade. No nothing.'

'Why? What have you heard? Did you know there was an explosion six days ago? The place has been blown apart.'

Eric glanced at Uncle. 'What did I say, man? Bad news.'

Cavendish was getting impatient. He scratched at the irritation on his hand. 'We've reports that there was a trekker who was travelling to Det-sen via Lukla. We checked her permit in Kathmandu. Her name's Victoria Waterfield. She's English. Do you know anything about her?'

'Jolly bad show, old chap,' enunciated Eric. 'Seen one trekker, seen 'em all.'

'Now look here . . .' Cavendish tapered off as Londqvist came through the door.

The Swede sidled up to the counter. 'I'll try one of your yakburgers,' he said to Eric and slapped five ten-*yuan* notes on the bar. He gave Cavendish a mocking wink.

Eric picked up the notes and sniffed them. 'Now that you mention it, man, there was a girl here. A couple of Sherpa brought her in. She was in a bad way. Bad burns. They ferried her back to Kathmandu.' He shrugged at Cavendish. 'Too bad. You missed the boat.'

Cavendish was determined not to be outdone. 'And was it her? Had she been at Det-sen?'

At this, Uncle began to chatter away. Eric was suddenly animated, trying to calm him down. He shook the old man, who never looked him in the face, but only stared fixedly at the floor. Under his tatty brown coat there was a flash of brilliant orange.

It was incomprehensible to Cavendish, but one word kept recurring. It sounded like *Travers*.

'What's he babbling about?' complained the second lieutenant. 'This is a total waste of time. Come on, Londqvist. There's no point in staying.'

The pilot followed him out into the street. As they marched towards the airstrip, he said, 'I think you are missing a few things.'

'Too bad. I want to get my report in.'

'The old man was looking for someone called Edward Travers.'

'Travers? Means nothing to me.' Cavendish was scratching again at his hand.

'He said that Travers had escaped.'

'Probably went off without paying for a hat. This whole business is a wild-goose chase. I've got my samples. I want to get back.'

'The old man was a priest,' called Londqvist. 'And he was blind.'

Cavendish halted and did a complete about turn. 'Do you have something to say?' he snapped.

Londqvist shook his head. 'It's your mission, Lieutenant. I'm sure it'll be in your report.'

'That's obvious, isn't it?' Cavendish complained. 'Good God, who in their right mind builds a monastery right on the side of a volcano? It's asking for trouble and that's what they got.'

The damned irritation on his hand was getting raw. He noticed that Londqvist was watching him scratch the skin.

'What about the attack?' the Swede asked. With a certain perverse satisfaction, Cavendish saw that he was scratching at his own wrist too.

'Frightened monks, that's all. They're mystics, aren't

they? So they're bound to tap unusual powers.' He would have thought that was obvious. 'I wouldn't be in UNIT if I didn't believe in the paranormal,' he snapped.

'I thought they tried to keep an equal balance of affirmed sceptics.' Londqvist paused, apparently no longer convinced by his own argument.

Cavendish was walking backwards towards the helicopter. His eyes never left Londqvist: a look that allowed for no argument. 'As for that trekker,' he said firmly, 'you hardly need worry about her. Sounds as if she was lucky to get away with her life.'

The pilot flexed his fingers as if something was clinging to them. He glanced up at the mountains and the sky as if the answer to something he could not remember might be hovering there. He said slowly, 'I am sure that you have made the right decision.'

'Good,' said Second Lieutenant Cavendish. They marched to the *Valkyrie* and climbed into their seats. Cavendish pushed his assignment file back into his holdall. 'I'm sorry, Londqvist. You never got your yakburger.'

Londqvist stared at the helicopter controls and grunted his agreement.

Cavendish clicked-in his safety harness. 'Never mind, old chap. It'll all be in my report.'

Duty Officer Rikki Patel, not one to miss a trick – not since the Tibet explosion fiasco at any rate – flicked through the previous day's computer lists. It was the usual log of Geneva's accessions and transactions, but three entries commanded his interest.

There were two enquiries to the personnel records database from Second Lieutenant Douglas Cavendish, and a third from Flight Lieutenant Per Londqvist of *Valkyrie* Flight.

Dashing Duggie had been far too cocky since he'd come bounding to the rescue with his Tibet report. He had certainly made it clear that Patel owed him one for that favour.

His first request concerned data on the name 'Waterfield, Victoria'. Access was denied – a formal instruction that suggested that information was held under a security lock. Apparently Cavendish did not have the clearance for this, since his enquiry went no further.

It was the next enquiry that made Patel sit up. Both Cavendish and Londqvist were requesting the same information. The input name was 'Travers, Edward (Professor)'. Access was given.

DO Patel logged into the database and entered the name himself. The system was slow – four years old and already out of date. The terminal whirred and clicked before finally disclosing its information. All the screen showed was 'Subject Deceased, 80/25/12. File closed.'

'So sorry, Duggie,' observed Patel in an Eton accent. 'Too frightful. The old bugger probably choked on a mince pie.' It was a fate he wished the precocious young officer might enjoy as well. But it was a long time to wait until Christmas.

3

A Day at the Zoo

As befitted the cold end of September, the zoo was deserted. The leaves were already turning and there was a bite to the air. Sarah Jane Smith was a little early for the photocall so she made a detour to go and talk to the elephants. There were no elephants to be seen, so she talked to a rhino instead. It was a one-sided conversation. She leaned on the railing and said, 'Hello, rhino,' and it ignored her and got on with some important munching.

'Your interviewing technique's going a bit rusty,' said a voice behind her.

She froze. 'Charlie!' She turned and flung her arms round his neck, hugging him tight. 'I thought you were in . . .'

'Paris?' he mumbled.

'No, Nepal! I thought you were plant-hunting.' She pulled back to look at him. Charles Bryce, sickeningly brown, with his golden hair bleached almost albino. 'You look wonderful.'

'So do you, Sarah darling.'

'I should have guessed you'd be here at this.'

'Why else do you think they put you on this story?'

'I see,' she grinned. 'Well, at least there'll be someone here worth talking to.' She looked round. 'Is Jill here?'

'Nah. She *is* in Paris, cataloguing my plants. It was a good trip.'

'You have a saintly wife, Charlie.' Sarah took his arm. 'Come on. You can tell me all about Yeti before all the bowing and scraping starts.'

As they walked across the zoo, they saw a large group of people standing on one of the lawns opposite the main restaurant – a motley mixture of civil servants and reporters. Sarah waved to Robin, her photographer, who was already milling among the throng.

'It's all gone very smoothly,' said Charles. 'Suddhodana, he's the father, he's already been flown back to Peking. But mother and child are doing fine.'

Sarah consulted her notes. 'That's Mahamaya?'

'Correct.'

'And what's the baby called?'

His smile drooped a little. 'Ah, well. That's due to be announced once the ceremony's underway.'

'Oh, oh.' Sarah had known Charles since college and could tell when a bombshell was on the way. 'Do I detect a spot of diplomatic chicanery?'

He had a sheepish smile. 'Everything's tied up with selling Hong Kong off to China.'

'And your poor old Yeti got caught up in the negotiations.' She hugged him. 'Poor Charlie. They should have asked you. You were the first person to catch one and bring it back into captivity.'

'Yeah, well, China got one soon after. But just recently I've seen reports of two being used as dancing bears in Russia.'

There was a general disturbance as a new group of Grey Suits made their way across the lawn. At the centre, Sarah recognized the Chinese Ambassador and, alongside him, the British Foreign Minister and, in a suit of cobalt blue, the Prime Minister herself.

One of the head keepers appealed to the reporters not to use flashguns for fear of frightening the Yeti cub. Then the zoo's director made a brief speech about there being three distinct sub-species of Yeti. Mahamaya and her cub were *Yeti Traversii*, belonging to the group that more closely resembled the bear family. They were very timid creatures and it was estimated that only a few hundred existed in the wild, which made the birth of the first cub born in captivity so important. (Mild applause.) The Yeti's diet consisted mainly of rhododendron leaves and flowers, although they were partial to honeycomb too when they could get it.

The liaison between China and Britain, which had brought about this happy event, was of major international importance. In recognition of that diplomatic concord, the yeti cub was to be named Margaret.

(Wild applause.)

A nervous young keeper appeared carrying a small bundle of fur in his hands. The cameras (minus flashes) began to click and whirr. The Prime Minister plainly saw this as the photo opportunity *sans pareil*. If one of her predecessors could do it with pandas, then she was certainly not going to flinch at a Yeti. She cooed regally over the wriggling bundle, determined to reinforce her maternal image.

She appeared less than enthusiastic, however, when the Zoological Society's director suggested she might actually hold the creature. Her cortège of Suits and PR men and the Chinese Embassy staff all looked on expectantly as the cub's nervous handler showed her the right way to hold his precious charge.

'Like handing Snow White over to the Wicked Queen,' murmured Sarah and got a sidelong look from Charles. He was surrogate father to the baby and was suffering as much as its keeper.

The Prime Minister angled her Tibetan charge awkwardly at arms' length and gave a rictus smile for the cameras.

Sarah, unable to keep a professionally straight face, slipped away from the crowd to look at the Yeti enclosure.

There seemed to be nothing at home, which reminded her of childhood visits to the zoo. The label would tell you what was meant to be in the cage, but the inmate was always indoors or curled up asleep in the corner, and no amount of shouting or chucking peanuts, in the days when you were allowed to chuck peanuts, would get it to stir. Sarah didn't have a rhododendron to chuck either.

She gasped as someone barged past her – an old man in extremely tatty and grubby clothes. He had a shock of wild white hair and a white beard and he gave off a musty smell like old cupboards.

'Pardon me!' exclaimed Sarah. Then she noticed the tapping white stick and realized her mistake. 'I'm so sorry. I didn't realize.'

The old man ignored her. His stick struck the safety barrier and he grasped at the rail with his free hand. '*Yeh-teh!*' he called out. The voice was commanding for someone who appeared so old. '*Yeh-teh!*'

He raised his stick and began to swing wildly across the barrier with it, clashing the implement repeatedly against the bars as he shouted.

There was a squeal from inside the enclosure. A massive grey bear-like creature came scrambling out from behind some rocks. It reared up on its hind legs and squealed again. It was nearly eight foot tall. It was pushing itself against the inner barrier, clawing at the wire.

Sarah ran to pull the old man away, but he pushed her clear with alarming force. She stared in disbelief. His face was dirty and his spectacles were cracked, but she was certain she knew him.

'*Yeti Traversii!*' he shouted and began to haul himself across the barrier.

Sarah ran to fetch help. She should have shouted, but she didn't want to cause an international incident. There must be trigger-happy bodyguards behind every tree. All of them ignoring events by the Yeti enclosure. She grabbed at Charles and pulled him away as quietly as she could, begging him to help.

He looked bemused. And even more so, when they reached the enclosure and there was no sign of the old man.

'All right, all right,' Charles kept saying. 'I believe you. Something's certainly disturbed Mahamaya.' The Yeti had dropped back to all fours, but was pacing up and down the length of the barrier, swinging her head from side to side in agitation.

Sarah was trying to stay calm, but she had to tell him or burst with frustration. 'I know who it was, Charlie. Oh, don't ask how, I just do.'

He tried to be patient. 'All right, tell me.'

She clasped and unclasped her hands. 'It was Edward Travers. *The* Edward Travers. The professor.'

'Don't be ridiculous, darling.'

'But it was. The one who discovered . . .'

He completed her sentence: '. . . who first discovered the Yeti in Tibet in 1936. How could it possibly be?'

Sarah shook her head. 'I interviewed him once for *Metropolitan*. I know it was him, Charlie. Please believe me!'

'Sarah, he was an old friend of mine. He's dead. He's been dead for nearly five years.'

She gave a huge moan of despair. 'I know.'

He put his arm round her shoulder. 'Come on. You had a shock and made a mistake.'

'I've had worse than that. And I wasn't wrong. It was so like him.' She bit her tongue.

'There you are then,' he said and there was a note of triumph in his voice.

A tuft of fur fluttered on the inner barrier.

'She's moulting,' Sarah sniffed. But the fur looked more like cobweb.

Charles offered her his huge coloured handkerchief. 'Come on, it's not like you to get so upset. When we're finished here, I'll take us out to lunch.'

'Thanks,' she said flatly. 'Sorry.'

But she did notice the nervous, even expectant, glances he had cast in every single direction while she was talking.

As they walked back towards the group, they heard a shout and a general disturbance among the crowd. There was another barrage of clicking cameras.

'What did we miss?' Charles asked.

'The cub,' smirked the nearest reporter. 'It just bit her.'

'Now do you feel better?' Charles muttered, giving Sarah's arm a squeeze. They peered over the heads, trying to get a better view.

One of the Suits was winding a handkerchief around the Prime Minister's hand. The nervous young keeper was hurrying his squirming charge away.

'It's all right. It's all right,' piped up one of the Foreign Minister's aides. 'Just a little nip.'

There was embarrassed silence as the entire British contingent stared at the Chinese party. Finally the Ambassador said loudly, 'More likely to offend Japan, I believe. Thank you for a most gratifying occasion.'

'No chance of rabies, I suppose?' whispered Sarah.

'Not a hope,' said Charles.

Sarah raised an eyebrow. 'Actually, I was worrying about the cub.' She waved to Robin the cameraman and then flounced away. 'Coming for a cuppa before you buy me lunch? Then you can tell me what else you brought back from Nepal.'

4

Home to Roost

He never got in touch, Victoria thought.

The front page of Mrs Cywynski's *Telegraph* was dominated by a picture of the Prime Minister, a pained look on her face, as she nearly dropped a small bundle of fur. The headline said PM DISCOVERS THAT DIPLOMACY BITES BACK. The report listed various comments from the dignitaries present and ended with a caustic quote from Charles Bryce, the British explorer who first captured a Yeti and brought it into captivity. 'No wonder the poor creatures keep clear of civilization. At home the worst thing they have to worry about is the occasional snow leopard.'

She had been back from hospital for two weeks, back at work for one. The hole in the pavement was *still* there and the house had taken on a musty smell. At the office, there were stacks of filing to do and letters to type. She felt as if her boss had deliberately done nothing while she had been away. She also still had no recollection of what had happened in Tibet. She remembered waking up in the hospital, but when she had fallen asleep she could not recall. The entire journey was a dream, littered with more dreams of journeys and things she might have only imagined or thought she remembered. It had become a gaping black hole from which blew cold, decaying air.

She even thought Charles might have been a dream until she saw the newspaper.

She *thought* she remembered waking up in hospital, but the more she thought . . .

'Thinking again?' the Duchess asked with another dig of her sharp little chin.

The words of a song began to circle in her head:

Row, row, row your boat
Gently down the stream –
Merrily, merrily, merrily, merrily . . .

And there was the letter from St John Byle. It had been waiting when she got back. She'd read it and taken it straight to Mrs Cywynski.

The letter curtly informed her that her father's will had been resolved. She was entitled to an undisclosed eight-figure sum of money. There were papers to sign, but no other complications.

'Who *were* your family?' Mrs C had said. 'Exiled Russian royalty?'

'I never even said he was my father,' protested Victoria. 'I don't want any money. Why don't they leave me alone!'

'You could always give it to charity,' the landlady suggested. The noticeboard in her kitchen was covered in leaflets from the local cats' home.

'I'll think about it,' Victoria had mumbled. That had been a week ago.

As she sat on the stairs between Mrs C's flat and her own, brooding over the paper, she heard a loud thump as if something had fallen. It had come from the locked room – the forbidden sanctum that was the late Mr Cywynski's shrine.

Mrs C was out at her bridge circle evening, so Victoria went and listened at the door. There was definitely something moving inside. On impulse, she knocked. The movement stopped.

Silence.

The musty smell that had permeated the house seemed at its strongest here. She called Mrs Cywynski's name and tried the handle. The door was locked as usual. She waited.

It must be a cat, she decided. It had got trapped inside. Heaven knows how long it had been there.

She went into the kitchen to fetch the key from the dresser. But it had been removed. Undeterred, she searched for something with which to force the door. She had settled on a large screwdriver when she heard the front door open.

Mrs Cywynski was hanging her hat up in the hall as Victoria burst out of the kitchen.

'Oh, thank goodness. I think one of the cats is trapped in there.' She pointed to the shrine door. 'I heard it . . .' She tailed off as she saw the old woman's face.

'What have you been prying after? That room, it is private.'

'I know. I couldn't find the key.'

'What have you been doing? You certainly weren't expecting me home so early. Coming down into my home like this!'

'But you always let me. I was worried about the cats.'

'The cats, the cats. Impossible. The door stays closed. They cannot possibly be in there.'

Victoria was stunned. 'Well, *something* is,' she insisted.

'Nonsense! Nobody goes in there. *Nobody!*'

'I'm sorry,' said Victoria and went miserably upstairs.

Half an hour later there was a knock at her door. She let Mrs Cywynski knock several times before answering.

The landlady was there, all smiles. '*Kochano.* It is I who should apologize. I have checked and that wretched ginger Thomas was in there all the time. Please forgive me. I've brought you some biscuits.'

Victoria took the plate of fresh *piernicki* and closed the door. She was not convinced. When she had been looking for the screwdriver, 'that wretched ginger Thomas' had been sitting outside on the kitchen window sill complaining that he had not been fed.

The next morning at the museum dragged itself so slowly that she thought it might expire totally before it ever reached lunchtime. She had taken to spending her lunch hour in the hallowed rotunda of the Reading Room. She still had a century of history and culture to catch up on and the library was too good a place to waste.

The usual gathering of academics and researchers were there poring over their various ancient tomes, but she found a corner and began to study a copy of Karl Marx's *Das Kapital*. She had seen a man cleaning daubed paint off the huge bust of Marx on a tomb at Highgate and had decided to find out what all the fuss was about.

She was just dozing off when there was a disturbance. From somewhere in the room, she could hear a droning sound, like someone chanting. There was a chorus of indignant shushing. Various researchers were staring across the library in the direction of the droning.

Victoria stood up to see better.

A dishevelled old man was sitting at one of the central tables, a heavy book open in front of him. He had unkempt white hair and a dirty white beard. He was staring blankly ahead as he ran his fingers lightly across the pages of the book. He looked like a blind man reading braille. His chanting was becoming more pronounced, like a hell-fire preacher damning all sinners to the flames.

It was years since she had seen the old man, but she knew him immediately. She went cold as she recognized Professor Edward Travers, late of the Yeti invasion in the London Underground, and further back on her original visit to Det-sen.

And somewhere more recently than that, she was sure . . .

She intended to wend her way through the academics, but suddenly felt very faint and forced herself to sit down again. Two attendants were already descending on Professor Travers. As they tried to remove him, the frail old man picked up a white stick and lashed out wildly with an extraordinary fury. The weapon caught one attendant on the head with a resounding crack. The second was caught across the stomach and keeled over in agony.

The white stick seemed to lurch to the left, pulling Travers after it. The occupants of the Reading Room fell back to let him pass.

Victoria hauled herself up from her chair and called,

'Professor Travers' after him. He faltered, his back to her. Then he threw back his head in wild unnatural laughter and vanished through the doors.

There were general looks of astonishment. Several people stood round debating what to do and one very hasty person began to help the two attendants.

'Extraordinary,' observed a professor with a green bow-tie, who was next to Victoria. 'I'd say you were absolutely correct.'

'I'm sorry,' she said weakly.

'Travers. Yes, absolutely incredible. Definitely Travers.'

Victoria was feeling faintly nauseous by now.

'Of course, you're wrong,' continued the professor. 'Couldn't possibly be him. Ted Travers died . . . ooh, at least a couple of years ago.'

'Four years,' added another professor. 'Went to the funeral. Same week that my paper on Etruscan viticulture came out.'

'Must have been some sort of double then,' suggested the first. 'Extraordinary. I wonder what the odds are on that?'

'Excuse me,' said Victoria and made her way slowly across to the table where Travers had been sitting.

'Ah, fascinating stuff,' commented another academic who was leafing through the yellowing pages of the volume Travers had been reading.

'What is it?' asked Victoria.

The script was in symbols resembling Sanskrit. 'All about the Bardo,' said the academic. 'The astral plane. Out-of-body experiences. It's *The Tibetan Book of the Dead*. In the original, of course. Do you know it?'

Victoria excused herself from work and went home. When she reached the house, she saw that the hole in the pavement had been filled in. There was now an uneven mound of earth bigger than the hole it had once filled. Someone had stolen the paving stones.

The house was unnaturally quiet with no sign of cats anywhere. All she wanted was to lie down and sleep, but she was frightened of where her uncontrollable dreams might take her. There was something lying on the stairs inside her front door. It glinted in the late afternoon sunlight – a shred of web. She was too tired to pick it up. She shut the door, only too glad to shut out the world. Once upstairs, she lay down on the ancient settee and tried to sleep.

She could hear the grandfather clock ticking downstairs and the familiar gurgle of the central-heating pipes. Nothing else seemed real. A sudden gust of wind tore copper-coloured leaves from the chestnut tree outside and threw them at the window. Then the wind subsided and there was a dead calm.

'*Victoria*,' whispered a voice.

Something moved downstairs.

'Mmm?' she murmured, only half awake.

'*Victoria!*'

She was wide awake. It was nearly dark outside.

'*I need you, Victoria. You promised you would help. You came to me . . .*'

She sat tightly on the settee, unsure if the voice was real or only in her head. 'What do you want?'

'*. . . so I have come to you.*'

'Where are you?'

'*Here. Waiting.*'

She rose and went to the door that led down to Mrs Cywynski's flat. It was open. She could barely see down into the hall below. A cold draught was coming up out of the darkness to meet her, carrying the smell of mustiness with it.

Everything was slow and smooth, like a dream she had dreamed a hundred times before. She turned away and walked into the kitchen. In a drawer, she found a candle and lit it from the gas cooker. Then she went back to the door and started down the stairs.

The candle flame flickered in the draught. Its glow caught on swathes of web that hung from the hall lamp and draped across the windows and walls. The candle guttered and went out.

An ashen light was seeping into the hall. It came from deeper within the house. Victoria reached the foot of the stairs. At the end of the passage, the door to Mrs Cywynski's 'shrine' was ajar. The unnatural light came from within. She advanced slowly and pushed at the door.

The room was filled with trophies for golf and bowls tournaments. On the sideboard, there were photographs of Mrs Cywynski and a man who must have been her Andrzej. His pipe was set there with the tobacco tin he had kept since the war. They were all covered in web.

Across the room, in a high-backed leather chair, his stick at his side, sat the old man from the Reading Room. His face was curiously young for someone so long *dead*. But it was not alive, it was animated. The head twitched up at her and he gave a strange cry, half moan, half laughter.

When she saw his watery eyes, staring blind through the cracked lenses of his spectacles, all her other thoughts and fears fell away from her. Charles Bryce, Roxana Cywynski, St John Byle, the Harrises, the cats, Jamie, the Doctor. She would not forget the past, but she must look to the future. She had made her promise to him, travelled to find him and release him. Her leap of faith was complete. She had things to do. A new world to discover. And there would be things he could teach her too.

She took his frail hand, icy against her own, and let him run his dead man's fingers over the contours of her face.

'Yes. Yes, you understand,' he croaked, a smile beginning to twitch at the sides of his mouth. 'It begins here.'

She smiled gratefully and said, 'Welcome home, Professor Travers.'

5

Geneva.
Deadline: The Intermediate Future

'Goddammit, Bonderev! What the hell's going on?'
'I think the machines are winning, sir.'

'What's that?' The face-shape on the phone-screen was in New York, but the interference scrambling the definition could be coming from anywhere between the States and Geneva via the UNIT ComSat over the Atlantic. 'We have a Level Nine security breach, mister. There's someone in your system. And it's taken a whole half-hour to speak to you. I e-mailed you four times. And your fax has a communication error.'

Major Semyon Bonderev glanced across the Comms Centre. In the dimmed emergency lighting, he could see a fax machine sitting smugly in a tidal wave of spewed blank paper.

'Sorry, sir. Nothing's responding to us. But we're working on it. I'll be . . .' He hit the 'hold' tab, hoping that New York Ops hadn't seen, and then hung up. Then he tapped up his second line, answered its incoming call and left both phones to talk to each other. He sat back, pulled on the stub of his Turkish cigarette and tried to access the Overview System.

The terminal froze again as it checked for trojans and variants. Seconds later, the screen went green and hundreds of tiny glyphs began to can-can cheekily across the surface.

Bonderev pinched the skin at the bridge of his nose tightly. There was a little red cursor flashing behind his eyes. Soon it was going to print 'MIGRAINE' all the way through his head.

He rebooted and tried another system. Why did you

join the Army? he wondered. So that you didn't have to spend all day in the Moscow queues for employment or bread, he reminded himself. And if he was seconded out to the UN, because Russia had to send somebody as part of its commitment to the Security Council, that was OK too. Better than being sent to shoot people in Grozny.

Toni Diaz slid in beside him. She planted two fresh bottles of mineral water on his desk. 'Well?'

'Lousy,' complained Bonderev. 'Our intruder's right inside the mainframe. All the servers are blocked so we can't get at them. I think I'll go back to Moscow now.'

'Great,' said Diaz. 'I can't go home to Mexico City. My granny would miss the Swiss chocolate.'

They sat and looked at the terminal screen. The can-canning glyphs had settled into a less manic, more stately berserker-mazurka. 'I don't know where to start,' confessed Bonderev. 'Where's the DO?'

'Nobody's sure. But there's a lift stuck between levels Eight and Nine.'

'Crafty bugger!'

'If he's any sense, he'll stay there,' chanted Diaz.

Her pager bleeped. She glanced at Bonderev, who shrugged his knotted shoulders in defeat. She replaced one of his phones and then answered it with her code. 'Sorry, he's busy,' she said, grimacing at the Russian. 'No. It just chucked us all out. We're still trying to get back in . . .' She paused and a look of astonished disbelief flooded into her eyes. '*Jesus Maria*, you're joking!'

She put her hand over the receiver and said flatly, 'New York say they're picking up top-security UNIT documents on the Internet!'

'*Bozhe moj!* What sort of documents?'

'Personnel records. They want us to shut down completely.'

'We can't shut down,' he snapped. 'Not like that. We don't know what damage it'll do. This guy's got a counter move for every situation. He could be leaving bombs and viruses all through the network.'

'They're frightened he'll breach the defence systems.'

'Ah.' Bonderev lit another cigarette, while Diaz argued with New York. Finally she put the phone down. 'They're going to shut down anyway.'

'We'll see,' he said slowly. 'Of course, if our friend got in through the back door . . .'

'Then why shouldn't we?' they chorused together.

They scrambled across the office to a spare terminal. Bonderev began to laugh as he logged into the e-mail system. 'This I always wanted to do. Hack my way into the biggest global security system.'

'It's your own system,' commented Diaz.

'Even better! Anyway I inherited it, so it's not my fault.' He was already pummelling his keyboard. Within seconds he was surfing. 'Look at that!' A series of menu windows was opening up already. 'I'm in. That's crazy.'

'Someone's going to have to rewrite the whole UNIT caboodle.'

Bonderev was grinning in shock. 'Oh, it's back to index cards for us.' He was in Overview by now. 'Our friend can certainly teach us a thing or two. This is much quicker than usual. Look, he's unzipped us like a banana! Torn right through.'

Overview displayed a graphic map of the entire network divided into coloured vertical blocks. It highlighted a white path that cut laterally across, jumping from system to system. 'He's using the liaison facility I set up,' announced Bonderev proudly. 'The one no one ever bothers with.'

'He's searching for something,' said Diaz.

'And he's squirting everything he touches out into the Internet. Maybe he's one of these open government crazies.'

Diaz nodded. 'Probably British then.'

'Look, it stops in Personnel Records. He's still there.'

'Can you get a fix?'

Bonderev was almost gurgling with pleasure. 'Ach, my friend. We have you.'

There was a sudden surge of power around them and the lights came on full. 'Oh, no,' Diaz hissed.

Bonderev swore loudly. 'He's gone. And he turned the lights back on when he went.' He flopped back in his chair, disgusted. 'So close!'

'You weren't supposed to enjoy that,' she said.

The terminal pinged at them. A tiny smiley face began to flash in the corner of the screen. Bonderev groaned. 'I don't want an incoming message. I want to know who this bugger in the system was.'

Before he could even tap in a reject, the screen was emblazoned with a logo: a letter W with a spinning globe of the world balanced on the letter's central peak.

WISE UP!

'What the Gorbachev is this?'

THE UNIVERSITY OF TOMORROW
IS HANDING OUT THE FUTURE
TODAY

The Cutting Edge of Further Education

The Course YOU Want in A Community You'll Like

'I don't believe this,' complained Bonderev.

No More Lectures or Essays or Tutorials

'I believe it,' said Diaz. 'I'm only surprised it hasn't happened earlier. Get rid of it.'

The screen had begun to flicker. It suddenly whited-out totally – an angry glare as if the terminal itself had taken offence at her judgement.

But the seething white had a fascination too. It dragged you in. Got behind your eyes. Bonderev could feel it pulling.

With a clunk, the screen went dead.

'That's enough of that,' Diaz complained. 'Bloody commercials. That's what I joined up to escape from.'

'You should have joined the Foreign Legion,' Bonderev said. He was gazing disappointedly at the empty screen. In his head, the little red cursor was suddenly scattering 'MIGRAINE' glyphs by the thousand. Spreading out, jumping systems. This lot seemed to be dancing a triumphant galop.

6

Putting it Together

New World University is famed as the first establishment for further education to employ tutorial methods run solely by computer program.

The University stands on the north bank of the Great Coker Canal to the North West of London. The 350-acre site, once an industrial estate, has been re-landscaped into pleasant parkland by Capability Green, the well-known firm of ecological developers. From the bank of the canal, planted with rushes and irises and stocked with waterfowl, the wide lawns sweep up through drifts of daffodils to the University complex itself.

This first 'green-field' university is designed in a style reminiscent of Sixties red-brick, but combined with an accessibility entirely in tune with the Nineties. Ranks of pyramidal ziggurats march triumphantly across the horizon – a fusion of nostalgia and hope, just as education must build on the past to lay out the future.

Extract from *Carbuncle*, The Architects' Monthly.

The event was going well. Maybe too well. There was always room for disaster.

Christopher Rice was starting to enjoy his role as *mine host* to a select throng of the academic *glitterati*, but perhaps that was just the champagne. The main hall of the university's Charles Bryce Memorial Gallery was exactly the right choice of venue. When the guests got bored with each other, they could admire New World's fine collection of paintings and ethnic Tibetan art.

A number of Fleet Street *gutterati* had also manifested themselves. Christopher had faxed the media and was gratified to find columnists from the tabloids in about equal numbers to those from the broadsheets. Students, who were cheaper than casual labour, moved in and out of the guests with trays of wine glasses. They were wearing their green New World sweatshirts and yellow New World caps as they would for any other study day. The guests plainly found this a novelty. 'Just as if McDonald's were doing the catering,' brayed one particularly asinine woman. 'I wonder if we could borrow a few for Marina's twenty-first?'

Christopher summoned up a smile for her as he passed. It was all façade, all pleasantries. Just below the surface, they were all piranhas. There was a shoal now, mainly tabloid, over by a set of computer art displays. They were milling hungrily around Anthony, who, Christopher was forced to admit, had to be today's focus of attention. With the opening up of New World FM Radio to the national wavelengths, they needed a high-profile front man. Anthony had done pirate radio in the Sixties, Radio 1 in the Seventies (briefly), and the graveyard slots on Radio 2 and London Broadcasting in the Eighties. He was only on a six-month contract anyway. After that, Christopher hoped, enough talent would emerge through the students for him to dispense with the old lag. If there was a DJ equivalent of the ham actor, then Anthony was at the Spam end of the range. 'Just read the scripts you're given,' he told him, 'and don't mention the word "Chillys".' The down-at-heel DJ was too grateful to argue.

Christopher left him to the frenzied carnivores and headed through the gathering, towards the buffet. There were a lot of Men in Suits, but he was looking for one man in particular: Desmond Pennington MP, Education Secretary and *frightfully keen on what you're doing here.*

Christopher had five suits of his own, but he never professed to wearing them. His position as Marketing Facilitator at New World called for a more genial and informal approach. They were forcing back barriers here, after all. He was the mover and the shaker and so he dressed in a selection of exclusive pullovers to complement his carefully cultivated laid-back image – even if the Vice Chancellor *had* stupidly implied that a formal suit with wing-collared shirt might be more appropriate.

She was his only trepidation. God knows, he had tried to instil some sort of business acumen into the woman, but she was a lost cause; too cautious, too old-fashioned and too wrapped up in her mystical beliefs.

She was also too lenient with erring students. Lately, several had been caught abusing the computer tutorial systems. One in particular, Daniel Hinton, a Virtual Studies student, was a regular troublemaker. The devious little shyster whiz-kid out to get as much out of the system as he could. When Christopher advocated sterner discipline, *She* had pleaded for more understanding. Daniel was a special case, and the computer agreed with her. The gifted were always difficult, so they must make allowances. Christopher had lost face over that and was still smarting.

The name *Chillys* was her fault too. In an initial interview, she had referred to the first students as Children of the New World. She apparently thought this was a rather romantic notion. The *gutterati* had fallen on the stupid remark like slavering hounds on a lame rabbit and nicknamed the students Chillys. Christopher had been battling the whole cult idea uphill ever since.

The real trouble was, of course, that *She* was in charge and held the purse strings. But he had been working on that. Maybe with a little help from the government's lottery fund . . .

There was still no sign of the Secretary of State. At least the Vice Chancellor was late too, which was refreshingly unusual for her. Christopher had just reached the buffet when he felt a hand on his shoulder.

'Young man, I want a word.'

He turned and recognized the Member for Burncaster North demanding his attention. 'How can I help?' he oozed.

'You're the young man in charge here, are you?'

'I'm the university's Marketing Facilitator, yes,' said

Christopher, nodding to the ID badge attached to his pullover.

'Are you going to tell me all about computers then?'

'Well, what would you like to know?'

'I've been reading this so-called prospectus of yours,' said the MP, flourishing the glossy brochure. 'And I'd like to know how you reckon that a machine can teach someone better than a person. That's for starters.'

'I'm so sorry,' pleaded Christopher. 'I don't believe we've been introduced. You are . . .?'

The MP bristled with gratifying irritation. 'Clive Kirkham, Education Spokesman for the Opposition.'

'Oh, I see. Thank you so much for coming.'

Mr Kirkham was plainly not a man for suits either. His brown checked jacket had worn elbow pads and an air of the Oxfam shop. 'I want to know what you think you're playing at, Mr Rice.'

'Christopher, please. We try to keep everything on an informal basis here at New World.'

'Oh yes, very culty. User-friendly, politician-friendly too, I expect. And grant-friendly, no doubt.'

'We all have to find our way in today's climate. Remind me Clive, what's your party's line on financing education?'

'We think pupils are more important than Marketing Facilitators.'

'Good,' said Christopher. 'So do we. But just tell me, with technology advancing so fast, what happens in ten years' time to children who aren't computer literate?'

'They'll know how to talk to real people, that's what. Their total experience won't be confined to the Information Super bloody Highway.'

'Nor will our students be.'

'Then who writes the syllabus?'

Christopher cocked his head to one side and allowed himself a satisfied smile. 'The computer,' he said.

'Computer bloody couch potatoes,' blustered Clive Kirkham, 'with Chilly sauce!'

Determined not to let his smile crack, Christopher

turned to the buffet and scooped up a tray of finger nibbles. 'Vol-au-vent?' he suggested, thrusting the tray under Kirkham's nose.

The MP glared. 'There's no such thing as a free lunch,' he declared and turned on his heel.

'Christopher.'

She was approaching through the guests, and, he had to hand it to her, she certainly looked the part with her new executive perm and new dark green executive suit.

'There you are at last, Victoria. We were beginning to wonder . . .' He had just seen that she was being accompanied by Desmond Pennington.

She leant in close to Christopher and whispered, 'You don't have to serve the food, you know. The students are doing that.' He hurriedly put the tray down and saw that she was giggling. When she was in a good mood, it was generally a cause for concern.

'I think you know Mr Pennington?' she continued. 'Desmond, you remember Christopher Rice, our Marketing Facilitator.'

Desmond Pennington, tall, suave, in his early forties and wearing a dark suit, shook Christopher by the hand. 'Victoria and I have been talking long and hard,' he said. 'Most profitable.'

'I think you'll be surprised,' Victoria said with a wink and started to usher Mr Pennington towards the podium.

God, thought Christopher, what the hell's she done now?

BOOM, BOOM. She was tapping the microphone and nearly deafening everybody. 'Ladies and gentlemen. Thank you all for coming today.'

Christopher saw Anthony bobbing up and down with astonishment, his MC material for the event already undermined by his new boss.

'It's an auspicious day for New World,' continued Victoria. 'We always look to the future . . .'

Bla, bla, bla, intoned Christopher to himself. Just get on with it. He glanced around at the attentive audience. There were flashes from the cameras. It was a perfect photo opportunity. If they only knew that the woman was obsessed. She and the Chancellor too – a Chancellor who was never on site. Her *éminence grise*, who issued dictums in private conference with her as if from some other plane. Or was it the computer? The Chancellor and the self-regulating technological miracle he had created seemed indistinguishable. The computer was a vessel of power, a twentieth-century grail, dispensing knowledge, but making strange demands as well. Almost mystical, thought Christopher, and he sneered as Victoria treated the machine with slavish reverence. But in the right hands, Christopher was sure that its potential could be irresistible.

He was certain Victoria was a witch of some sort. Maybe one day the papers might get hold of that, but not quite yet. He still had things to do. The Chancellor needed information and he was the one who could provide it. He had wheels in play. In the meantime, he could humour Victoria Waterfield because she trusted him. And that way he would soon have the control and position he wanted.

She was still expounding her hopes to the politely petrifying gathering. Christopher looked up at the balcony overlooking the gallery. At first he could not make out the figure standing there. It was in the shadows at the back, staring down at them. A youth wearing what looked like a school uniform. As their eyes met, the youth registered a brief second of startled recognition. Then it simply melted away into the air like a ghost.

Christopher blinked several times, unable to take in the image. The figure was too young and did not wear glasses, yet it bore a striking resemblance to that devious whiz-kid Daniel Hinton.

There was a loud burst of applause as Victoria stepped back from the microphone and was replaced by the smiling Education Secretary. Christopher listened in mounting disbelief as Desmond Pennington announced that New World University was being formally recognized by the government as a Centre of Excellence.

(Enthusiastic applause.) Furthermore, it would be receiving a substantial research grant in recognition of its achievement. (Exultant cheering.)

'Good for you, Victoria,' he muttered aloud. 'But that doesn't solve your other little problem, does it!'

7

The Watch

Gordy sat on the bed and edged his head round the curtain. His mum was on the phone and too busy to notice. She had told him not to look, but that made it much more exciting. It was no good her telling him that it was all over, because he could still hear the sound. Even when it got dark, he could hear it. It went on and on.

Sshp, sshp, sshp, sshp without stopping, and it was starting to make him cross. He wanted to break something or throw something. *Sshp, sshp, sshp.*

He couldn't sleep either, so his mum had got cross too and shouted at him and he shouted at everything because he hated it and he could shout much louder than she could. So she started to cry.

He was looking again now, when her arms slid in behind him for a hug. He snuggled back into her long yellow hair, but she wasn't looking at him anyway: she was looking out of the boat window too.

They were still there across the water. Kate could see the two figures in yellow and green, sitting motionless on the boats at the other side of the basin to the *Mananda*. That damned tinny beat from their headphones went on and on, driving her crazy.

'No, Gordy.' She pulled him away from the window and plonked him down on the floor of the cluttered cabin. She took a deep breath and tried to stay calm. 'I told you to play down there while I'm talking.' She tugged the curtain shut and gave him a book to look at. Then she picked up the phone again.

'Sorry, Beth. Distractions.'

Her friend Beth, another one-parent family, was

probably used to these phone calls by now. All Kate expected was to hear sympathetic noises from the other end of the line, but at least Beth was a listener.

'Look, Beth, they're still there!'

'Who's that?'

For God's sake, thought Kate. I've told you before. 'Two of those New World weirdos.'

'Chillys?'

'Yes, whatever they're called.' She wasn't sure that Beth believed her. Her voice had taken on a *terribly* patient tone.

'Now what about the police? Have you tried calling them?'

'Of course I've called the police again. And the council. They think I'm crazy.'

'Now come on . . .'

'But the Chillys just vanish when anyone comes.'

There was a pause. 'I see,' said Beth.

'But they're soon back. I mean, why pick me?'

'Are you really sure it's you? You have been under an awful lot of pressure lately.'

'Of course it's me,' Kate snapped. 'I'm not imagining it!' She remembered Gordy and moved further down the boat to the bathroom. 'I don't know what they want. And I don't know what to do, Beth. I've no one else to talk to.'

'Right.'

Kate looked through the window. The Chillys were still there, staring across the basin at the boat. *Sshp, sshp, sshp.* Then she realized that Beth was saying something. There was an inordinate burst of crackling on the line.

'. . . if you're that desperate.'

'What? Sorry, this line's terrible.'

'I said, your father. Maybe he's the person to get something done.'

The idea brought Kate out in a cold sweat. 'My dad? Oh God, no. I couldn't do that.' She groped for excuses. 'It's at least six years since I even spoke to him.' She sat down on the closed loo seat and started to wallow. 'Look, the computer keeps crashing, so I can't work from home. And that damn noise all the time from their headphones. It's just wearing me down.' She lowered her voice. 'And it's disturbing Gordy. He can't stay here.'

'Oh, well that's simple enough,' said Beth. 'He can come here for as long as he likes.'

Kate hadn't even hoped for anything other than a little moral support. 'Would you? I mean really, Beth?'

'Course. The demolition duo'll be made up. They love sleepovers. For as long as it takes. No worries.'

'You're wonderful, Beth. But soon, please. He can't stay here. He just can't.'

'Soon as you like. Just throw his essentials into a bag. But you should come too.'

Kate shook her head. 'No, I can't. I must stay put. That would be like giving in.'

'No surrender, eh Kate?' said Beth. 'Jesus, you're a fighter. Must be in the family.'

'I don't know,' Kate said. 'Look, thanks. I'll have him ready by this afternoon. Thanks, Beth. We'll see you.'

She clicked off the phone and almost ran the length of the narrow boat. 'Gordy? Guess what? You're going to have a real treat . . .' She stopped. The main cabin was empty.

She flew up the steps out of the door.

Gordy was sitting on his swing on the bank. He lifted a stick and took aim. '*Kerpow! Kerpow!*'

Kate saw red. This was her family. This was what she hated. She yelled, 'No, Gordy! Not that!' And she was off the boat and grabbing the stick from him before he could even grin. He knew what he was doing. She forced her anger back in. She had to be reasonable. 'Come on, darling. Not guns. I told you before. Please, no guns. Now play inside until Auntie Beth gets here.'

She bundled him unceremoniously back into the *Mananda*. Across the oily water of the basin, the two watchers sat staring, unmoving. 'Bloody Chillys!' she yelled. She grabbed a piece of wood from the deck and flung it uselessly in their direction. 'Leave us alone!'

They stared. *Sshp, sshp, sshp, sshp . . .*

Kate turned away in frustrated despair. 'Leave us alone,' she repeated to herself.

It wasn't easy to wave him off. He had dragged Aloysius, his bear, round the boat, saying goodbye to everything as if he was going for ever. 'You know how to play on this, don't you?' complained Kate.

'Goodbye bath, goodbye bed, goodbye computer.'

'Don't worry, they'll still all be here when you get back.'

'Goodbye Grandad.'

Grandad sat on a shelf in a cheap plastic frame, schoolmasterish with a clipped militaristic moustache and a look that appeared preoccupied with business elsewhere. Typical, Kate complained. She wasn't quite sure why he didn't live at the back of a bottom drawer. Yet she had even got quite upset once when Gordy had knocked Grandad to the floor with his football.

'Sorry, Grandad,' said Gordy, who was upset too, and gave Grandad a dried apricot.

Today, rather to her horror, Grandad looked terribly solid and reliable.

As she bundled Gordy off the boat with his bags, the four-year-old (nearly five!) looked across the water and said, 'Goodbye . . .'

She clamped a hand across his mouth. 'You dare!'

'I was saying goodbye swing,' he complained emphatically.

Not daring to look back, she prayed the Chillys would not follow. When she reached the car park at the top of the towpath, Beth was already waiting in the car with the demolition duo.

'That phone call,' Beth said. 'You know which one. Just make it, will you?'

Kate hugged Gordy tight, both reluctant and relieved to let him go. He clambered into the back giggling with the others and didn't even turn to wave goodbye to her as they drove away. Only Aloysius stared, button-eyed, through the receding back window.

Kate walked slowly back down to the narrow boat. Aloysius had been her bear before Gordy purloined him. He was battle-scarred now, but she could remember when her dad had won him in a shilling raffle and he was as big as she was.

She passed the other boats on the basin, none of them occupied just now, as if there was a curse on the place. When she reached the *Mananda*, she was almost relieved to see the Chillys still in position on the other side.

So it wasn't Gordy they wanted.

8

Eye Spy

A tinny jingle erupted from the car radio, followed by a gush of slushy background mood music, all of it with an irritating ground bass beat. The DJ was tying himself into knots of unctuous fatuity.

'And it's a Mega-morning to all you slickers out there. You're jacked into N Treble U – the ones who share – bringing you our daily show on National FM Radio. I'm Anthony and this is where the jazzy bright day starts. A New World coming soon. The way it always will be.'

'And I mean that *most* sincerely,' jeered Sarah Jane. She swung her bright yellow Spitfire into the fast lane and broke free of the standard M25 snarl-up – at least for a couple of miles.

Undeterred, the DJ continued, 'You know, we want to share that with you all. Meantime it can be a *meeean* time out there, so let's unlock the beat right now.'

Bleahh, went Sarah. 'You've got to be joking. Give K9 some air-time and a few CDs and he'd do better than that.'

The music settled into a bland pop number by the latest teeny idols Fizzy Milk, which seemed coincidentally to continue the background beat, already an obvious hazard of listening to this station. In hope of something soothing, Sarah switched to Radio 3, but the Composer of the Week was Stockhausen and he was obviously not at his best on Thursdays. As a last resort she turned to Classic FM and hoped to stay awake until she got to the university.

She still hadn't decided on her line of attack. New World had employed her after all, but she was going to give them only about an eighth of what they wanted.

And, having listened to the bog-standard quality of their radio station, she couldn't work out what they could possibly want it for. Maybe she'd be better off investigating them. The fee was fine: they told her there would be an article in it for her too. It was the content that worried her. It had seemed simple enough: trace the people on this list. Some twenty-five years before, they had all been present at something called 'The London Event', but it would have helped if someone could define what the 'Event' actually was. No one seemed to know.

The official channels started clamming up immediately. They were almost racing ahead of her, slamming doors and shutting up shop before she even turned the corner. Sarah had plenty of strings to pull and favours to call in, but the more she uncovered, the less she knew. She began to run out of strings. Of the people on the list, several were dead, at least three had vanished without trace and those surviving seemed in truth not to remember.

She even knew two of them personally. The veteran TV presenter Harold Chorley of *Yours Chorley* fame had been delighted to see her again, but couldn't remember her name properly, let alone what story he had been covering in London a quarter of a century ago. He called her Sandra and kept staring over her shoulder as if he expected a cue card to materialize out of the ether.

What concerned her most was the large number of army names on the list. And the name of one colonel in particular. At that point, she decided it was definitely time to give New World University a good going over.

There was also another name, which, although not on the prescribed list, had emerged when she started to conduct her own research. There was no ID photo on the MoD report, old enough to be held only on hard copy. But the description of a male, aged approximately 50 years, height five foot nine, with long dark brown hair and eccentric dress, plus the almost deliberate lack of any other information, only confirmed his identity. It matched her own brief memories of one of several gentlemen that her best friend had once introduced her to. He said that they were manifestations of himself, but her best friend had the knack of talking scientific or philosophical nonsense. Or just being bloody-minded for that matter.

Anyway, that situation had been absurd, and it was much too complicated to explain to her university employees. The MoD report simply called him 'The Doctor', but that name, allied to that of Colonel Alastair Lethbridge-Stewart, was enough to set her blood tingling.

From a window high in the techno-studies block, Danny Hinton watched the yellow sports car pull up outside the reception block. Its driver, a woman with thick auburn hair, wore a smart fawn suit and startling cherry pink accessories. She was carrying a briefcase and hurried into the foyer as if she was late.

Danny closed the blind with a snap and turned to the terminal on the desk beside him. He had about an hour before anyone was due to use the room. An hour elsewhere; other places to access, snapping the blind shut on one existence as he jumped to somewhere better. All you needed was a key to unlock each door. Danny had the whole bunch. He knew how to find things – his special trick. Just visualize their location in his mind and go and collect. But that wasn't enough. Running away, they always said; the boy lives in his head. Well, maybe one day he'd log out of reality for keeps.

The screen, reflected in the lenses of his glasses, made him look unnecessarily studious. He wore a dark wool coat over his Chilly uniform, but he had swivelled the yellow baseball cap into reverse. He wore the headphones only when he could be seen. Even then, he never connected them to the radio receiver strapped to his belt. He didn't want his head full of that beat, that slow incessant pounding that all the others seemed to need. It wasn't a cosmic heartbeat or an aid to meditation or clear thought. To Danny, it meant slavish conformity like the metronome beat of the drummer on the galley ships.

He resented the cumbersome terminal and its keyboard. It let him go surfing when he liked. Easy. It unlocked the way into another world where the impossible could be everyday. But it was limited, man-made. The net could get tangled. He still had to log out and come back down to earth.

It was the same when he went flying, projecting himself out-of-body onto the astral plane – another trick. Soaring at will amid the congregations of stars, freed from responsibility and continuous assessment and lack of cash. Winning through to ever higher levels, higher etheric planes where he saw such beauty and wildness as his mind could not encompass. And once, hovering even higher through pearly clouds in some spiritual sky, he thought he had seen an immortal being, an arch-seraph or even God, its hundred wings beating like feathered torches.

But no matter what world he projected into, etheric or man-made, his physical body stayed anchored to what passed for reality. He was bound. He wanted to sever the silver cord and fly on and on for ever.

Working at the terminal, he consulted a crumpled piece of paper, tapping in codes that had taken weeks to visualize and find.

The screen presented a sequence of status reports on checks for viruses and trojans. Then a synthetic voice read aloud what was being printed.

'*Good morning.*'

The time and date appeared in the corner.

'*Please insert your identity code.*'

Working from the paper, Danny input a fresh set of codes. Almost immediately, the screen cleared.

'*Welcome to NEW WORLD.*

'*Have the Best One yet.*'

This is where we take the plunge, he thought. He tapped in a sequence that would take him into the administrative database. He had got caught here before, but that was because he had the sequence wrong. For that he had been hauled up before Queen Vic herself.

He'd always had this problem with authority. He

blamed the start of it on his dogmatic parents, whose inability to show affection resulted in a home run like a corrective institution. He was the only boy in the history of School House who volunteered to stay at Brendon for the holidays. Once he chained himself to his bed in the dormitory rather than go home for Christmas. Matron and one of the junior masters had to restrain him physically until his parents, none too pleased, were summoned to collect him. After that, all authority figures reminded him of his father.

Yet his hauling over the coals by the Vice Chancellor, whom he had expected to be the most repressive of all of them, turned out to be about as severe as a barbecue with a favourite aunt. Yes, Miss Waterfield admonished him, but all the time there was a wink behind her tone. It made her sermon seem at worst half-hearted, something to be got out of the way before she broke out the lagers. She had been far more lenient than he would have been with himself. She asked about his family – dodgy subject – and, considering his abilities with computers, how he rated the university mainframe? It was a bit like meeting the real Queen and finding out that she played the lottery and ate takeaway curry like normal people. He came away understanding why Victoria had this great reputation with all the other students. She had a sort of innocence that had no business in a business suit. It was at odds with everything in the place.

Which was more than could be said for the Marketing Facilitator, Christopher Rice. From the moment Danny had first seen the guy, there was an instant dislike. Rice was a poseur who liked to throw his weight about. Danny had been working on his terminal after hours and had surfed into something, he couldn't remember what now, that made him burst out laughing. At that moment, he saw Christopher Rice watching him across the ranks of terminals from the far doorway of the computer room. Christopher had said nothing, but the next morning there was an e-mail message warning all students that the computer room was out of bounds after session hours.

Every time Danny had encountered Christopher since, the unspoken look was, 'I'm watching you, you little creep.' And they hadn't even spoken yet.

That was why Danny had to know more.

The terminal pinged angrily at him.

'*Authorization Failure.*'

He nervously tapped at his teeth with a fingernail.

'*You have 10 seconds to enter Stage Three Security Key.*'

He consulted the paper and began typing. No. It was all wrong – a trick. He deleted it and stared into the screen for a moment. He visualized the mainframe and found what he wanted.

Speak the same code aloud. 'Waterfield.'

Aural response. The screen turned blue.

'*You are attached to Priority Zone Zee.*'

A line-graphic pyramid appeared and began to spin in the centre of the screen.

'Yes!' Danny made a little fist of triumph. Good game.

By the time Sarah Jane reached New World reception, she was considerably irritated. The university's one-way system consisted of enough junctions and circuits to fill a computer. There were Chillys everywhere, all neatly uniformed in green and yellow, all studious, all plugged into their headphones. Sarah guessed that Student Accommodation provided them all with neat pigeonholes in which to live and sleep. Further education had started to take on the attributes of the battery farm. Yet there was also an air of cheerfulness about the campus. The students all looked happy. Sarah found that doubly worrying – probably something in the tea. She began to wonder what exactly she had walked into.

She crossed the airy foyer where a group of Chillys sat motionless on expensive leather sofas. The crass beat of N Treble U FM was being piped in from somewhere.

The girl at the reception desk was another typical example of the breed. So bright and friendly with her 'Hi. Welcome to New World. How can I help you?', that Sarah thought it would be more appropriate to order large fries and a strawberry milkshake. Plainly there were no administrative staff here – the students were expected to run the place themselves.

'Sarah Jane Smith of *Metropolitan* magazine. I have an appointment to see the Vice Chancellor.'

The receptionist was staring at her computer screen while she tapped away at her keyboard.

Sarah added, 'I am expected . . .'

'At eleven o'clock,' completed the receptionist. 'Would you like to take a seat.' She handed Sarah a yellow pamphlet and indicated the sofas. 'Have the best one yet.'

Sarah gave a surface smile and sat down. On the speakers, the DJ started to babble something inane. The pamphlet contained the same New World hype that had made her switch off earlier. She glanced across at the waiting Chillys.

With one concerted movement, their heads swivelled to return her stare.

'Ms Smith?'

Startled, she saw a man standing beside the reception desk. He had slicked black hair and his smile oozed sincerity. Somehow it all matched exactly with the Bransonesque pullover.

'Welcome to New World. I'm so sorry to have kept you waiting.' As she stood, he took her hand firmly with both of his. 'I'm Christopher Rice, the Marketing Facilitator.'

'Good morning,' she said, somewhat taken aback.

'I hope you've brought the files.'

She tapped her bag. 'Yes.' Her heart wasn't in it. She was sure he could see right through her little subterfuge.

'Then come on up. Miss Waterfield, she's the university's Vice Chancellor, would like to thank you personally.'

He ushered her into a waiting lift and pressed the button marked eight. They stood side by side, she avoiding his eyes.

Once the doors had closed, he said, 'I think the sum agreed was twelve K, assuming all the personal profiles are complete.'

Sarah took a deep breath. 'Not quite.'

He still looked straight ahead and she suddenly realized that he was watching her reflection in the polished metal doors. 'Ms Smith, when we were advised of your reputation, both Miss Waterfield and I were impressed. We thought, what's a few red-tape barriers to a journalist of this calibre?'

She smiled at his reflection and said curtly, 'But you didn't tell me some of this data was government classified.'

The doors slid open with a thunk.

Without another word, he led her along a passage and ushered her into a spacious office. Its large windows and white curving walls should have made it starkly clinical, but the minimal furnishings gave it a surprising warmth and character. The hi-tech desk that dominated the room was surrounded by several strategically placed antiques: a walnut bureau, a tall and beautiful Chinese vase, a glass cabinet. There were also a number of framed photographs depicting scenes from the last century and several items that Sarah recognized as originating from Tibet: the head of a Buddha and two silver prayer wheels.

Miss Waterfield was sitting behind the desk in a high-backed leather chair. She looked over the top of her spectacles as they entered and then rose to greet her guest with a smile that was more formal than friendly.

Sarah had expected the Vice Chancellor to be older than this smartly dressed career woman. She felt uncomfortable because, although she was used to interviews, it was usually she who was in charge. She was sure that these two, who looked for all the world like mid-morning TV presenters, were going to leave a lot to be desired as far as their interviewing technique was concerned. She simply handed over the disk of information she had compiled and waited with increasing agitation as they flicked silently through the files on a screen she could not even see.

She knew the data well enough. A series of reports on personnel present at the 'London Event'. She could make out the ID photos reflected in the lenses of Miss Waterfield's glasses.

Annoyed at being ignored, she finally said, 'Look, I still don't know what New World wants these people for.'

Christopher, who had been studying the screen from over the Vice Chancellor's shoulder, smirked. 'Afraid of unearthing a scandal?'

Sarah was not going to be thrown. 'Half of them vanish off any records. And what's this "London Event" that connects them?'

'What do you know?' parried Christopher.

In for a penny, thought Sarah. If that's the way you want it. 'I've found records implying that about thirty years ago central London was evacuated in an industrial accident. They say it lasted three months. But there are no extant reports. No actuality. No one even remembers. How can that happen?'

Christopher never lost his superior air for one moment. 'The London Event was a wasted opportunity – the world missed out on interface with a higher plane of existence.' He shrugged. 'It's no big deal. Other chances come along.'

'It was totally misunderstood,' insisted Miss Waterfield. She turned away from scrutinizing the data and fixed Sarah with an equally intense stare. 'We all stumble about in the unknowing darkness. New World seeks to light the first candle.'

Sarah just managed not to laugh. The woman's sincerity was genuinely touching. 'Oh, come on. New World's more than just a New Age Sunday school. You've got fingers in more pies than Robert Maxwell.'

At this, Miss Waterfield looked slightly hurt. She glanced at the screen for a second and then reached forward to open a large painted box that sat on her desk. Inside, nestling on a couch of blue satin, was a mirrored metal globe.

'I'm afraid we've wasted your time, Sarah,' she said.

This time Sarah did laugh. 'You already knew all this. I should have known better,' she accused. 'New World has the solution.'

The Vice Chancellor nodded. 'That's our motto.'

'Our *program*,' corrected Christopher sharply.

Sarah was incredulous. 'But if you've got such high-flying sources, why employ me?'

Christopher slowly turned the gold ring on his index finger. 'There's still one name missing from your list.'

'Not to my knowledge,' replied Sarah.

'But much to ours,' said Miss Waterfield. She was intent on gazing into the depths of the globe as if it were a crystal ball.

Sarah had been wondering which story was worth more. The ease with which she had obtained classified MoD information, or the university that was prepared to pay for it? Whatever she decided, it would all have added up to a nice little exposé for her. That was until the names of people she cared about had started to emerge. And, of course, the information she had passed on was just the tip of the iceberg.

Even so, she was beginning to get the sense of a hornets' nest about New World University. She started to feel for the handle of her briefcase in the vain hope of making a scoot for the door.

'United Nations Intelligence Taskforce is a paramilitary espionage squad,' began Christopher as if he was kicking off a lecture. It was plain that they were testing her, so Sarah tried to feign disinterest.

'It's the old MI5 story,' he angled. 'Everyone knows it's there, but no one knows what its real agenda is.'

'Even those who work for it,' added Miss Waterfield.

Sarah returned their accusing stares and noticed a reflection in the Vice Chancellor's spectacles of the monitor screen on her desk. An old black and white image, instantly recognizable, of Brigadier Lethbridge-Stewart in his UNIT uniform.

Christopher blinked slowly. 'Colonel Alastair Gordon Lethbridge-Stewart figures largely in its setting up in the Seventies. He's a Brigadier by then with a remarkable active service record.' He leant forward slightly. 'And then he vanishes.'

'You must have known him during your time at

UNIT,' said Miss Waterfield.

Sarah shook her head wearily. 'Sorry to disappoint you, but I'm just a journalist.'

'With no "official" records of him, you could easily imagine Lethbridge-Stewart was dead,' continued Christopher.

The Vice Chancellor half turned to him. 'UNIT looks after its own.'

'What's this "Brigadier" supposed to have done?' Sarah enquired.

There was a sudden look of pain on her employer's face. 'He has committed a great crime,' she said. She plainly took this offence personally. Christopher edged towards her, almost as if to console her, Sarah thought. Miss Waterfield suddenly pulled up and said, 'There are other ways of seeking him.'

Simultaneously, there was a flare of light from the screen and a shrill bleeping sound began. It came from the silvered sphere. Beside it on the desk, a small white ivory pyramid began to pulse with an inner fire.

Cracking the Waterfield system had been a doddle, but now Danny was inside, there was nothing to do but nose through the files. It seemed to be all administrative records; nothing immediately political or in any other way damning. Even Victoria's diary was only a list of the future meetings she had to attend. Danny couldn't believe that she could really be so boring. He was skimming through the items faster and faster until he reached a file titled 'LOCUS'.

He edged in and found a series of documents flicking up onto the screen. Some were headed 'Ministry of Defence', others marked 'UNIT'. A number carried ID photos of military personnel. Danny tried to control the flow of images, but the function keys refused to respond. He guessed that he was monitoring another screen elsewhere on the same server.

The parade of documents continued as Danny tried to puzzle out why anyone needed to know about 'ARNOLD, George Albert – Staff Sergeant (DECEASED)' or 'EVANS, Gwyn Ivor – Private'. Then the screen went blank.

Danny tried the keys again, but they refused to punch down. They physically resisted. No exit. No escape from the file. He started to try other combinations, but the keyboard was jammed solid. He started to bite at his finger until the nail tore painfully.

The screen flickered into life.

Danny studied the new image for a second and gawped. It was a UNIT file and the ID photo was of Old Stewpot. Or, rather, Young Stewpot. Lethbridge-Stewart, the Brigadier, his old maths master at Brendon, but *much* younger. He was in full military uniform as he invariably was on School CCF Inspection Day.

School was three years back for Danny, although it seemed about a century. Three years since he was expelled for dabbling in the occult – or was given what the headmaster called 'early career benefit opportunities'. Danny's father was more concise with his condemnation. The school did its damnedest to avoid the publicity. Even so, the Brigadier had argued strongly and surprisingly in Danny's support. It had been of little avail, but in return, Danny had inwardly promised to be eternally grateful.

His parents had sent him here to New World as a last resort. A course in Virtual Studies. His father thought the university sounded 'just the job'. His mother didn't have a say. Danny thought it was a right-wing holiday camp. It was the last place he expected to re-encounter the Brigadier.

The image on the screen had begun to flicker, forcing Danny to screw up his eyes against the glare. The screen suddenly flared to a blinding white – a white that crackled out at him like a bolt of indoor lightning. He tumbled back in his chair shielding his eyes.

The light was howling at him like a trapped beast. Behind it he could hear a shrill repetitive bleeping. Through the gaps between his fingers, he saw that the monitor screen was turning slowly back and forth on its pivot like a deadly eye searching for a victim. He began to edge the chair backwards as twice the 'eye' passed over him. It seemed to be blind.

Something clouded his vision. With a gasp of revulsion, he saw that the fingers on his left hand, the hand closer to the monitor, were covered in strands of sticky web.

He sent the chair clattering as he hurled himself across the room and out through the door.

9

Flight

Sarah sat in her chair bemused by the sudden effect of the alarm on her interrogators. She seemed to have been all but forgotten. It might have been a good opportunity to escape, but she was fascinated and the cassette hidden in her briefcase still had twenty minutes' record time left.

'Someone in the secure system,' muttered Christopher.

Miss Waterfield seemed to be staring into the middle distance, a look of rapt concentration on her face. 'Daniel Hinton,' she pronounced.

Christopher smirked. 'That devious little . . .' He reached down and reverently lifted the bleeping sphere from its box.

The Vice Chancellor watched him apprehensively as he started towards the door. 'I don't want him hurt, Christopher.'

'Of course,' he smiled, and went.

On the desk, the ivory pyramid was still pulsing with light. Somewhere an alarm was sounding. Victoria Waterfield, now abandoned by her accomplice, sat staring at her monitor screen.

Sarah, determined not to waste this opportunity, moved quickly in on her subject. 'What is New World University?' she asked urgently. 'You don't have lectures. You don't even have tutors.'

Miss Waterfield turned slowly and regarded her with a look that was defensive and surprisingly vulnerable. She looked very small in the huge winged chair. 'All the tuition is conducted by the mainframe – a personalized syllabus for every student.'

'Since when did computers get personal?' complained

Sarah. 'Come on, what are the Chillys really for? Some sort of fascist hippy cult?'

Miss Waterfield shook her head gently. She began to remind Sarah more of a nun than a Vice Chancellor – all very laudable, but totally impractical. 'The wicked world is full of lost children: the aimless, the lonely. We follow the Det-sen disciplines that our Chancellor shares with us. We *really* do care.'

This compassion was very persuasive. Sarah did her best to resist. 'Where is he then?' she said. 'Why can't I see him?'

'The Chancellor *sees* no one. He has taken the Path of Truth.' The light of the pyramid was catching in her eyes.

Sarah thought back to the documents she had brought with her. In the context of her present situation, one name stood out. 'Victoria Waterfield,' she said. 'That's you on the list, isn't it? At the London Event?'

The result was immediate. The Vice Chancellor was plainly startled.

'You must have been very young then,' Sarah added.

Victoria nodded. She had recovered her composure startlingly quickly. A teasing smile spread over her face. 'Considering I was born over a hundred and forty years ago.'

Sarah half laughed. 'Peanuts, I used to know someone . . .' She cut herself short, embarrassed and confused. 'No. Sorry, I mean . . . you don't look a day over . . .' She mugged and saw to her relief that Victoria was giggling too.

'But I don't *feel* a day over . . .' She mimicked Sarah's grimace and they both burst out laughing together. They regarded each other for several moments, caught in a sudden unfathomable rapport, even affection. Sarah wanted to ask her to ring for some tea, then they could talk properly.

Victoria's smile suddenly faded. Her eyes were drawn back to the screen.

Sarah followed and saw that the text was endlessly printing:

Find the Locus
Find the Locus
Find the Locus

To the side was the image of the Brigadier.

Victoria's hand gave a little reflex jump. Her fingers seemed to reach out of their own volition to touch Sarah's face.

Sarah jumped back with a gasp. The air was suddenly cold. Victoria's voice had become cracked and hard as if someone or something else was using it. 'We all have pain to face, Sarah. But the Revelation will be soon.'

Startled by the sudden change, Sarah began to edge away from the desk. She picked up her bag and left the office.

Victoria shuddered. The voice in her throat croaked out again, reiterating its demand: 'Find the Locus.'

Victoria clutched at the sides of her desk. She gasped for air, her head pushing up to stare at nothing at all or something she saw in the ether. Her own voice, no longer usurped, whispered in fear. 'Daniel!'

The whole corridor pumped with the beat. It was pounding into Danny's head as he ran. His legs were going in time with it. He tried to stumble, tried to break the rhythm. Time was slowing up. He was nearly flying already.

Anthony, that's who he had to reach. The DJ would listen. He'd been complaining in the cafeteria the other day. He'd been there a month and he wanted to know what was going on. Danny had listened to him then, now he could listen back. He had contacts. He wasn't sucked into the system yet. He'd know how to reach the Brigadier.

'*You're jacked into N Treble U from New World. The people with the solution.*'

That was Anthony now. The beat went on, but Danny managed to career against the wall and slither to a halt in a doorway. It was a shock to realize that the beat wasn't feeding directly into his brain.

A bouncy jingle burst out of the speaker above his head. Danny eased open the door a crack and peered inside.

'*If you can't get your head round life, no hassle. There's over 300 different courses here at New World. So there's got to be a right one for you.*'

The room inside hummed: a deep growl like the chanting of Tibetan monks. It was the meditation hour. Row upon row of desks reached to the back of the computer room. Each desk had a terminal and at each terminal sat a Chilly, cap and headphones on, intent on his or her input. All neat rows of neat little automatic people. All with identical graphic patterns swirling on neat little screens.

Danny shuddered. His fingers were stinging where the web had clung on. With one concerted movement, every student in the room turned to stare at the crack in the doorway. Their eyes were ice cold, unseeing.

Danny ducked back and started to run again. He reached a stairway and saw two Chillys making their way up. He dodged back and headed for the fire escape.

Outside, he was away from the beat. He began to clatter down the corkscrew escape route. Halfway down, he heard a shout.

Christopher Rice was standing on one of the overhead walkways that linked the New World buildings, pointing up across the gap at the fire escape. From Danny's vantage point, he could see Chillys converging from all directions. Above him, there was the clatter of descending footsteps.

Alarms started to jangle. Alarms with a cosmic disco heartbeat. Danny reached the foot of the escape and started to belt along the concrete walkways.

Twice he faced them head on, but he knew the system. He could cut corners, jump levels, clamber across roofs, running them in circles until they dropped and he got maximum points.

He careered another junction and skidded to a halt. Gliding out of a side turning came a small silvered globe. It echoed the alarm beat with its high staccato bleeps. It paused and then changed direction, seeming to glide rather than roll towards him.

Danny panicked. He started to backtrack, desperate to reach a stair up to the next walkway before the pursuing Chillys. This wasn't what he had planned. He was going to be sandwiched. Already there were more of the students gathering behind the gliding sphere, content to follow as its entourage.

Danny tore at a group of bikes parked by the stairwell, scattering them across the walkway, blocking the sphere's path. He started to run up the steps, heading for the ramps that lead to the university generator rooms. Behind him, the globe reached the scattered bikes and began to weave to and fro, momentarily confused by the tangle of metal. The Chillys began to clear a path for the sphere.

There was no one on the next level up and Danny, his legs already giving out, made for the generator service area. He need only go a little higher to reach the feeder ramps and then down away off campus. But God only knew how he was going to find the Brigadier.

He struggled up to the crest of the walkway on what felt like his last breath and looked down towards freedom. A group of Chillys were heading up towards him. He looked back and saw more emerging from the stairwell. He ran to the edge and looked over. It was high. There was nowhere to run.

Both groups stopped short, one at either side of him. They waited as if afraid to upset the balance of which he was the pivot. The beat had stopped, but he could still hear from somewhere the high repeating pips of the sphere. There was a disturbance on the stairwell side and Christopher came pushing through the Chillys. He advanced, all cool smarm.

'Come back, Daniel. Nothing to be afraid of.'

Danny nearly laughed, but it choked in his throat. Christopher was coming closer. Danny climbed up onto the parapet. The ground below him swayed.

'Come on, Daniel. We're here to help you. You were chosen.'

The Chillys' fixed stare unnerved him. It was like invisible hands holding him there on the edge. He braced himself against it. 'It's a sham! The whole thing! It'll get you all!'

Christopher seemed almost nonchalant. 'It already has *you*, Daniel.'

Behind him, the Chillys parted and the sphere glided, bleeping hungrily, through the gap.

'Daniel the Devious,' grinned Christopher and stepped back for the sphere to approach. The object began to rock back and forth as if gathering power for a sudden leap at its prey.

Danny looked down in despair. Tears were gathering on the lower rims of his glasses. He felt a new rage stinging and burning up inside him. He didn't want to finish it here.

'Go on then,' suggested Christopher. 'There's no escape. Not even that way.'

Danny flung his arms out wide and threw himself into the air.

He felt the world rushing up and wind hitting him, whistling between his fingers. Everything was whirling past in a maelstrom of concrete and sky and branches. And somewhere he heard a voice, her voice, calling his name.

'*Daniel.*'

The air seemed to cradle him and carry him. The rushing fall became a cushioned swoop. Like the dreams of projection, like surfing, like flying. The ground no longer sprang up to smash him, but slid beneath him as he ploughed down into leaves and brown-smelling earth and darkness.

Game over.

The sphere jumped up onto the parapet, weaving back and forth on the edge. Beside it, Christopher, with Chillys gathering around him, stared down into the depths. There was no sign of the body.

The Marketing Facilitator watched the silver globe.

Even in defeat it was impressive, he thought, this mobile manifestation of the New World computer. And now it was having its own little temper tantrum. That's how advanced it was. Frighteningly advanced. Maybe a little possessive too, but then it had power to protect. It was already rewriting its own systems, outstripping anything humans could do. So he must stay close to the power. He had his contacts outside, that was why it needed him. But he must come closer, closer. No one else must be as close. He must make himself invaluable. Only Victoria stood in the way. And her beloved Chancellor, always so conspicuous by his absence. And this endless search for something the computer needed so desperately. This indefinable *Locus*, whatever that was, or the elusive Brigadier Lethbridge-Stewart. But he was happy to deal with that too. It was an expensive task, but Victoria was always ready to sign blank cheques for anything he needed. Her purse was the most important asset they had and it would be suicide to get rid of her just yet.

10

By the Sea

The wind was freshening, whirling little sand devils out of the dunes and across the wide, wild expanse of the beach. The tide had dragged the sea far off into the distance. It left a flat exposed area of grey, rippled mud broken only by the occasional pool in which bits of upside-down sky had got trapped.

Somewhere a telephone was trilling. It mingled with the jaunty *oompah* of a distant military band. If there had once been bathing machines, they had all been dragged away by the tides of time.

From the dunes, the Brigadier, clad in his favourite tweed jacket and cap, surveyed the beach with a look of satisfaction. In the distance, he could make out a group of blazered schoolboys – or were they uniformed squaddies? – kicking a ball about. He drained the cup of tea he was carrying and started down onto the beach.

The air was very bracing here. It took him back to his own childhood visits to the seaside – long family walks and building complex strategic fortifications in the sand that never withstood the advancing forces of the smallest waves.

He stopped to look at a large piece of flotsam, a London Underground sign for Piccadilly Circus, that lay half sunken in a pool surrounded by more trapped bits of upside-down cloud.

He sniffed, rather appalled at the stuff that got dumped overboard these days. He was pleased, however, to find that his cup was replenished with tea once again and drank it down smartly.

Dark storm-clouds were building on the horizon. The Brigadier was sure that somewhere that phone was ringing again. Nearby, a small boy with matted curly hair was building a pyramid out of sand.

The Brigadier smiled indulgently. There was a sudden violent animal roar and he ducked, spilling the remains of his tea, as a shadow swooped in low over him. There was nothing in the sky, but when he looked down at the sand, he saw a monstrous footprint.

Distant thunder grumbled out to sea. The Brigadier crouched and ran his leather-gloved hand across the contours. The footprint had four massively clawed toes. It took him back. The roar of lumbering brutish machines echoing through pitch-black Underground tunnels. Luminous heaving web, dead men walking and the roar of the angry Yeti. It dragged him right back to the beginning.

He stood up, alert, eyes darting round for danger, his hand pulling his revolver from inside his UNIT uniform.

There was nothing he could see. The beach was suddenly deserted, and the sand all around him was blemished only by the single clawed footprint.

Convinced that there was no immediate threat, he tried to replace his revolver in its holster and found that he was spilling tea down his tweed jacket. He shrugged off his foolishness and set off on his constitutional with a spring in his step. He wasn't sure what he was making for. It didn't really seem to matter, even when he realized that in the unblemished sand he had left no footprints of his own at all.

He headed down towards the sea and gazed out across the breakers as they thundered out on the open water. By the time they reached the shore, they had turned to submissive little ripples at his feet. A lone seabird, its head capped with blue, was wheeling and swooping above the tumult. Its cry was a lonely protest against the blustering wind. The UNIT symbol was emblazoned on its khaki wings.

Distant thunder again. A tiny spark of light flickered repeatedly on the horizon. A lighthouse or lightship or guttering star, he decided. He turned and began to walk back inland.

There was a dark figure on the dunes, too far away to be clearly defined. It seemed to change shape, expanding and shrinking without altering position. Even at this distance, he could sense its fierce scrutiny. He headed towards it.

'Sir? Please, sir?' said a voice at his shoulder. A moon-faced young man in his mid to late teens was watching him intently. He was dressed in a scruffy Brendon blazer. The Brigadier grappled for a name.

'Hinton? Good Lord. What are you doing here?'

The boy had sand in his gelled hair. 'Hinton, D. A., sir. School House '91.'

'Yes, of course.' The Brigadier glanced back at the dunes, but the figure had vanished. He studied the boy instead, trawling his mind for memories. 'It must be a good three years since you got yourself expelled.'

'Yes, sir,' Hinton admitted sheepishly. 'But I need to talk to you now, sir. It's important.'

The Brigadier sighed – a reflex reaction. Whenever boys wanted advice, he was always in the thick of marking or writing reports. 'Well, make it snappy then.' He was relieved to find that they were already sitting in deckchairs. He sipped his tea while Hinton looked awkward and ummed and ahed round the point. The way the wretched boy always behaved when he was in trouble. It had been exactly the same three years ago. It took him back.

'Frankly, Hinton, I don't know how you could throw it all away. You excel at maths and computer work.'

The boy pulled a long face. 'The headmaster says I'm "a disruptive influence", but it wasn't deliberate, sir.'

'No more than losing your CCF kit or skiving off games,' observed the Brigadier. 'This occult nonsense. Dabbling in black magic is a dangerous business.'

'It was a seance, sir. Not black magic, or drugs.'

'No?'

'I've done it loads of times. I suppose it's a gift.'

'You have no idea what you're playing with.'

Hinton grinned. 'No, sir. Not natural, is it?' As if

realizing his impertinence, he gazed wistfully out to sea. 'Do you have family, sir?'

Lethbridge-Stewart gave him a weary and withering look. Somewhere he thought he heard a phone trilling. He glanced round at the beach. The shape on the dunes had reappeared. It was closer and he could see that its undefined form was caused by a dark cloak that billowed in the wind around the hooded figure.

'You realize we're under surveillance,' he said, but the wretched boy's deckchair was empty. He stood to face the distant figure and once again felt a power emanating from its presence. It was a challenge, he was certain of that. He stood firm and defied it.

The figure did not move. Two tiny figures on an empty beach, buffeted by a wind that blew in from a sea, carrying memories from the past or dreams of the future. Two defiant wills locking horns in a vying for power.

The Brigadier was listening to words torn by the wind. '*Where is the Locus?*' The whispering of a woman or siren.

'Who are you?' he barked.

The surge of power from the figure grew in strength. Bracing himself, he heard the roar of a wild beast again. The figure seemed to split as a second massive shape rose and strode out of the first.

'Yeti,' he muttered and reached again into his military tunic for his gun. He pulled his hand out in disgust. Web was clinging to his fingers.

The power surge had begun to obliterate everything else. It funnelled at him, swirling round him like blown sand. He was physically forcing against it. The beach was starting to tilt top-heavy towards him. It was rearing above him, tumbling in. He could not bear the weight alone. Sand and light were choking into his face. A high-pitched silvery note whistling in his head like a cord pulling him down, down, down . . .

The television flickered balefully in the corner. Its empty, white screen had become a monstrous eye, a cyclops that fed on the minds of its subservient prey. It crouched, transmitting nothing yet still horribly active, emitting a continuous high tone of triumph over its prostrate victim.

The Brigadier floated by the ceiling watching himself slumped asleep in his armchair in front of the television. He looked a world-weary and lonely figure, a saucer and overturned teacup balanced on top of his pullover. His appearance was dishevelled with several days' stubble on his chin. His moustache needed trimming. He snored and twitched. A bad show all round. He was letting things slip. There were cobwebs up by the cornice. Somewhere he was aware of a phone trilling.

A voice clunked in, a tinny, formal imitation of himself that he should have renewed some time ago. Abrupt, martial, no nonsense, and still thoroughly uncomfortable with these blasted machines.

'*This is Alastair Lethbridge-Stewart at School House, Brendon. Leave your name, number and message after the tone and I'll call you back as soon as possible.*'

A series of pips followed. Then a woman's voice on a very crackly line said, 'Oh hello, Brigadier. This is Celia.'

As if yanked by a winding cord, the floating Brigadier rushed down into his prostrate body with a snap. His eyes came open and blinked several times. He stared up at the ceiling, which seemed considerably more familiar than usual.

The voice of the school secretary still clucked out of the answerphone. 'The headmaster was very concerned that you missed the meeting about your retirement party this morning. We've also had several rather strange phone enquiries about you. Could you get in touch ASAP? Thank you.'

There was a short burst of tone which mingled with the other continuous note from the staring television. The Brigadier swallowed. His mouth tasted like dry cardboard. He sighed. For some reason, he had been certain he was in Cromer. He rubbed his grizzled face and looked at his watch. It was just past thirteen hundred hours on Tuesday.

Tuesday?

'Nonsense.' The curtains were still drawn, but light was seeping in from outside. 'You stupid machine,' he muttered to the watch and hauled himself out of the armchair. He had never really got the hang of setting the thing. Always the wrong date or wrong time or the alarm going off in the middle of the school concert.

His joints were stiff and creaky. He switched off the irritating television and pulled back the curtains. The sun was very high in the blue sky. The wallflowers in his window box were wilting. Ridiculous, he had only watered them yesterday. It couldn't have been that hot.

He peered across the avenue. There was a gas van parked a short way along. Odd. He had somehow known it would be there, as if he had already seen it. The image of the van in his mind was from above as if he had flown over it. The man who should have been sitting in the driver's seat was gone at any rate.

He pressed playback on the answerphone and pottered into the kitchen while the tape wound back and back. The milk in the fridge looked a bit suspect. He sniffed it and grimaced. It was cheesy, but the fridge was quite cold. He looked at his watch again and tapped at the dial in annoyance. From the kitchen he could see the front door. On the mat sat a handful of letters and at least three newspapers.

Another voice came from the answerphone. A much younger woman who sounded awkward and distraught. 'Look, erm . . . it's me . . . Dad.'

That stopped him in his tracks. He stared at the phone and the framed picture beside it. A girl of about twenty with shoulder-length blonde hair and giggling eyes. 'Kate?' he said.

'I'm sorry . . . I know that it's been a long time. This'll be a shock and all that . . .' She swallowed. This was plainly an agony for her, and that was an unforgivable and unnecessary suffering. She was pacing the words slowly and deliberately. ' . . . but can I see you? Soon please, Dad. Sorry. It's 0122 69046. Erm . . . thanks.'

The Brigadier was immobile for a moment, going back. How long? Five? Six years?

'*Saturday. Threefortyfour p.m.*,' said the answerphone.

'Stupid machine. Can't have been asleep that long.' He could not take it in. He could deal with aliens, dinosaurs, even the British public schoolboy, but this left him in total puzzlement. He pushed the newspapers aside and opened the front door. There were five full milk bottles on the step. This was absurd.

A clipped voice with a public-school swagger was next to emerge from the answerphone. Officer material, he thought instantly.

'Greyhound is asked to call Trap Six. I repeat, Greyhound to call Trap Six.'

It was the UNIT emergency call sign. In a reflex movement, his hand went to check for his gun, a movement for which he immediately reprimanded himself. He hadn't worn a gun since he left the UN.

'*Monday. Tenofive a.m.*'

'Monday? What happened to Sunday?'

The answerphone clicked again.

'*No further messages.*'

He reached out to a door frame for support. Nonsense. No one slept for three days. Something was up. Something serious if UNIT were calling him in. He was still standing in the open front door. Along the avenue sat the empty Gas Board van. They were always digging up the pavement out there. Replacing faulty pipes or laying cables. He flexed the fingers on his other hand. They itched as if something had caught on them. He studied them with a suspicion that this had happened before.

The phone trilled again.

Now what? He was reluctant to answer. Suddenly he was under fire. A bombardment of things from the past. It would be easier to ignore them all and stay put in his comfortable rut. Why did they need an old fuddy-duddy on the verge of retirement? He hadn't seen active service for almost twenty years. He was a schoolmaster now, so why didn't they just leave him alone?

The phone kept trilling. He had switched the answer-phone off. He looked the length of the hall at the host of army photographs and his displayed collection of medals. It was no good. He knew he was talking out of his hat. He wasn't half as old as he felt . . . yet. He picked up the phone.

'School House, Brendon,' he said, carefully avoiding his name. There was a slight burr on the line. 'Who is this?'

As soon as Sarah Jane reached her car, she checked the cassette in the hidden recorder. About forty minutes of tape had been used. On the campus, the alarms were still ringing. Several groups of Chillys ran from one of the main blocks, heading along the walkways out towards buildings close to the university's perimeter.

Sarah was torn between instincts: either to find out what was going on or to get the hell out of the place. Forcing herself to think rationally, she picked up the car phone and called home. Predictably, it was scarcely a second before the call was answered. There was a slight electronic burr on the line.

'Mistress?' said the tinny, slightly precious voice.

The instant recognition always disconcerted her, but of course the receiver had monitored the incoming number. It was part of one of his innumerable programs.

'Hello K9, I need a telephone number.'

'Yes, mistress. I have one hundred and ninety-six thousand, seven hundred and thirty-nine numbers available.'

'Oh, good. It's the Brigadier's number. Brigadier Alastair Lethbridge-Stewart. His home number. He's teaching at a school somewhere, but I can't remember which one.'

'Checking files.' There was a whirring noise, which meant that K9 Mark III's electronic ears were waggling. Sarah glanced out of her window. The campus was suddenly deserted, but the alarms continued.

A signboard she had only just noticed pointed the way to the Charles Bryce Memorial Gallery. Her heart always sank when she saw Charlie's name. The circumstances of his death had been hushed up, but people whispered. Even so, to see his name here was so much at odds with the coldness of the place. To Sarah, he was always laughing, even if at times that laughter was desperate. Why was it always the least deserving and most alive who were carried off? Her hand reached for the ignition.

'No number available, mistress.'

Sarah smacked her hand on the steering-wheel in frustration. 'K9, are you logged into the Internet?'

'Affirmative, mistress.'

'Could you access ex-directory numbers?'

Another brief pause. 'Affirmative, mistress. Number located. School House at Brendon College in Hertfordshire.'

'Oh K9, you're a retriever in a million. Can you put me through?'

'Affir . . .' The line whooshed as if the wavelength was changing. Music began to pump in. Sarah recognized the mindnumbing beat immediately.

'You're listening to New World FM. Your daily curriculum of fun and food for thought.'

Sarah started to shake the phone. 'K9? K9, are you still there?' The beat was mingled with hissing and burbling through which she could hear her faithful computerized hound calling for her.

'Mistress? Mistress? Please respond.'

'This is the station that beats time. A New World coming soon.'

'Mistress . . .'

'New World has the solution.'

The two voices were becoming interchangeable. K9 was fading. Sarah found herself incapable of tearing the phone from her ear. The beat was losing all its bass and accompanying jangle, paring down to a single repeating high note that began jabbing into Sarah's thoughts. She felt sick and gasped for breath. Her shaking hand grabbed out, knocking the contents of her case over the car floor.

There was another whoosh and the line cleared again.

. . Mistress?' she heard K9 saying.

K9. Thank heavens.' Her heart was racing. She wound down the window and took a deep gulp of air. The alarms on the campus had stopped.

'Interference on line dispersed, mistress.'

'Don't get me that number yet,' she said. 'I want to get out of here first.'

'Number already ringing.'

She heard the line trilling and glanced warily round. The area was still deserted.

'School House, Brendon,' barked a familiar voice. 'Who is this?'

'Hello? Brigadier? This is Sarah Jane Smith.'

'Good Lord. Miss Smith?'

Her mouth had dried. She gulped at the air again and said urgently, 'Yes. Look, just please listen. You could be in danger. I'm at the New World University . . .'

A grating blare of tone cut across the line.

'Hello? Brigadier?' There was no answer. A shadow fell across the side window. A Chilly was staring intently in from only a foot away. She heard the tinny beat from his headphones.

She grabbed for the key and turned the ignition. The engine fired into instant life. She put her foot down, took the corner far too fast and sped out of New World on scorched and screeching tyres.

'Hello? Hello? Miss Smith?'

The voice cut out into the gloom of the silent office. Blinds had been drawn across the windows. The hard light from the monitor turned Victoria into a statue, silver reflecting as her unblinking eyes returned the stare.

'Miss Smith? Sarah? Are you there?'

A strand of web from the shrouded monitor drifted across her face.

'We have him,' she whispered, her voice as cold as space.

11

Neighbourhood Watch

He ignored the ringing of the doorbell. He was about to get into the bath when it started, closely followed by a rapping at one of the downstairs windows.

'Brigadier,' called the letterbox, which had a redoubtable female voice. 'Brigadier? Try to call out if you can't move.'

No blasted peace for the wicked! He pulled on his well-worn dressing gown and stumped downstairs. The headmaster's secretary, known as Twickers by the boys, was standing agog on the front doorstep surrounded by milk bottles.

'Celia,' said the Brigadier flatly, his usual charm wearing even thinner than his dressing gown. 'What can I do for you?'

'Thank goodness. I thought you might have been lying unconscious in here for days on end.' She barged past him, eyeing the newspapers that still lay inside the door. The navy cardigan draped over her shoulders flung its arms wide in shock as she started her whirlwind inspection. Why was it that whenever she popped in, an increasingly frequent occurrence, he felt as if he was on full dress parade? At this moment, he needed a visit from her even less than one of the cakes she seemed to have developed a habit of bringing him.

'Well, as long as you're up and about,' she continued. 'Did you get my telephone message?'

'Yes, I heard it. I'm sorry, I've been busy. I've been away.'

To his annoyance, she was casting about in the front room, plainly looking for the bottle he had been hitting.

'How nice to go away on the spur of the moment. Where have you been?'

'The seaside,' he snapped. 'It *is* the Easter holiday, isn't it?'

'I thought perhaps you were having a party. All that milk.' She stood waiting for some explanation.

'Celia, the phone calls you've been getting. Who was it?'

'I've no idea. The man didn't leave a name or a message.' She had picked up the newspapers from the hall and was threatening to start tidying up. 'He just asked for Brigadier Alastair Gordon Lethbridge-Stewart. I'm sure it wasn't a parent. And since I won't give out direct numbers and told him so, he just hung up.'

'I've had some strange calls too,' said the Brigadier.

'What you need is a cup of coffee,' she said and he was just in time to block her path into the kitchen.

'I was about to have a bath.'

'Were you, dear? I thought I could hear water running.'

He made a dash up the stairs for the bathroom and began mopping the floor. It was no use arguing with Twickers; the old busybody was already tidying up downstairs. That was humiliating in the least. Just, he suspected, what she had always hoped for, but he had other more bewildering things on his mind. He had his bath, as long a bath as possible, until the water was tepid. It gave him half an hour of seclusion in which to take in events and plan his strategy. He shaved, dressed and went back down to the coffee Celia had waiting.

'Do you remember Daniel Hinton?' he asked.

'Hinton D. A.,' she said, dunking one of his ginger biscuits. 'That boy was never out of trouble. Very twitchy. Finally expelled three years ago for terrifying the fourth-year dormitory with some black-magic nonsense. And quite right too. Matron's cat never got over the shock. Why do you ask?'

'I don't know,' frowned the Brigadier.

Celia shrugged her cardigan with irritation. 'That's all right. I don't expect to be told anything. I'm sure you think I'm interfering, but if you need to talk . . . Oh,

Brigadier, please stop pacing up and down like that . . .'

He kept glancing out around the side of the curtain. 'I have to go out.'

'But you only just got back. If you'd wanted some shopping done . . .'

'I'm quite capable of getting in provisions myself.' He was squinting out of the window. 'Good Lord.'

Celia stepped up behind him, but he pushed her back.

'No, no, no. Keep down.' He angled a finger at the school field across the avenue. 'There. Do you see? On the far side by the pavilion.'

A figure was there. A woman, tiny, but the black hooded cloak made her stand out against the stark vista of the field.

'Where?' asked Celia.

'Over there. On the boundary. I'm sure I've seen her somewhere before.'

'Are you sure?' she said, but she was looking at him.

'Yes, definitely familiar. Recently too.'

'I'm sorry, Brigadier.' Her hand touched his arm. 'I can't actually see anyone.' Her look was one of sad concern.

'Just there.' He looked where he had pointed and saw that the figure had vanished. 'Well, she's gone now.'

'Yes,' said Celia slowly.

'I'm not imagining it you know.'

'No, of course not.' She looked along the avenue. 'I wonder when they're going to start digging things up. That van's been there for days.'

The Brigadier frowned and peered through the window at the Gas Board van. There was a figure slumped in the front seat. He appeared to be asleep.

'Perhaps I should ring the Gas Board,' Celia suggested. Any stranger seen loitering around the school grounds was a cause for concern. 'Or even challenge him.'

'Not just yet. I don't think the Gas Board will know.'

Celia took another swig of coffee. 'Brigadier, is this all to do with those phone calls?'

The Brigadier smiled. 'Nothing to worry about, Celia.

Just some old army colleagues trying to get in touch, I expect.'

'They have a strange way of going about it, I must say.'

'Well, must get on.' He started to usher her towards the door.

'The other reason I came round was the retirement meeting?'

He was suddenly flustered. 'Sorry, I was forgetting. Can't be for a few days yet. I may be away again. I'll give the headmaster a ring and apologize.'

'You *will* be back before term starts?'

'Oh, yes. Not to worry, Celia. Just some business I have to attend to.'

He finally closed the door on her and watched from the window as she marched towards the van, cardigan flapping. It had come as no surprise when he had discovered that Twickers was merely a conflation of Celia's original nickname, Old Tweed Knickers. For sheer formidability, she earned every stitch of it.

The van's occupant had sensibly disappeared, but Celia made a note of the number plate and set off in the direction of the headmaster's house.

Sarah waited until she got home before she rang UNIT. She was not prepared for the changes that had occurred to the once familiar organization. Security had been radically upgraded. She was subjected to a series of identity checks. Her name was recognized by the personnel system, but when it was established that she was a journalist, all the doors started to slam shut.

'How did you get hold of this number?' she was repeatedly asked.

She was tempted to tell them that her dog had found it. 'I always used this number when I spoke to Brigadier Lethbridge-Stewart. You can check on your files.'

'Yes, Miss Smith, but according to records that was nearly twenty years ago.'

'How many other breaches of security have you had lately?' she asked.

'Why are you ringing, Miss Smith?'

'I have important information. I told you, I used to work with Brigadier Lethbridge-Stewart.' As an afterthought she added, '*And* the Doctor.'

'Just one moment.' There was a long pause.

'I think we've rattled them,' she muttered to K9. The angular metal dog was parked beside her chair, monitoring the call intently. His tail wagged slowly in positronic appreciation.

'Miss Smith.' A suave male voice on the line. 'Captain Cavendish of Virtual Ordnance Group. Perhaps I can help.'

'I hope so, Captain.'

'I gather you used to work for UNIT.' He sounded condescending and a little bored.

'Yes, in a periodic capacity.'

'I see. That would be with Brigadier Lethbridge-Stewart.'

'Yes. Look, perhaps I could speak to your current CO. Is it still Brigadier Crichton?'

'I'm sure you can pass any information you have on to me, Miss Smith.'

'I'm not sure that I can,' she said. 'It *is* very urgent. It concerns UNIT security.'

'Right. Perhaps I should say that if there is a security breach, we will be addressing the problem.'

'You mean "no comment".'

She had to hand it to him. His voice stayed absolutely smooth. 'I'm sure that if there is a need, then a press statement will be issued.'

'Oh, come on. This is about the Brigadier . . .'

'Naturally Brigadier Lethbridge-Stewart's safety is receiving our full and discreet attention.'

'Why?' she demanded. 'What sort of trouble is he in?'

'Perhaps you'd like to come in and tell us what you think you've uncovered.'

'I didn't say that.'

She could hear him smile. 'Even so, as a former employee . . .'

'I was never "employed" as such.'

'I could arrange an appointment.'

She was starting to get very wary of this persistent crocodile charm. 'Thank you so much for talking to me, Captain Cavendish. I don't think I'll come in if you already have everything in hand. My dog wouldn't like it. Good morning.'

Sarah put the phone down and breathed a sigh of exhaustion. 'Oh, K9. As long as they don't decide to pay us a visit in return.'

The robot dog retracted his aerial from the telephone. 'No worries necessary, mistress. The call was re-routed through my personal transmitters and is therefore untraceable.'

She rubbed her hands across the back of her neck. 'I only hope you're right. Something was very wrong there. You don't think, I mean it's stupid but . . .'

'Mistress?'

'No. Well, I mean, I had this sudden thought. I mean supposing UNIT had been nobbled.'

The phone trilled. Sarah nearly choked on her tea.

12

Anthony

Anthony, his temper up, emerged from the lift and aimed a savage kick at the doors as they snapped hungrily closed, just missing him. 'Hah, better luck next time!'

He headed towards the Vice Chancellor's office. The trouble was that all these corridors looked the same. All Sixties-style breezeblocks, which the architect obviously assumed gave the university a historic traditional feel. '*Very Malcolm Bradbury, Very Sanderson*,' he complained on frequent occasions, but no one under twenty-five got the reference.

A couple of Chillys, plugged into their walkmans, approached. 'Hi kids,' he sneered. 'Been in any good deprograms lately?'

They ignored him, drifting past like zombies.

'Want any autographs?' he called after them. 'If you can read, that is,' he muttered. He had deserted his post, leaving a syntho-pop medley playing on the grams. It was pumping out into the corridors all over the campus. Yet the Chillys weren't even listening to it. Their headphones played a simplified version of the beat. He had tried it, but it literally gave him a bad head after only a few seconds.

He already hated the place. The students didn't behave like students. No illegal parties. No oversleeping, not even oversleeping in each other's rooms. No jailbait available. They were seriously dead, these Chillys. So chilled out that their minds and other faculties were frozen solid. Stepford Students. *I'll just die if I don't get that degree. I'll just die if I don't get that degree.* Students should be radical and dishevelled and late for lectures – he had been. Gigs for students should be like playing to a load of Krypto-Metal fans.

He reached the entrance to a computer room and stopped to listen to the deep growling hum that came from inside. It sounded like the chanting of Tibetan monks.

He scooped up a mangled piece of paper from the floor and smoothed it out. It was covered in codes and numbers with a line drawing of a pyramid. It was the note Danny had shown him in the canteen.

Anthony had been sitting at a table, bemoaning the lack of a Union bar on the campus, when Danny had come up and spoken to him. The kid was unlike any other Chilly he had come across. He displayed emotion. In fact, he was very upset, even disturbed, but Anthony was glad to talk to anybody else, however deranged. The only other people he spoke to were the right-wing fascists and loonies who called on the daily chat show lines.

Compared with them, Danny seemed completely rational. Danny was convinced that something was going on at New World University. It was all too easy. Everyone was too taken in. Danny wanted to know how the computer that seemed to control everything really worked. He had elaborate plans to hack his way into the secure areas of the mainframe and find out what was behind it.

Anthony wasn't even sure he wanted to know. He just wanted to work out his short-term contract and go back to being unemployable. Even so, he liked the kid. There was no one else in the place to like. 'Let me know what you dig up,' he said to Danny, 'and we'll see what we can get out of it.' The kid obviously thought this would make the Big Time, and he sidled off looking happier. Anthony had thought that this might have been his good deed for the decade.

Here and now, looking at the crumpled paper, he wasn't so sure. He rubbed his fingers. There were strands of something resembling cobweb on them. He ducked back as the door opened and Christopher, resplendent in another new pullover, emerged.

'Something you want, Anthony?' he oozed.

Anthony rose to the challenge. 'A producer with a sense of humour?' He shrugged. 'I want a word with the High Priestess.'

Christopher closed the door behind him. 'The Vice Chancellor's busy.' He started steering Anthony back along the corridor, but the DJ pulled free.

'Hello, first-time caller to Christopher Rice. Your jazzy-bright DJ has a problem.'

'You had a salary rise within a month of starting.'

Anthony was not deterred. 'I was top of my year at drama college, right?'

Christopher nodded. 'Nineteen seventy-two.'

'Listen up, buster. The conviction I give your propagandist crap should win me a BAFTA. Instead, I get chucked out of my office so you can move in more bloody computer hardware.'

'It's part of the transmitter automation programme.'

'Then get the transmitter to read the scripts. There's no real people left in this goddamned place. Just hundreds of empty offices, full of computers and squatting Chillys!'

Christopher locked eyes with him and smiled. 'I'll tell Miss Waterfield.'

They had reached a stairwell. Anthony glared for a moment before he started down. At the first landing, he stopped. Out of reach. 'Tell her I want action now. Not when orders arrive from our Glorious Sponsor, wherever he hangs out.'

Having delivered himself of his tirade, he set off back to his glass dungeon. If they didn't react he would do a DLT live on air and see how they liked that. He still had Danny's crumpled note in his fist. He rubbed at his fingers where they were irritating.

13

Shapes

A rush of stale air and the approaching roar of another engine.

The presence inhabiting Travers pushes his shape into the low angle between the wall and the floor. A niche for itself, confined to the extent of the body's substance, anchored by gravity to the Earth.

The sound of bodies moving. A threnody of a thousand footsteps clattering, dispersing, echoing away.

The thing in the blind old man's body listens to their shapes. Light and heavy shapes, clumsy, old and young shapes.

A human voice shouts, 'Mind the doors.'

A shrill alarm of bleeps. A slide. A thud. The engine's roar fading into the distance and a rush of air pressing against Travers's surface skin.

Footsteps approach and pause. A chink of metal pieces on the ground in front of it. The footsteps move on again.

The presence feels itself in every region of Travers's body, held in the stasis it has imposed. It knows every ancient blood cell moving sluggishly in every ancient vein. Every hair and follicle, every nerve-ending. Its own pounding thought-beat overwhelming the dull double thud of Travers's heart. It can make him jerk with spasms as it flexes inside his body. But laughter, cruel and mocking, is exhausting. And it is still *so* weak. A scooped-out pulp without its own shell.

It has no shape. That was lost long ago. Does it recall what it was once? Was it huge with massive claws to crush and maim? A bloated spider-mind filling every cavernous gap with billowing web? Was it a mountain? A bank of mountains looming and rumbling like clouds in another sky or on another continuum? A comet scattering thoughts when it surges through the junctions and circuits of the New World computer?

It is there now, resting while it projects out of that body into Travers's body, where it has had a hold for years.

In truth, it cannot remember what it once was. That was so far off, in another dimension, another form of now.

It struggles to hold its thoughts together. A mass of thoughts is all it is. But such substantial thoughts. More than just an idea. A mass of thoughts with one single thought. The Doctor reversed the energy flow. Reversed everything. The power that enabled it, *It*, the *Great* Intelligence, now binds it. Now *it* is the pawn. It is blinded. It cannot escape.

It is still weak, but it has a new web now: a web of wires and fibres where it has soothed and healed its wounded mind. The new web reaches and connects with other webs. The Intelligence has spread slowly, bridging interfaces, breaching firewalls, hiding in other commands and texts. The new web already circuits the Earth. All systems are converting to one command system. Search and retrieve that focus that binds it. That Locus must be recovered and destroyed!

And that is not enough. The rigid web binds it too. It must have solid form and substance. Not to exist solely as blind impulses of data. But does it have the strength?

Something squeaks nearby.

The Intelligence feels a shape brush against its foot – against Travers's foot encased in soft animal skin. It reaches out its will, temporarily abandoning its aged host.

It feels itself inside the new shape. A hairy little body with a long febrile tail and a tiny racing heart. The little creature stops, terrified by the sudden enforced blindness of the invader. The blind Intelligence revels in the creature's heightened sense of smell – vividly and colourfully pungent. The creature squeals and rolls over and over, all but bursting apart from the monstrous existence inhabiting its tiny form.

The intruder loosens its inner grip, allowing the puny creature's instincts to scurry it forward. From its new-found whiskers, it senses the narrow crack that the animal enters. At home in the acrid darkness. The presence feels rough wood and mortar below the creature's paws and then something smooth, unnatural, fed with a charge of electricity.

The Intelligence abandons its tiny host and enters the cable, surging along it, a long finger of thought stretching thinner and thinner. It remembers this place and seeks the tinny voice at the end of the cable.

'Victoria! Victoria!'

It hears startled reactions below: 'What are they on about?' 'This is Piccadilly Circus, isn't it?' 'Nah, change at Green Park for the Victoria Line.'

The address system gives a burst of hysterical demonic laughter that echoes away into the tunnel. 'My strength is returning.'

The Intelligence gives a leap of imagination back into the well-tried and hateful prison body of Travers. It needs him now. There will be no more waiting.

A nearby voice is saying, 'Come on, old man. You can't sit begging here.'

Travers's shoulder is gripped by a human hand. He is being pulled upwards. Flat circles of metal are being pushed into his palm.

'Here you are. Take your money and push off.'

Travers, old and worn out, is grunting in confusion.

'Come on,' says the voice. 'Don't you have a home to go to?'

With a rush, the Intelligence takes full possession again. Travers gives a bear-like snarl. His stick lashes out and strikes something hard.

There is a scream from nearby.

The stick swings wide, searching its way, dragging blind Travers behind it.

Victoria's conference with the Chancellor was part of her daily ritual. First the office was darkened and she would sit in contemplation before the screen of her monitor.

Concentrate – relax – concentrate . . .

Increasingly it became important to gather her inner strength before they spoke, if only to withstand his rages. As it was, he often left her weeping. The Chancellor was old, a reclusive hermit, driven by a great will that would one day provide the greatest revelation to them all. Victoria never saw him. He spoke to her through disciplines inlaid in the New World computer, his creation, which the students nicknamed the Om-puter. He spoke from somewhere distant and unknown, but with such intense conviction that when she heard him, she knew nothing else. He held the key to the future and she was chosen to help him.

Relax – concentrate – relax . . .

He had shown her how to pilot her mind from perception into imagination and rise out of her body; to project herself into other etheric states; to see the world in overview, from a witch's-cradle of thoughts.

Contemplation, however, had its drawbacks.

'Thinking again?' her father would say. 'Too much of that and you'll forget how to talk.'

She had achieved so much, but was she content?

No. Contentment was as much a fallacy as perfection. Yet they all strove for it.

She was driving her thoughts, concentrating. Then thinking of blue, deep infinite blue. Drifting back again. Back, back into dream memories.

Eastbourne holidays. Watching the sailing-boats with her mother and collecting shells and starfish on the beach when the tide was out. The wind blowing her bonnet into the sea from the promenade and the fisherman who fetched it back and got thrupence from her father for his trouble.

Sunday dinner with boiled leg of mutton and caper sauce. Stewed greengages with egg custard. Cook in a fluster when Disraeli the spaniel stole the vanilla blancmange. Mother taking camomile medicine for her poorly stomach.

It always ended in sadness.

Suppose they had fled the house near Canterbury? She and her father. Away from the horror and cruelty of the Daleks who imprisoned her there. Brutal monstrosities, forever screaming orders at her and pushing her to and fro while they engaged in their horrible experiments.

Where would they have gone? Back to London? Or even Oxford? Would she have married? Would she be running her own household, bearing a baker's dozen of children and having two dozen more grandchildren playing around her skirts? Would that be fulfilling enough?

The modern world had become almost unrecognizable. Moral codes that had been strictly dictated by Victorian society were now more and more in the domain of the individual. Even so, her students were devoted to their studies. Perhaps too much. There was little of the wildness that seemed to dominate society at large. She was almost glad when one of them did rebel a little. That was why Daniel Hinton must be cared for.

The world still frightened her by the speed with which it changed. She was forced to rely on Christopher for guidance. She didn't like him, but he was single-mindedly brilliant at organizing and promoting the university. Even if the results were strange, she trusted him because the Chancellor said he was the best man for the job. In modern terms, Christopher had the twentieth century sussed and she was left on a shelf in the antiques market. If only he didn't *lunch* quite so often.

Her privilege was to liaise with the Chancellor. Her task was to find the thing he craved, the vital Locus that had been missing for over twenty-five years. His voice had lately grown more fierce, his endless demands more wearying. The staring white eye of the monitor, his blind eye, burned out at her as his harsh whisper echoed into the shadowy office. The voice dislodged other sounds that scattered around it as he tore angrily at the injustice of the sacrifice he had made. The suffering was great for those who sought Enlightenment. Only she could offer consolation.

'The Locus must be recovered now!'

He was bad today. Ranting accusations at her. It was as much as she could do to stay calm. She was on a knife-edge. 'I gave you my word. Soon.'

On an impulse, she reached for the box on her desk. It was a surprise and a relief to see that the silvered globe was back in its place, although she could not remember how it had returned.

The voice gave an almost inhuman groan of pain. 'You know nothing of this blind, empty outer darkness where I am bound . . . It is unendurable!'

Victoria closed her eyes and said quietly, 'I do not belong in this world. My family and friends are all lost in time.'

There seemed to be something there that he understood. His rage subsided. He sounded broken and alone. 'We are both outcast, Victoria.'

'That's why we work together. I built you this place with the money my dear father invested one hundred and thirty years ago. In return, you promised us the Light of Truth.'

There was a burst of hollow laughter. 'There is no Light.' Again the voice settled, but there was a threat behind it. 'I trust you, Victoria.'

She rose from her place and walked to the window. Daylight was seeping in from a gap at the edge of the blind. 'And I trust you,' she said.

The monitor eye was suddenly aware that she had moved. The terminal began to turn back and forth, searching blindly for her. 'One Locus still binds my . . . power. The others were dealt with long ago. The last one must, *will*, be ready for my return.'

She blanched as the glare swept over and past her. At last, the screen dimmed. Today's conference was at an end.

Victoria clutched the back of a chair to steady herself. Was the Chancellor returning now? How much time did she have? Brigadier Lethbridge-Stewart must know where the Locus was. Everything pointed to him. She had been searching, surely the Chancellor knew that. What else could she do? And Daniel Hinton must be found before he got into serious trouble. It was up to her to find them. Always up to her. She must redouble her efforts. She had a feeling she wanted to scream.

14

Twickers' Big Day

The Brigadier unlocked the drawer and extracted the Browning from its case. It was the gun he had kept since the old days. It fitted his hand like an old friend. He raised it and checked the chambers for bullets.

The telephone line to London had been diabolical, but he had made all the necessary calls and had a full campaign strategy drawn up in his mind.

He had slept fitfully that night, part through worry, part through not being in the slightest bit tired. In snatched moments of sleep, he knew that there was something outside. A huge brooding shadow in the dark that lumbered round the house, pushing at the walls and windows. It scrabbled at the front door, its massive silhouette filling the stained-glass windows. He heard its low growl and saw a pair of eyes like burning coals. Whenever he woke, all he saw was the crack of orange light from the streetlamp that sneered under the curtain.

He had been keeping an eye on the van as well. The poor blighter assigned to keep him under tabs did not seem to have been relieved of duty at all. The Brigadier wondered whether to invite him in for cocoa, a house speciality based on RSM Benton's original recipe.

He had reckoned to leave the house by nine, but was up and ready to go at least an hour earlier. He decided to make a show of normality and went out to bring in the milk that he had forgotten to cancel. There were footprints in the flowerbed, but no sign of the windows being tried. His dark green Range Rover was parked outside as usual. Across the sunny avenue, beyond the wall and line of plane trees that bordered School Field, long glittering arcs of water circled slowly above the cricket pitches, newly prepared for the summer term – his last term.

He glanced to the end of the avenue and saw to his surprise what looked like the *Twickermobile*, Celia's ancient cream Triumph Herald. It was parked further down, beyond his friend in the Gas Board van. For a moment, he thought he saw Celia's head bob up above the dashboard. He was getting a fan club he did not want. He cursed as he hurried back inside.

Getting away without being followed was going to be the problem. He had wondered about putting bullets through the van's tyres, but didn't think the neighbours were ready for a shoot-out in the middle of their avenue. Especially since that blasted interfering woman was involved.

He put on his tweed jacket and cap and picked up his car keys. He was locking the front door when he realized that, of all things, he had not picked up the gun. He fetched it from the drawer and slid it into the holster inside his jacket. It felt uncomfortable there without his proper uniform. Resigned to the makeshift arrangement, he marched back out of the house.

He ignored his own car and turned along the avenue. The van still appeared empty when he passed it, but he kept going until he reached the Triumph Herald.

Celia appeared to be busy with a road map. She jumped when he rapped smartly on the windscreen. A pair of ornate opera glasses sat on her lap.

'Good morning, Celia,' he said. 'If you're going sightseeing, I suggest you try somewhere else.'

She looked quite mortified. 'Brigadier, I've spoken to the Gas Board and they know nothing about that van.'

'Very perceptive,' he said tetchily. 'Now please go back to the safety of your office. I'll speak to you later.'

'If you're in danger, Brigadier . . .'

'I said "go"!'

There was no arguing with the command, although she looked incensed. She started the car without another word and drove off up the avenue.

As he passed the van on the way back, he slammed his fist against the side and shouted, 'Good morning!' He looked in at the dirty windscreen. There was no tax disc. The seats were old and torn, and were covered in rubbish. From inside, he heard the sound of a baby crying.

The back door slammed. A young woman with a thin, weathered face and greasy hair climbed out. She wore a faded 'Hobbiton Rules' tee-shirt.

'Can't you leave us for five minutes?' she snarled.

This wasn't a surveillance unit. It was travellers or squatters. The Brigadier was about to give the woman a good basting on moral responsibilities, when he heard a car approaching at speed.

A black-windowed Porsche cut straight in at him. He grabbed the woman, pulling them both behind the van, out of its path. It shot past, so close it was a blur.

'Bloody fascist yuppies!' yelled the woman and hit at the Brigadier too. 'They're the trouble, not us!'

'Get inside and stay there!' he ordered. He ran across the avenue to his Range Rover. He was an idiot thinking that techniques hadn't advanced in the past twenty years. He didn't even know who these people were, or what they wanted.

'*Where is the Locus?*' said a voice in his mind. A voice he thought he had dreamed.

He turned the ignition. Ahead, further up the leafy road, the Porsche was turning to make a return run. The Brigadier put his foot down and started away.

The Porsche came straight up the middle of the avenue. Straight at him. He saw the open gate in the school wall and swung the wheel. The Range Rover went straight through the gap out into the wide arena of School Field.

He heard a screech of brakes behind him. A second later, the Porsche shot into view through the opening. It came at him like a homing shark. He did another high-speed turn, which sent a shower of earth up from the pitch. Water sloshed onto his windows as he cut through the range of the sprinklers. He tried to weave back and forth, but the Porsche followed his every move and was cutting down the distance.

The Brigadier cut sharply to the right and kept turning as if he was on the tightest of hairpin bends. Every loose item inside avalanched across the car. For a moment, the vehicle was turning on two right wheels only. He nearly stalled in the process, but the manoeuvre caught his pursuer unawares. The Porsche sliced narrowly past him, its brakes screaming.

Making the most of his chance, he headed for the gate again, but as he approached, he saw another car coming in through the gap towards him. A cream Triumph Herald with Celia at the wheel. As he swerved to miss her, he saw her astonished face.

'Stupid, blasted woman! You'll get yourself killed!' he shouted uselessly.

The Porsche was already gaining ground. The Brigadier tried to zig-zag, but the steering-wheel jerked as if a third hand was controlling it. His engine roared like a wild beast. Something was pulling on the car. A force dragging against it. In his mirror he saw, ever closer, the black malevolent reflection in his pursuer's windscreen. The Porsche started to pull alongside. He pumped his foot on the accelerator, forcing his protesting vehicle straight on. He began to make headway, but he was running out of field. Ahead, the school assembly hall was looming.

The Range Rover left the field and mounted the footpath. In desperation, his foot still on the gas, the Brigadier jammed the handbrake hard on. The car skidded wildly, the dragging influence suddenly released. There was no road. He angled sharply through the first arch of the school cloisters. The Porsche came behind him.

They tore along the stone corridor under the ancient arches, rattling classroom doors as they passed. Notices were ripped from their noticeboards. Litter bins were sent clattering. The school Chaplain, drawn by the noise, dived for cover into a doorway as the cars thundered through.

The steering-wheel began to jerk again, trying to force

the Range Rover against the walls. With a crash, a wing mirror smashed against an arch, but the Brigadier had a firmer grip now. He kept on a steady course.

Ahead, the far entrance to the cloisters led out into the Chapel yard. It was blocked by the council dustcart and a group of binmen who were staring at the spectacle.

He didn't dare slow down. The binmen scattered as he reached the end of the cloisters. He crooked the wheel left instead, accelerating out onto the field again.

Celia's car was parked on the far side. She had emerged and was standing watching with her opera glasses. She started to wave desperately, but he was too involved to respond. He heard the loud report of a gun. In the mirror, he could see an arm extending from the driver's window. It was aiming a pistol at the wheels. He swerved again as he heard another sharp report.

With an apologetic thought to the head groundsman, who had been a close friend until now, he turned the car in another shower of turf and headed straight towards the sprinklers. The turning arcs of water rushed nearer. As usual, the Porsche was on his tail – moving in for the kill. He saw the gun levelling at him.

With a whoosh, the Range Rover shot over the sprinklers. The big vehicle cleared the spinning machine and its water jets easily. There was a loud crunch from behind as the Porsche hit the metal carousel and skidded wildly. The broken hose reared like an angry snake under the force of the water. It flailed against the Porsche as the car's engine choked in frustration.

The Brigadier wasted no time in heading for the gate. Celia was already back in her car and moving in from the side. She was waving from her driving seat, gesticulating for him to move faster. She was putting on speed too.

In the mirror, he saw that the Porsche had righted itself and was moving in on him fast. He put his foot down and headed for the gate.

As he shot out onto the avenue, he saw Celia's car screech to a halt right across the entrance. He heard another set of brakes screaming and a loud crash. One of the plane trees beyond the wall shook and a cloud of smoke rose from the hidden base of its trunk.

The Brigadier jammed on his brakes and ran from his car back to the gate.

Celia was standing by her undamaged vehicle. 'One for Twickers!' she cried with a look of fierce triumph.

The Porsche had swerved to avoid the blocked gate and hit the tree head on. The Brigadier moved round the smoking chassis, ready to meet any attack. The driver's buckled door hung open. The car was empty.

Impossible. The black car couldn't attack him by itself. Could it? Of course not. He had seen a hand angling the gun.

'There,' called Celia. She was pointing further along the wall. He just glimpsed a figure disappearing over the top.

People were running in across the field. Soon this would be a public affair. He leant inside the car. There was some sort of web on the seats and dashboard. He pulled back his hand.

Web on his gun hand and the clawed footprint in the sand of some huge animal like a Yeti.

He scooped up a card from the floor by the accelerator. It was a parking permit with a serial number, but there was no name. It was embossed with the UNIT logo. He pocketed it and stood up to face Celia.

'Celia, you take charge of this,' he snapped as if he was addressing his sergeant. 'I've urgent business. Tell them, I'll be back later.'

For the first time in his experience of her, Celia was too dumbstruck to answer. He cut the approaching Chaplain dead and ignored the binmen. In the distance he could hear a police car's siren. He strode out through the gate, climbed into his car and drove off in the direction of the city.

15

Gridlock

The computer located Christopher in Modem Room Three. It offered to take a message, but Victoria needed to talk to him face to face.

To reach the Modem Room, she had to pass through the Computer Studies Room, disturbing the students who were working there. As she walked down the central aisle, the students she passed started to rise and applaud her. It was just what she did not need. By the time she reached the front of the class, they were all clapping her. It was always the same, she brimmed with pride and was buoyed up by their show of genuine affection. Through the window, she could see Christopher watching her coldly from the terminal where he was working.

She turned and acknowledged the warmth of her students, signalling them to return to their work. When she finally got through the door to the Modem Room, her face dropped like a stone.

'The Brigadier's on the move . . .' began Christopher, before he saw her agitation.

'Daniel Hinton,' she said firmly.

Christopher smiled sheepishly. 'He "fell" from the building.'

Her hand went up to her face in shock. Out of the corner of her eye, she saw a sudden movement through the glass. All the students in the Computer Room had looked up simultaneously. 'What are you saying?'

He shrugged. 'Just jumped. Right off the top walkway. There was no sign of him below.'

Victoria was shaking, trying to keep her back to the students. 'But no one could . . . Why didn't you tell me? Poor Daniel. We must find him!'

Christopher's head nodded to one side. His smile froze solid. 'Let me explain again. He's vanished. His program's ringfenced. He can't deprogram himself.'

His patronizing was as much as she could take. 'Horrible modern terms.' She had had enough.

'I do have an appointment, but if you want me to deal with it for you . . . ?' he said silkily.

She pursed her lips and squeezed her eyes shut to stop herself crying. She nodded. 'Yes. Yes, find him please.' It was playing right into his hands, but what choice did she have? 'I have my own task. To prepare the way.'

To her annoyance, he didn't even thinly disguise his scoffing. 'Not found the Locus yet then?'

She tried hard to pull herself together. This, after all, should be a time of celebration. 'Christopher, the Chancellor is coming home. It seems the time is now. I must find the Locus, before Daniel's misguided hopes wreck everything we've worked for.'

When the alarms started sounding, Harrods had been picking through one of the bins at the back of the gallery buildings. The things people threw away, especially what students chucked, were a source of constant satisfaction to him. He had furnished his garage entirely with discarded items. And very presentable it looked. The best pickings were always at the end of a semester, when all sorts of stuff got ditched. He'd got blankets and a pillow that way. Almost clean. Oddly though, the Chillys hadn't taken a vacation over Easter – perhaps the government had banned holidays – but at least that meant there was more food about.

The Chillys normally ignored him, but he kept clear of them anyway. They'd only ever challenged him once. They'd held him against a wall and had gone through the pockets of his long military coat. He'd struggled and shouted, 'Sir, sir, I'm a mature student, I am!' But they'd soon let him go and he'd had no trouble since. Still, they were a netful of cold fish, the Chillys. Not natural.

When the alarms started up today, Harrods was

balanced on the edge of a skip, fishing out some wire coat-hangers that might be useful sometime. He clambered down and was knocked sideways by two bloody Chillys, who hared past like a couple of dogs on the scent of something defenceless.

He set off after them, keeping to the bushes under the walkways, where no one ever came. He could follow people the length of the campus down there.

There were Chillys running in from all directions. All making for the far side of the maintenance block. He could see their yellow caps bobbing along the top sides of the walkways. There was some sort of gathering going on. Then the alarm racket switched off. It went deathly quiet.

He heard a scuffle and looked up. One of the Chillys had jumped up onto the walkway parapet. He swayed there, glancing behind and then down at the forty-foot drop. He yelled something Harrods couldn't hear – more of a scream of anger or fear – and launched himself into the air.

Harrods's yell dried into a croak. Instead, he started to laugh and clap. The boy didn't fall. He glided, his coat billowing around him, his arms outstretched like a bird of prey. He hovered in the air for a moment and then slowly circled down, his face a mask of disbelief. He passed right over Harrods' head and finally came to earth, none too cleverly, in a mound of rubbish right under the walkway.

Heads had appeared on the wall above, staring down. But they hadn't seen the bird-boy, or where he'd landed, face down and senseless in the garbage.

'Sir,' croaked the vagrant, scampering up. 'Can't leave you here, sir. They'll be after you. They'll put you in a cage, they will, sir. You come with me. I'll see you right, sir.'

He lifted the insensible boy, who proved as light as a bundle of feathers, and carried him home. His home – a disused garage with all mod secondhand cons: collections of knick-knacks, music-hall posters. All of it recycled, most of it nicked.

'You stay there, sir.' He laid the unconscious boy on his bed and pulled down the sacking that covered the garage door. *They* would be out hunting, he was sure of that. But this was his prize. No one else's.

The boy moaned a little, but he was still out to the world. Harrods began to rifle systematically through the boy's coat pockets. There was precious little to speak of: a couple of pens and a crumpled hanky. He found a mobile phone, which he pocketed, although he had no one to call. Then his fingers closed on a tightly packed bundle. It was a wad of tenners held tight with a rubber band. Harrods couldn't believe his luck. The boy was bleeding loaded.

His hand suddenly clamped round Harrods' wrist. The tramp dropped the money and struggled. He was held in a vice.

'Bloody Chilly, I'll break your fingers.'

The vice squeezed tighter, but the boy was still asleep, his head turning fitfully in the grip of an unknown nightmare.

The traffic was the worst the Brigadier had ever seen. Bumper to bumper all the way into the City. He had sat in the same position for twenty minutes. He was already late and he couldn't even move far enough to reach a side street where he could park and walk.

Ahead, the traffic lights were flickering through their sequence like demented seaside illuminations. The air was getting thick with exhaust fumes and the blaring of angry car horns. The offices seemed to be emptying of workers, who were thronging the streets like sightseers. Tempers were flaring among the stranded motorists.

He tried to listen to the radio, but the reception was terrible and he could pick up only one station. The pap-brained presenter kept burbling on with traffic reports. London was in total gridlock, extending from the central zone out as far as the suburbs. To compound matters, the entire Underground system had failed and was closing down.

Victoria Waterfield (Deborah Watling).

Right: Brigadier Lethbridge-Stewart (Nicholas Courtney).

Above: Daniel Hinton (Mark Trotman) and the Brigadier.

Above: Kate, the Brigadier's daughter (Beverley Cressman).

Left: Victoria as she appears in the Brigadier's dreams.

Left: Anthony, the New World DJ (John Leeson).

Below: Professor Travers (Jack Watling).

Above: Harrods (Geoffrey Beevers).

Left: Captain Cavendish (Miles Richardson).

Above: The Brigadier holds a Yeti at gun-point.
Right: Sarah Jane (Elisabeth Sladen) and Kate hide from a Yeti.

bove: Victoria,
e Brigadier and
arrods surrounded
y Chillys.

Right: A Yeti
stands watch
at the New
World
University.

Sarah Jane Smith (Elisabeth Sladen).

'Well, is it Friday the Thirteenth and they didn't tell us?' wittered the presenter. 'Seems like that case of computer flu I told you about is spreading. They've just announced they're shutting down all major airports and that's on top of the rail networks. Can you believe it? Don't know how you're gonna get home tonight. That's if you got anything at work to work with. So why not stay tuned for news and chaos updates with New Wor . . .'

The Brigadier snapped the radio off and closed his eyes. The sun through the window and the heavy air were making him drowsy. His head started to nod.

A loud blast on a nearby car horn brought him up with a start. Ahead of him, through the stationary cars, he saw a figure standing on the busy pavement. She stared across at him as the wave of commuters surged around her. He shuddered, her black cape marked her out as a portent of evil. What nonsense, he reprimanded himself.

And a thought whispered into his head. *The Locus.*

The figure had vanished among the streaming pedestrians.

'It's coming closer,' the Brigadier muttered.

A voice from behind him said, 'Perhaps you have something it needs, sir.'

The Brigadier stared into the driving-mirror. Young Daniel Hinton was sitting on the back seat in his school blazer. Apparently the wretched boy was now ready to continue the conversation that he had so abruptly cut short on the beach. 'After all this time? I doubt that, Hinton,' he said.

'But you remember what it is, don't you?'

The Brigadier wound down his window and surveyed the beach. It was still deserted. Blown sand whipped around the car, which seemed to be parked on the crest of a dune. In answer to the boy's impudent question, he snapped, 'I'm not as blinkered as people think. It's a sort of mind parasite. The first alien force I ever came up against.'

'Sir?'

All these stupid questions. Lethbridge-Stewart opened

the car door and stepped out onto the beach. He surveyed the terrain, looking for trouble. 'In those days it called itself the Great Intelligence.'

Hinton lowered his window and peered out. 'And?'

Despite provocation, the Brigadier no longer really cared whether the information was classified or not. 'It had no physical shape of its own, so it enslaved humans as its pawns. And it deployed a squad of strategic robots camouflaged like Yeti.'

He knelt and dusted at a footprint in the sand. When he turned, the boy was leaning against the wing of the car. 'Was this in Tibet, sir?'

'No. London about thirty years ago. It invaded the city like a virus, using the Underground network as a sort of nervous system. No shape of its own, so it steals others. Grisly business. I thought we were rid of the blighter.'

Danny looked out to sea, where dark clouds rumbled on the horizon.

'It's still out there,' he said. 'On the Bardo, the astral plane. Trapped outside our physical existence.'

The Brigadier nodded grimly. 'Is it indeed? And what does it want?'

The boy shrugged. 'Don't know, sir. It's you it's hunting.'

'What's this got to do with you, Hinton?' It was the Brigadier's dream and he didn't see why the boy should be dictating events to him.

Daniel Hinton looked ruefully at his teacher. 'Just don't trust anyone, sir.' He turned and started walking away across the sand-blown flats.

'What?' called the Brigadier.

The boy glanced back. 'No one at all.' But he kept walking.

'I'll thank you, Hinton, not to treat me like a total . . .' It was no use. The boy had rapidly vanished into the sandstorm.

The Brigadier was suddenly startled by the close blast of a horn.

* * *

He jolted awake with a start in the driving seat. A chorus of horns was blaring.

The face of the hooded woman was staring directly through the windscreen at him. Her clear blue eyes were fiercely penetrating. He felt her searching into his thoughts. She was angry and accusing. And it was time he put a stop to it.

He opened the car door, but by the time he had scrambled out, she had vanished once again.

There was a furious animal roar behind him. He spun round, reaching inside his jacket for the gun. A huge brown and shaggy creature reared above him. Just what he expected. Its eyes blazed with scarlet fire. Its massive claws raked the air. The Brigadier raised his gun to shoot as the Yeti lashed at him.

Its roar mingled with a fresh barrage of car horns.

The monster had vanished. The Brigadier was alone in the traffic, gun in hand.

He mustered a charming smile for the family in the next car – two astonished parents and their fascinated daughter.

'Damn traffic. Brings out the worst in you, doesn't it?'

The father, a look of disgust on his face, slammed his fist against the horn.

The Brigadier hurriedly slipped the gun away and got back into his car.

16

The Summons

'It's coming closer,' murmured the boy in his sleep.

Harrods clapped a hand over his mouth. Outside, something was moving. A steady tap-tap-tap sound that was coming nearer. Harrods' eyes darted round his garage at the dozens of 'useful' things he had collected. An old magpie, he was. Never knew what he might need next, so best to have plenty of things just in case. But what to save if they caught up with him?

The boy was still asleep under Harrods' hand, shifting his body restlessly. A real fight he was having.

The air had gone chill, although the watery sun still shone in at the garage entrance. From outside came the tap-tap-tap and the shuffling of worn-down shoes. Something was wheezing like a landed whale. A hunched shadow lurched across the sacking that hung in the entrance. It stopped, turning back and forth, searching.

The boy sat up with a yell. His eyes staring, wide awake. He was shaking. Harrods, one hand still on the boy's mouth, shushed him quiet and nodded at the door.

They stared at the silhouette on the sacking. A bulky figure of a man, slowly sweeping a stick before him. Harrods thought of a metal detector.

An unearthly voice broke the stillness. A dry ancient whisper that was full of weariness and hatred. 'Daniel Hinton. You are summoned.'

Harrods felt the boy's body go so taut it might snap.

The shadow stick jerked forward and the rest of the silhouette followed. The shadow focused darker as the figure approached. The sacking was pushed aside and the light flooded in.

'Daniel,' commanded the figure.

Harrods could not make out the features against the glare, but the white hair was like a halo.

The tramp and the boy scrambled backwards to the wall as the intruder entered, his stick swinging as if *it* was searching rather than the old blind man. Something like web seemed to be drifting in around him.

Harrods edged back further. The stolen phone dropped from his pocket with a clatter.

The stick swung in on him and pinned him to the floor.

'Daniel Hinton?'

Harrods lay there terrified. Strands of web were gathering on his coat, in his hair. 'Get off me, sir! Sir, get off!'

With a yell, the boy barrelled against the old man, toppling him against the wall, sending a cascade of Harrods' belongings to the ground. The stick dragged him up again, swinging wildly, beating against the fallen objects.

'Daniel Hinton. You were chosen. I claim you now. My summons binds you!'

The boy pushed Harrods towards the door. He paused and glanced back at the phone lying on the floor. He dashed at it and snatched it away as the stick cracked down in its place.

As they turned to run, the figure, still disorientated, was blundering about among the detritus of Harrods' violated home.

The Brigadier had had enough. He was less than a mile from his first appointment and he was going to be late. No traffic had even crept in the past twenty-five minutes and it was plainly not going to get better. There had been a punch-up across the street between a taxi driver and a policeman whose radio had gone wrong. A lone cyclist kept biking up and down the rows of stationary traffic, laughing loudly. Further along the street, he had seen several people abandoning their vehicles.

That was it. He got out of the car, locked it up, tipped his cap to the family in the vehicle alongside and joined the steady flow of pedestrians.

He cut through towards St Paul's and Fleet Street via Watling Street. Ahead, through the crowds, he saw two youths in yellow baseball hats and green sweatshirts. Logos emblazoned on their fronts proclaimed the 'New World University'. They were distributing leaflets. As soon as they saw the Brigadier, they made a beeline for him.

As they approached, he could hear the irritating tinny beat of their headphones. 'Excuse me, sir,' said the first with a sickly smile, 'can I tell you about the New World?'

'I'm not interested.' The Brigadier tried to push past, but they were very persistent.

The second youth barged in front of him, catching his sleeve. 'We want to tell you about our good news, sir.'

'I said, I'm not interested,' the Brigadier snapped. He angrily pushed between them and hurried away. Behind him, he heard one of them call, 'Have a better one!', but he was in too much of a hurry to argue.

Christopher Rice sat back and drank in the elegant, history-steeped surroundings. The House of Commons dining-room, overlooking the river, evidently kept an extensive cellar. 'White Burgundy?' suggested the immaculately coiffured Desmond Pennington and ordered the Criots-Bâtard-Montrachet, '88 vintage. 'We had a bottle at Glyndebourne last year and I've drunk nothing else since. But then I'm very unadventurous once I find something I like.'

Christopher smiled. He glanced around again, counting the number of famous political faces with whom he was sharing the dining-room. People with power.

He had *borrowed* the university's helicopter to get to his lunch date. There had been no choice. He had flown over a frozen city. Every road was a seam of trapped metal. The trip was a gamble, but he doubted that Victoria, obsessed with the imminent arrival of the Chancellor, would even notice. Anyway, he'd tell her it was business, which, of course, it was.

'You're one of the first people to use the new helipad,' said Pennington.

'I'm duly honoured,' Christopher nodded humbly. The half lobster in cream and brandy sauce was a marked improvement on the food served by the university caterers.

'Good.' The Education Secretary had restricted himself to a light salad. 'Your Miss Waterfield was . . .' he searched for a word, '. . . enthusiastic, shall I say?'

'Naïve?' suggested Christopher, but Pennington frowned.

'That doesn't disallow her heart to be in the right place. Even so, I felt that she does not really grasp the sheer potential of New World University.'

'Exactly my feelings,' said Christopher.

'Then you must tell me what its real agenda is.'

New World's Marketing Facilitator helped himself to the wine bottle. 'The computer is the cutting edge. That's where the real potential lies. Its mainframe is self-analytical. It makes other computers look like counting-frames.'

'I think we've had enough of computers today,' said the MP.

'It's not affected,' Christopher reassured him. 'It has built-in immunity. It hasn't been touched by all this virus business.'

'Then who controls it?'

'Anyone who's in charge. It was designed by the university's founding Chancellor, but it's outgrown the initial programming long ago.'

'I see.'

'It redesigns itself as it goes along.'

'Fascinating.'

'And with more extensive funding the sky would be the limit.'

Pennington tapped his fingers on the table for a moment. 'There is, of course, another consideration. The computer's British. And that's extremely important.'

Christopher took another swig of the Burgundy. 'I think it could prove a real powerhouse for the government . . . in the right hands.'

'Yes,' Pennington said slowly. 'But there's one thing

that still bothers a lot of us. This mystical business that goes with the New World package. It's Tibetan, isn't it? These days, Britain is a multi-cultural society. God knows, we're never allowed to lose sight of that. But the power base is still C of E. And hippy chanting instead of morning prayers won't go down too well in the Home Counties.'

Christopher smirked. 'It's a quirk of both the Chancellor and the Vice Chancellor,' he admitted. 'But I'm sure I can deal with that. Miss Waterfield always listens to me.'

'Ah.' Pennington suddenly appeared to shrink in his seat. 'Word gets round fast in this place. I'm afraid we may have company.'

Clive Kirkham, the Burncaster Bruiser, was standing in the far doorway surveying the diners. He was still wearing his brown checked jacket. As soon as he saw Pennington he started to weave through the tables.

'Well, this is very cosy, I must say,' he gibed. He studied the remains of Christopher's crustacean. 'Good afternoon, Mr Rice. If everyone at that New World reception of yours returns the compliment, you'll be eating out till next Christmas.'

Pennington made a show of topping up Christopher's glass. 'No one to have lunch with, Kirkham?'

'Plenty, thanks. Do I take it we're going to see another radical reform in teaching structures after this?'

'Meaning?'

'All schools and colleges, sorry *universities*, furnished with a single national curriculum computer?'

'We'd have to ask parents and teachers first.'

'Oh. Oh. You've heard of them, then?'

Pennington had been beating a Devil's Tattoo on the table. 'If you want to make a spectacle of yourself, Kirkham, why not do it in the Chamber and get a bigger audience?'

A look of gleeful smugness slid across Clive Kirkham's face. 'Not seen this evening's *Standard* yet, then?'

Pennington sighed. 'I suppose you've written a piece for them. I hope they paid your expenses.'

'Bloody typical!' exploded Kirkham. 'The government

negates its responsibilities by letting New World take care of privatized education, just so they can do less and less!'

Christopher watched Pennington turning a bright shade of scarlet. He decided it was time for him to step in before blood or, worse, wine was spilled. He coughed lightly. 'Mr Kirkham, I think you may be jumping the gun a tadge.'

'Oh, you reckon that do you, laddie? I warn you now, don't overestimate the big boys. They don't let just anyone into their playground.'

Pennington opened his mouth to speak, but Christopher held up a hand. 'Let me explain it in simple terms. Desmond asked me up here to establish exactly what New World's agenda is. As you pointed out, Mr Kirkham, we're pretty unusual. There's bound to be suspicion over any new innovation, and we at New World, to coin that hackneyed phrase, are the cutting edge. Desmond here is simply concerned as to where this might be leading.'

Desmond Pennington was studying the stem of his wine glass.

'Absolute tosh,' protested Kirkham.

Christopher, who reckoned himself a dab hand at seeming reasonable, was not abashed. 'We're an open book. And you're more than welcome to visit at any time.'

'I might take you up on that.'

'Good. I look forward to reading your article in the *Standard*.'

When Kirkham nodded, his whole body bobbed as if it could scarcely contain his furious excitement. He turned on his heel, narrowly missed a waitress and left the dining-room.

'Hyperactive little twerp,' muttered Pennington. 'Well done, Mr Rice; you fielded him like a pro. Perhaps you should consider a career in politics.'

17

Web on the Line

'It's competition time! Since we can't go over to the national news at the moment, let's have a little quizette to keep the airwaves humming.'

Anthony sat alone in his studio. He was drowning. All the back-up feeds from outside sources were failing. No news, no traffic reports, no weather. He wanted to pull the show, but the producer was relentless. He had to get as far as the handover at fourteen hundred, then someone from Jesus FM could cope.

'Just ring in to us with the name of the founder of Tantric Buddhism, and you could win an N Treble U prayer mat. But, and here's the hard bit, you have to spell the guy's name too. And if you want a clue, he was said to have been born in a lotus bud. Perhaps his mother was a budding gardener. No, but seriously, give us a call.'

He paused to wait for the calls to come flooding in.

Nothing happened. He glanced at the transmission lights to see if they were still on air. The light was still green, and the producer without a scrap of pity. But what did you expect from a computer?

He scratched at an irritation on his hand. On the console beside him was Danny's crumpled scrap of paper. The strands of web attached to it glistened. He thought they twitched, but it was just the air-conditioning.

'And if you've got problems you want to talk about, why not give us a call? I've got problems too. Ring in your phone number and I'll call you.'

'*0135 666 416. Caaall Noo Wooooorrlld,*' sang a jingle.

'Come on, somebody. Anybody. You can't all have switched off. Is there anybody there? One rap, yes. Two raps, no. If there's anybody out there, even by mistake, give me a ring.'

At last the Line One light began to flash.

'And who's calling us on Line One?'

Through a curtain of crackles he heard a voice say. '*Anthony, it's Danny.*'

'And where are you calling from, Danny?'

'*It's me. Danny Hinton. I'm still alive.*'

Anthony froze. 'Danny?'

The kid's voice sounded terrified. '*Listen. It's coming. It's already coming for me, but it wants all of us! You've got to warn . . .*'

Anthony's hand hit a button.

'*This is Noo Wooooorrlld,*' sang the jingle again. Anthony listened as his own recorded voice began to babble inanely. 'New World Radio, the ones who share.' Music fed into the transmission channel.

He let the emergency insert play and cut back into Line One. 'Danny. You bloody idiot, what's happening? I knew you'd get caught. Where are you? You've got to get help before . . .'

The unobtainable tone cut in on the line.

'Danny? Danny!'

Anthony slammed a fist on his console. He pulled off his cans. The tone on Line One was breaking up, becoming a series of high-pitched staccato blips.

Danny's paper was bubbling up with a sort of frothy web. The stuff had spread like a malignant growth onto the console. Anthony pulled back and moved towards the door. It was jammed. He pulled and tugged at the handle before he realized that the fire lock had been operated automatically by the computer.

The endless run of blips was getting louder and louder. Behind him, the frothing web hissed and spluttered with a voracious glee.

The stream of blips knifed into Danny's ear. He yelled and flung away the mobile phone. It struck a rock and cut off. Danny dropped to his knees and retched. As he caught at his breath, he heard the tramp behind him shouting and complaining.

'What you after? Bloody Chillys! I'm going to get the law.'

'Think they'd believe you?' Danny snapped without looking up.

They had got well away from the campus, out onto an abandoned allotment that bordered the canal. The tramp, who was well-known round the university – a sort of joke or mascot – had helped carry him after they had escaped the garage, but Danny had to make the phone call, if only to warn someone. There were things he had discovered at New World. Things he'd unearthed, but didn't understand. And now the things, whatever they were, were coming for him.

'Sir, I never hurt no one. Not me, sir. Not old Harrods.' The old guy, filthy-dirty and crazy as he was, seemed to be genuinely concerned. He was scrabbling down to reach the phone.

'Don't!' shouted Danny and the tramp cringed.

Then a wicked grin cracked over his sun-baked face. 'Sir, flew right down, you did. Glided right down out of that place.' He spread his arms like a kid being a jet-plane and whistled himself down. 'Don't need jets no more, sir!' He cackled and capered a little dance. Then just as suddenly his eyes were full of fear. He glanced back at the distant ziggurats of the university. 'And then he comes after us, like an old spidery man.'

'He's coming for all of us,' declared Danny and grabbed Harrods by the coat. 'That money you nicked from me's no good to anyone. Period. Not unless you help me.'

Harrods' eyes narrowed. 'You got more?'

Danny shot him a look of withering contempt and he started to whimper. 'Sir, I got principles. I'm very particular.' But he kept his hand on the money in his pocket.

'You've seen what's coming,' said Danny and they both stared again at the distant buildings.

'Yes, sir.' Harrods twisted his head and looked up at the young man with a sense of wonder. Danny was squinting into the depths of the upper air.

'That's only half of what I can see,' he said. 'There's someone we have to find fast.'

18

By Appointment

It took the Brigadier three-quarters of an hour pushing through oncoming crowds to reach Great Portland Street. He cut up through Covent Garden – the old market streets where he had once led a squad against the invading Yeti. The robots had had no apparent strategy. They were like shaggy tanks, formidable and virtually unstoppable killers. The trendy piazza with its fashionable shops seemed a world away from the battlefield where he had lost so many men.

It was going to be a day for memories. He reached Great Portland Street at last and headed into the august portals of the Alexander Hotel. He could remember when the building had been a gentlemen's club. The Victorian Gothic façade remained, but the inside had been gutted and renewed. The once agreeably fusty reception area was now all mirrors and chrome. Pleasantly vacuous music was being piped in from somewhere. The smiling girl at the reception desk with her 'Hi. Welcome to the Alexander Hotel,' was as innocuous as a strawberry milkshake.

'Lethbridge-Stewart to see Cavendish,' he announced.

He noticed that the receptionist, who was wearing headphones, was seated at a computer which actually seemed to be working. She indicated the double doors across the foyer beyond a mêlée of Japanese tourists. 'If you go through to the lounge, Brigadier, you'll find Captain Cavendish waiting for you.'

From the expansive windows of her office, Victoria watched the university helicopter sink down behind the outbuildings. Christopher's absence had not gone unnoticed, but she half hoped that he was actually returning with the Chancellor.

Her thoughts had been flying far away, searching for the Brigadier, but his location eluded her. Desperation drove her now. She was not sure she could physically face the Chancellor's rage at her failure to find the Locus. Perhaps she was looking too hard. All she saw was spreading chaos, further signs that modern society was teetering on the brink of collapse. No wonder the Chancellor had chosen this moment to return.

She saw Christopher crossing the quadrant alone. While she waited, she gazed from the windows at the extensive grounds of the university she had inaugurated. Everyone else reckoned it an amazing achievement, but it was far from complete and that final resolution rested on her shoulders. Sometimes her thoughts got confused. Things happened that she did not always understand.

There were people she wanted to talk to, to ask if she had got it right. Where were they all? The Harrises and Roxana Cywynski and poor dear Charles and the Doctor. Surely the Doctor would know what was right or horribly wrong.

'Now Victoria, you know that this is a decision you have to make for yourself,' he would say gently. How she wished he was here to say that now.

She was aware that Christopher had silently entered the office. She could sense his presence moving in behind her like a serpent. He coveted her position, she knew that, but she could not progress without him. A wave of self-pity and nostalgia for things lost began to well in her heart.

John Jerum, soldierman,
Is searching high and low.
The only secret he can keep
Is one he doesn't know.

She sighed. 'My father used to say that. He'd have hated this.'

Christopher's voice was very quiet. 'You haven't a clue,

have you? It's your precious Chancellor who's got the real power. Power we can all profit by. He's not just a father substitute for you.'

She shuddered, but retained her composure. 'He works for the world's spiritual good.' She faced him. He was gloating over something, slowly turning the gold ring on his finger. She wished she had the courage to banish him forever. 'You'd even sell your own soul.'

He laughed. 'That's marketing.'

Victoria smiled too. She was, after all, still his employer. 'All "ringfenced", no doubt. Just like your expense account.'

His fingers froze on the ring. His glare could have inflicted physical injury on lesser mortals, but she revelled in it.

Without warning, the PA system crackled into life. 'Victoria Waterfield? Can you hear me?'

It was her turn to freeze. Anthony's voice sounded more than half crazed, full of insane mockery. 'Miss Waterfield's our boss, ladies and gentlemen. The big cheese at N Treble U!'

Victoria groped for the edge of the desk to steady herself. 'What's he doing? Make him stop!'

'And she's today's surprise guest on *Lift the Lid*. So ring in those questions now.'

'Stop him!' yelled Victoria, but Christopher clutched her arm and laughed in her face.

'It's Revelation Time, Vice Chancellor!' ranted the presenter.

Christopher gave her arm an extra-hard squeeze before he ran from the office. She watched him hurrying towards the studio block, but there was no stopping Anthony's ravings. By now he sounded close to tears.

'Forget anything I said before. It was lies. New World's just a big front. But they pay well, don't they, Miss Waterfield?'

What was he saying? She didn't understand. From the window, she saw groups of Chillys standing and listening. The broadcast was feeding right across the campus.

'What about all the people who disappear, eh? Danny was right. New World doesn't give a toss for you. Something's coming. Victoria Waterfield'll tell you!'

Music cut in over the voice. It was smooth and pleasantly vacuous. Victoria sat in the security of her chair. She clung to one of the high leather wings. 'Of course, something's coming,' she said. She couldn't understand what poor Anthony was saying. 'It's what we've all been waiting for.'

Christopher had cut in the music as soon as he reached the studio control room. He could still hear Anthony in the studio booth, but the glass panel between them was opaque, tinged with a pale green light. The inside was covered with a skein of glinting web that rippled as if it was horribly alive.

Anthony's voice was close to breaking point. 'She'll tell you. She knows what's coming. And it'll finish everything.' He finally cracked in a flood of hysterical tears.

From the window in the door, Christopher could see Anthony's shape through wreaths of web. The presenter was rocking to and fro, caught like an insect in the tangle. The substance had spread through the booth like a malignant, rampant plant. The strands of web were flecked with luminous froth.

Christopher smiled. This was abominable, but fascinating. He tested the door to ensure that it was locked. Satisfied, he set off back to Victoria's office with a jaunty gait.

19

Blunder Days

The young man rose casually as Lethbridge-Stewart entered the hotel lounge. He had sleek dark hair and classically handsome features. The Brigadier had taught dozens of boys like him. The public school and military aura was inbred, indelible despite the sharp business suit. Sandhurst, the Brigadier decided before they even spoke.

'Captain Douglas Cavendish, Virtual Ordnance Group at UNIT. Good to see you, Brigadier.' He indicated an armchair for his guest. In one hand, he clutched a tumbler of whisky. 'Can I get you a drink?'

'Not for me, Cavendish,' the Brigadier said firmly. He felt like adding, 'Not on duty.' 'Sorry if I'm late,' he said instead. 'The whole transport system seems to be fouled up by this wretched computer business.'

'Quite,' agreed Cavendish. 'It's better to meet here. The security boys get stressed out over ID checks.'

The Brigadier smiled. 'UNIT hasn't changed much since my time then.' He glanced round at the lounge. Many of the old features had been retained from when he had once met Air Vice-Marshal Gilmore here in this same room. Even several of the paintings of illustrious military forbears remained, their ferocity restored by the cleaners. He must have seemed like a young whippersnapper to Gilmore then, just as Cavendish appeared to him now. But he hoped he had displayed many degrees more civility.

'I doubt if there's much left you'd recognize,' said Cavendish. 'Razor-smart weapons. All on computer these days.'

'Oh, I used to leave the technology to the experts.'

'Yes, of course.' Cavendish took another swig of

whisky. He had cut-glass eyes that watched over the rim of the tumbler. The Brigadier wondered just how much the Captain had drunk while he waited.

'You know they call your era "The Blunder Days"?'

'What?' retorted Lethbridge-Stewart.

Cavendish smirked. 'Blood and Thunder. Well, you took on some formidable opposition. Cybermen, Daemons . . . Yeti.'

'No worse than jumped-up officers with tuppenny-halfpenny commissions,' the Brigadier observed.

The atmosphere went cold. 'Right,' said Cavendish and studied the contents of his tumbler.

'Why exactly did you call me up to town, Cavendish?'

'Information . . . sir.' He glanced round the lounge and confided, 'Of a personal nature, you understand.'

'Meaning?'

'Someone's been hacking into files at Geneva.'

'*My* files, I take it.'

There was a pause where Cavendish seemed to be gazing into space. He suddenly smiled. 'There aren't many who can remember back before UNIT's founding.'

The Brigadier studied him for a moment. He wondered what on earth it had to do with UNIT. 'That's all covered in old army reports.'

'The MoD were never very forthcoming when dealing with UNIT. Besides we need more personal details.'

'We? Are security in the dark on this one too?'

Cavendish's manner suddenly became less nonchalant, more sneering. 'Strange that you never rose higher than Brigadier, wasn't it?'

The Brigadier showed no reaction whatsoever. 'Internal politics,' he said. 'I didn't realize there was a market for my memoirs. I'll send you a copy when I get round to writing them.'

He was not exactly warming to Cavendish. He reckoned the Captain a bit of a lounge lizard, just the sort of person to run a black-windowed Porsche. He had been trying to ascertain what exactly the officer's game was. It was unorthodox, that was certain, and he knew that he was not going to play along.

Instead, he regaled Cavendish with one or two stories of his days at UNIT. Exploits that he was sure would be generally accessible to the current staff, if not apocryphal by now.

He deliberately strung the young man along, hoping to catch him off guard somehow. Cavendish was becoming increasingly familiar, probably due to the drink, and laughed out loud at the punchline '. . . so UNIT got blamed for blowing up the church.'

The Brigadier glossed over the strength of public outrage at the Aldbourne incident; questions in the House; a near riot at the General Synod. Only the secret capture of the Master had swayed the committee of enquiry's verdict in UNIT's favour, but relations between the UN and the MoD had never been lower.

'Are you sure you won't join me?' Cavendish enquired again as a waiter delivered another whisky.

'Not for me, Cavendish.' The Brigadier was watching the ornate clock, wondering about his schedule, when he glimpsed in a large wall mirror two youths in yellow baseball caps waiting outside the lounge doors.

'You must've picked up the odd souvenir in your time,' said Cavendish.

The Brigadier regarded him without a trace of emotion. 'I counted them in and I counted them all back out.'

'No special keepsakes? Things *do* get mislaid.'

'If you lose things, you can lose men too.' The Brigadier glanced at his watch and the mirror. He was still under surveillance. He stood abruptly. 'Well, it's been good to talk to you, Captain, but I have another appointment.'

He could no longer see the doors, but he heard them opening behind him and caught the sound of a tinny repetitive beat.

Cavendish stood, suddenly nervous. 'So soon? I was concerned, Brigadier.'

'So was I.' In the angled glass bordering the mirror, the

Brigadier saw a flash of green and yellow. He sensed the presence behind him and saw Cavendish's eyes flick over his left shoulder. He pulled out his gun and backed round to the right.

The two youths he had encountered in Watling Street had been right at his back. One was holding up a pair of headphones that emitted the tinny pulse of sound.

When they saw the gun they faltered.

'A taste of blood and thunder for you, Captain,' the Brigadier warned. 'Now back off. I'm leaving.'

The youths glanced to the Captain for instruction. After a moment, he nodded them away.

The Brigadier moved sideways to the doors, keeping his assailants firmly in his sights. The strawberry-milkshake receptionist was there, barring his retreat. She backed off from the gun too, another one with cold, cut-glass eyes.

The Brigadier ran across the foyer, dodging through the milling Japanese tourists, and out into the busy street.

Behind him, he heard Cavendish's distant yell. 'Get after him!'

20

Arrivals

London was laid out like a toy city below her. When she swooped lower, she saw that a tide of bodies was swarming through the streets around and between the endless lines of stationary vehicles.

She moved along between the buildings, just above the level of the streetlamps, but even now she knew that her task was impossible. The air was full of thoughts, anxious and stressful: thousands of instincts and concerns that the daily rhythms of the city, perhaps the whole world, were so disrupted. The air was angry. Some disaster was imminent. She could sense its lowering approach, but its nature eluded her. She could no longer focus. The object of her own quest slipped further and further out of reach.

Hope did not desert her. She had vowed to *him* that she would find it before *he* returned.

She felt the tug of the silver cord. Reality rushed at her as she coiled back into her body.

She snapped awake and saw Christopher at the other side of her desk, staring intently across at her, exuding all that smugness for which she so despised him.

Bewildered, she said urgently, 'There's still time. I must find the Locus.'

Christopher smiled. On the desk top, the small pyramid of opaque glass had begun to pulse with rhythmic light. A voice erupted out of the air. *His* voice.

'*Victoria, I am here.*'

The old man who was Travers stood where the stick had brought him. His unseeing eyes stared from behind grimy spectacles with cracked lenses. He was gaunt and stiffly erect, barely containing a fearful coiled energy like some fearsome bible-brandishing preacherman. His threadbare clothes were filthy and torn. His tangled white hair and beard had not grown in a decade. His face was a mask dragged like scrim over bony features frozen by one driving thought.

He stood waiting in the centre of the university reception, his hand resting on his immaculately vertical white stick. A dozen Chillys, drawn by the thoughts they heard from their headphones, gathered round him in wonder and fear.

One girl slid a scarf from her neck and wrapped it with reverence around his shoulders.

The old man shuddered at her touch. The mouth twitched and the throat growled out its question. *The* question.

'Where is the Locus?'

The Brigadier hunched up and stared at the pavement, trying to stay as inconspicuous as possible. He had stood for fifteen minutes in a telephone queue of people trapped by the transport system breakdown. Ringing home, ringing the office. Damnation. Why didn't they hurry? He was a sitting target standing here.

When he finally reached the phone, the line was appalling. He was surprised to reach Sarah Jane Smith so quickly.

'Hello?' he barked. 'Miss Smith?'

At first, he thought he was through to some sort of answerphone. A robotic voice said, 'Your telephone call has been received and your voice print recognized. The mistress is being summoned. Please remain on the line, I am boosting the reception differential.'

The quality of the line improved radically and the Brigadier heard Miss Smith saying, 'Who is it, K9?'

The other voice replied, 'Brigadier Lethbridge-Stewart, mistress.'

'Oh, thank goodness,' he heard her exclaim.

'From a public callbox situated at the junction of Great Titchfield Street and Foley . . .'

'Yes. All right. Thank you, K9!' Her voice was suddenly close in on the line. 'Brigadier?'

'Miss Smith. I need your help.'

'Oh, I'm so relieved to hear you.'

'Please, just listen.' He glanced along the street and saw a youth in a green uniform about fifty yards away. 'I want you to contact UNIT for me.'

'But I've already tried that, and well, I thought there was something very wrong. I spoke to someone called Cavendish.'

'Cavendish!' The Brigadier hunched up further as the young man in green ran past the phonebox. He was followed by a tramp who seemed to be having trouble keeping up.

'Yes. Captain Cavendish. Do you know him?' she asked. 'He sounded like a right little charmer.'

'Miss Smith, just ring the regular UNIT number. Ask for Brigadier Charles Crichton and quote them the following codes: NN and QQ.'

'NN and QQ. Right, got you.'

'Tell Crichton what you told me. It's a risk, but we must reach someone we can trust.'

'But Cavendish said . . .'

With a click, the line went dead. It was replaced by a series of high pitched bleeps. The Brigadier's thoughts swam. He slammed the receiver down hard. Leaning heavily against the side of the booth, he tried to extract his phonecard from the machine. It seemed to be jammed. As he watched, there was a crunching sound and the card was slowly extruded, its shape mangled and bitten.

He pocketed the object and left the phonebox, forced to concentrate on every step, making his way north.

A pack of five Chillys were moving up Regent Street, heading towards Portland Place. Danny and Harrods ducked behind an abandoned bus until they had passed. The traffic lights at the junction with Mortimer Street were dementedly flashing all their lights at once. From somewhere they heard the echoing sound of police loudhailers. The West End was apparently being sealed off.

'Well, sir?' whispered Harrods.

Danny was nervously tapping a finger against his teeth. 'I don't know.' The certainty of what he was seeking had gone. It was part of his gift – seeking and finding an object; visualizing it and then simply going to collect. But he was seeking a person, not an inanimate artefact or a computer code; not his sister's watch hidden in the garden, or his father's car keys. He couldn't visualize. He just didn't know any more.

'This way,' he said and they hurried west towards Wigmore Street. The cafés and shops were deserted, the roads clogged with abandoned vehicles. Danny ran, his head turning this way and that, vainly searching for some clue. His head was starting to swim. He was removed from his thoughts, flying above their surface, but unable to reach them. They flashed and rippled mockingly like sunlight on water.

He saw a cluster of huge white eyes flickering and glaring. They drew him in. In his head, he heard a high pulsing beat. He went to it, but an invisible wall barred his way. Arms stretched out, he pinioned himself against the barrier, trying to force a way through.

In his head he saw a toy – a lumpen carving of a bear creature. He couldn't get past it to see the Brigadier.

Fingers dug hard into his shoulders and Harrods pulled him away from the shop window. Inside, a dozen television screens were flickering balefully, their reception reduced to blank white light.

Clive Kirkham sat in plush surroundings of the Millbank studio at Westminster waiting for something to happen. The BBC's hospitality was beginning to wear a bit thin. The young upstart correspondent they had assigned to interview him about New World University kept apologizing for the delay. There was meant to be a report to accompany the interview, but the top brass at New World were unavailable for comment and the camera crew were stuck in traffic between Westminster and Shepherd's Bush.

'Gone to the pub if they've any sense,' muttered Kirkham.

Initially, the producer had said that the interview was for the evening news. Now, in between bouts of blasphemy, she was muttering that the news might not go out at all. If it did, it would wholly concern the technological meltdown that was infecting every major computer system around the globe.

Millbank's link to Television Centre had gone down. All TV and radio stations were currently running on their own generators and several of the transmitters had failed.

'Christ,' the producer complained, 'what the hell's going on out there? The licence-payers complain we spend too much time speculating, but how else do you cover the end of the world? Get Kate Adie to summarize Armageddon *after* the event?'

'It'll never get the ratings,' crowed Clive Kirkham.

The producer gave him a withering look and retired from the studio to the bedlam of her control room. The correspondent apologized again. The lights went out. With no internal phones working, they were isolated and literally in the dark.

Kirkham stayed put, determined to have his say no matter what. He sipped his BBC tea, enjoying the dimly lit sight of the world's most prestigious broadcasting organization reduced to grovelling about trying to change a fuse.

Twice, a secretary from the House came in to see if there was any news. The second time, she announced that Parliament was to be recalled for an emergency debate.

The back-up generator came on. Clive Kirkham grabbed at the microphone boom and glared at the producer through the glass window of the control room. 'Young lady, are you listening? If you want this interview, I suggest you get it now. Or maybe you can afford to get me back at a time more convenient to you.'

Within minutes, Kirkham was facing the camera and

unleashing his tirade against New World, neo-Nazism, the Education Secretary and the irresponsibility of the government in general.

As the correspondent nodded dutifully, there was a shout from the control room. The lights flickered and dimmed. Several of the cables that lay across the floor twitched and undulated. There was a deafening screech of feedback.

Kirkham gaped as the whole camera podium, operator and all, lifted gracefully away from the floor. The cameraman flung himself sideways. The camera hovered and then threw itself straight at Clive Kirkham. The MP ducked as the massive piece of technology sailed inches above his head and smashed itself into the wall behind him.

There was a loud clunk as someone cut the power.

Technicians and PAs clustered round the astonished Kirkham. All he could think to say was, 'Bloody hell. You didn't tell me you had a poltergeist.'

Sarah was getting increasingly frustrated. 'No. No. I said codes NN and QQ.'

She threw a glance at K9, who was waiting by the desk, monitoring the call to UNIT HQ. The voice still told her that Brigadier Crichton was unavailable, but at least she was not talking to Cavendish.

'Q . . . Q! It's urgent!' She shook the phone angrily, trying to clear the crackling interference. 'I'd get more sense out of the tea lady.'

The voice on the other end of the phone burbled something which she didn't even imagine she had heard correctly.

'Sorry? Have I encountered any what? What have Yeti got to do with it?'

There was a pause.

'Mistress?'

She groaned. 'Not now, K9.'

'Yeti, mistress?'

'What?'

'I have references to Yeti which also mention Colonel Lethbridge-Stewart and the London Event.'

'K9?'

'Mistress?'

'I'm sorry for what I said when I tripped over you this morning.'

'Apologies are unnecessary.'

'You're a wee gem, K9, and I won't ever threaten to put you in kennels again.'

'Hello,' said a new voice on the line. 'This is Crichton.'

'Oh hello, Brigadier. My name is Sarah Jane Smith. I used to work with UNIT a long time ago. But I'm ringing about Brigadier Lethbridge-Stewart and the London Event and New World University.'

Victoria rose from her desk as the old man appeared in the doorway. He advanced slowly, his white stick sweeping the floor before him.

'Chancellor,' she said, and came to meet him.

He stopped, sensing her presence.

She ignored Christopher's stare and gazed adoringly up at her mentor's ancient, bedraggled features. 'Welcome home, Professor Travers.'

His head did not turn and his voice was icy. 'I am still in the wilderness. Only my will to survive keeps me from despair.'

Victoria took his free hand and lifted it to her face. 'You have lit a flame of hope in all of us.'

He gave a little groan and started to run his bony fingers almost tenderly across the contours of her face. Then, with a grunt, he caught her chin and held her with sudden ferocity.

'Is it as I instructed? My shape. Symmetry. A form at last. Shaping out my future. When will my new web stretch out across the Earth?'

'Web?' She struggled to break his grip as his face came closer. He was drooling into his filthy beard.

'Not until I have the Locus!'

21

A Reunion

The Brigadier followed the canal west from Regents Park. He was hungry. He had not eaten since breakfast. Eventually he saw the figure of his daughter seated on a bench, staring out across the water at the cemetery on the other bank. It was a day for memories. The blonde hair she had inherited from his own mother still reached down to her shoulders, just as it had done since she was little. He thought she looked distinctly lonely.

He had almost reached her before she noticed him. She stood up, looking embarrassed.

'You're late,' she said.

'I was delayed. The traffic and this computer business.'

It seemed a world away in this desolate spot. They eyed each other warily, both awkward, not touching, each not sure if the other was an enemy.

'Are you all right?' she asked politely.

'I can't complain. How are you?'

She paused and then turned away. 'Look, this is stupid. I'll just go. I shouldn't have called you.'

'Kate?'

She was instantly back. 'Yes, Dad?'

'Have you eaten? We can go and get a meal.'

She shook her head emphatically. 'No. I just . . .' She sat down in frustration.

He sat at the other end of the bench, looking out over the water. 'All right. We'll sit here.'

'Sorry.' She was tight with emotion. Without turning towards him, she said, 'You look tired.'

He glanced round for trouble. 'I've had a difficult morning.' He turned to her. 'It's been six years, Kate. What's the matter? Is it money?'

'Not especially,' she said.

'Your mother, then?'

'No, I don't see her either.' She kicked out her feet. 'Sorry. It sounds stupid, but well . . . I'm being harassed.'

'Who by?'

'There are these Chillys.'

'Chillys?' As usual she was miles ahead of him. He felt like the High Court judge who had to have compact discs explained to him.

'You know. Children of the . . .'

'Children?'

'No. I mean they're called *Children*. From that New World techno-cult.'

'Ah.' He maintained his look of concern, silently relieved that at last some pieces were falling into place. 'Nasty customers in yellow and green.'

'Two of them,' she went on. 'They just sit opposite the boat all the time.' She had turned to look at him at last, her face taut with despair. 'Look, I'm just being stupid.'

'No,' he said firmly.

Tears were welling in her eyes. 'But they just won't go away. And they're frightening . . . they're frightening me.'

He nodded, wondering what name she had nearly blurted out. He did not like sitting here. It was too exposed. Not for him, but because he had always shielded his family from the implications of his job. He was the one the Chillys were after and now Kate was involved because she had his name.

He had another abiding image of her as a little girl. She had huge sad eyes and said, 'Come back soon, Dad.' He was always being called away at crucial moments, and it was usually a certain Scientific Advisor's fault. Ridiculous that they had never met, because he was sure that the Doctor would be wonderful with children.

'Can we walk a bit?' he said.

She started to lead back the way he had come and he guessed she was taking him away from her home.

Showing emotion had always been a problem. That shrink woman that they sent him to after his breakdown at the school had told him as much. He couldn't imagine why. It had never been difficult to shout at the men, or at public schoolboys for that matter. That was letting off steam wasn't it? But the shrink, who was a very charming woman, he recalled, said he had been bottling it up for years. That was nonsense, of course. He never took family problems onto the parade ground, and if he never talked to Fiona either, then there were good reasons for it. He had duties and other commitments. Anyway, Fiona had never talked to him either, not for years. So that evened things out a bit.

He fished for something to say to Kate. She used to have a partner or boyfriend or lover, but he had never met the chap. Probably some sort of activist of whom he would never approve. 'What about . . . whatsisname? Doesn't he help?'

'I split up with Jonathan two years ago.'

'Ah. I'm sorry.' He watched a pair of geese that were winging like arrows along the stretch of water. 'I'm getting old, Kate.' He felt himself starting to wallow and immediately changed the subject. 'Perhaps you should get off that boat.'

'It's not the boat,' she snapped. 'It's them!'

He stopped walking. 'And me too?'

Kate froze where she stood. When she was little it had been the prelude to a tantrum. He braced himself, but her voice came surprisingly quietly and was twice as cutting.

'Army families get to live together. So why didn't we? Was your career that important?'

It was a familiar argument she had inherited from her mother.

'It's something I can't explain, Kate.'

'Mum used to think you were some sort of spy. We used to *hope* it because at least that would be interesting. But it's just soldiers, isn't it? Training to kill people with big guns.'

He could remember a golden-haired little tiger who played cowboys and indians with the rest of the children. He also recalled many sleepless nights over the Christmas

Monster that lived under the stairs. She said it gave her nightmares – presents wrapped up in the old Christmas paper in which it made its den. But he kept his silence on that.

'I had other responsibilities,' he said to her.

'Who to?'

He smiled. How could he explain? 'To . . . everyone.'

'What?'

'That's all.'

There was a woman in a dark cloak standing on the other side of the canal. A solitary figure like a ghost risen from the cemetery.

'Who *do* I trust then?' said Kate.

She was there alone among the gravestones. Another memory. The woman who had been plaguing his thoughts.

'Who *do* I trust then?'

He turned back and found that he was standing with young Hinton. The world was misty, lowering, turning into a bowl in which he was trapped. The trees were leaning in over him.

Hinton seemed frightened and spoke urgently. 'Don't trust anyone, sir. I told you, no one at all.'

He was no longer dressed in his school gear. He wore a dark coat and under it there was a flash of green and yellow.

'Trust no one at all.'

The cloaked woman was suddenly there behind Hinton. Her clear eyes pierced him. He shuddered under their assault. He put them out of his head. The world opened out again.

'Well?' said Kate.

Confused, he snatched at a straw. 'Are you sure you don't want any money?'

A look of sickened despair settled over her face. 'Just forget it,' she said and started to walk away.

'Kate!' When he shouted her name, she started to run. She was already disappearing up a side track. He tried to follow, but could not begin to match her pace.

As he ran, two familiar figures in Chilly uniforms emerged ahead of him from the side of the towpath. The first blocked his way with a surly grin.

'Hello, grandad. We want you.'

The Brigadier felt himself grabbed from behind. Arms pressed in on his chest. He struggled as the first Chilly raised his spare set of headphones and advanced on him. He recognized the repeating bleep from the speakers. A sound that had once accompanied the Yeti when their forces occupied London.

The Chilly started to force the phones over his head. The signal began to swamp his thoughts. He fought to keep his own will. Swooning, he reached out with his hand and yanked the Chilly's own headphones off his attacker's head.

The youth gave a yell of pain and his knees gave way. He sprawled on the path, shaking his head in shock.

Somewhere in his head, the Brigadier heard a shout. He staggered and saw both the Chillys taking to their heels along the towpath.

His head was going numb. He dropped to his own knees, unable to catch his breath. He fell sideways supporting himself on one hand. Kate. He wanted Kate.

There was a figure running towards him, running downwards out of the sun, scuttling down the side track, a heavy coat flapping round it, a dark scarf flying behind it. The light made a halo of wild curls round its head. And the face, the nut-brown face, was too close, staring too hard. He couldn't make out the face in the shadow of the golden halo. It could be anyone he was half expecting.

'Good Lord,' he slurred. 'Is that you? Have you changed yourself again?'

Too much light. Too much. He couldn't make out the face.

He keeled over into darkness.

22

Light of Truth

The mix of dream and reality that she had learned to juggle, slid between her fingers. The canal snaked away below. The silver cord that anchored her astral body to her physical shape stretched, threatened to tear. Faster and faster. An irresistible current was dragging her down into a Charybdis vortex of flying faces and flying mountains. Victoria was carried in the grip of a wave of her own despair. The lost shapes of things never born snatched at her; ideas yet to find thoughts; shadows hungry to be cast. All the hidden life that waits to squirm and wriggle through any crack into reality.

The wave broke and washed her like jetsam onto the empty beach. Endless fields of computer data scrolled across the livid sky. The wind flung squalls of sand in her face. The dark shape of her despair still gripped like a vice, a clawed hand, wreathed in web, clamped at her arm. She struggled to escape as its shadow rose above her.

'I needed time!' she protested to her judge.

'*I needed freedom!*'

She struggled to free her arm. The wind was tearing at her hair, tangling it into wild streamers. 'You're not Professor Travers. For pity's sake, let me go!'

A burst of laughter echoed through the clouds like thunder.

'*Your task is done. Now I take control. I'll find Lethbridge-Stewart . . . my gaoler!*'

Victoria turned for help, any help. She saw the Brigadier himself, in uniform, walking away across the flats. She reached for him, but he was too far, fading in the veils of blown sand.

Other fingers were reaching in to her. Thousands of

beseeching hands. Promises she had made, expectations she could not fulfil. They all bound her, a hideous anemone of human yearning.

'Let me go!' she cried to the huge shadow. 'Who are you?'

'*Remember me, Victoria?*' Again its laughter boomed. '*Who's blind now?*'

The shadow reared above her. It raked the air with heavy claws. It had a shaggy pelt of ruddy fur and eyes like burning coals. It filled the sky and its roar of anger made the beach tremble.

23

Crichton

Brigadier Charles Crichton flipped yet another plastic coffee cup into the bin and snapped irritably at his adjutant.

'Nothing on Miss Smith either?'

Sergeant Beagles looked ready to duck. 'No, sir. There's nothing we can do, not without Central Records at Geneva.'

'Damned computers!' exploded Crichton. His normally immaculate jacket had been discarded. He was down to shirt sleeves with the rest of them. UNIT HQ had been pandemonic since the early hours. Twice in the morning, Crichton had fielded calls from Clive Kirkham. The opposition MP was demanding to know why, with the overwhelming plethora of inexplicable events, UNIT was doing nothing. Something had better be done because the government wouldn't lift a finger.

Crichton refrained from telling him that they didn't know what to do because they couldn't access the UNIT computer net. He had been inordinately grateful when the phone lines had crashed as well. But it didn't solve the Lethbridge-Stewart problem.

'Sir?' Sergeant Beagles was still standing in front of his desk. 'Apparently there are some old records in the security vault, sir. Still on hard copy.'

'Sir!' Corporal Ishani dashed in from the outer office and came to an abrupt halt. 'Sorry, sir.'

Crichton fished a key out of his pocket and proffered it to Beagles. 'Out of order, I know, Sergeant, but go and see what there is.'

'Sir.' Beagles hurried away, obviously relieved to be out of the firing line.

'Yes, Corporal?'

Ishani handed an envelope to the Brigadier. 'Just arrived by courier, sir.'

Crichton tore open the envelope and produced a letter printed on Home Office stationery.

'Good God,' he announced as he started to read. The letter was recalling all British troops attached to UNIT '*in the event of expected civic disorder following the global breakdown of the technological infrastructure.*' It was personally signed by the Home Secretary.

'They want us to stop the public looting Sainsbury's.'

'Sir, the courier's waiting for an answer.'

Crichton tried to concentrate through the machine-gun barrage of a resuscitated electric typewriter in the next room. It occurred to him that mankind's evolution had peaked and from now on they were devolving backwards down to the primal slime.

Someone in civvies sauntered past his office door.

'Cavendish!' yelled Crichton.

The nonchalant head appeared round the door. 'Sir?'

'Ishani. Wait outside and close the door.'

The corporal disappeared as Cavendish came to attention in front of the CO's desk. Crichton had the Devil's very temper when roused and knew how to play on its reputation.

'You're supposed to be on surveillance, Captain,' he barked. 'Who's keeping tabs on Lethbridge-Stewart?'

'Grieve's taken over, sir.'

'And?'

'Nothing unusual to report. Brigadier Lethbridge-Stewart was still at home when I left. He lives alone.'

Crichton flicked at a paper on his desk. 'No callers, Captain?'

'Only the school secretary.' He smirked. 'She seems to drop in on a regular basis.'

'No phone calls either?'

'Only one incoming call in the past week, sir. I've the report here.' He presented Crichton with a file and pointed out the caller details. 'It's the school secretary again.'

'Hmm.'

The Captain glanced round the office, apparently checking that they were alone. 'Is there a problem, sir?'

Crichton nodded coldly. 'I've just been contacted by a Miss Sarah Jane Smith. She used to be attached to UNIT in the early days. She says she's been talking to Lethbridge-Stewart. She also says he's in London.'

Cavendish, decided Crichton, was a supreme example of UNIT training. Faced with this accusation, he managed to look convincingly surprised. 'That's impossible, sir. Why hasn't Grieve alerted us? Unless it's this computer business.'

'Miss Smith also said she spoke to you here at HQ.'

Cavendish gave a little laugh. 'Hardly, sir.'

It was too much. He was so infuriatingly smooth. 'What's going on, Cavendish? And what do you know about New World University?'

There was a knock. Crichton glowered. 'Come!'

Sergeant Beagles appeared in the doorway. He was carrying a battered cardboard file. 'Excuse me, sir, but I found this in the security vault. It's a full MoD report on the London Event of Sixty-eight.'

He reached in front of Cavendish and placed it on the desk. 'Like I said sir, it's pre-UNIT, so I doubt it exists except on hard copy.' A twinkle came into his eye. 'And there's a lot here about Yeti, too, sir.'

It was the first time Brigadier Crichton had smiled that day. 'Well done, Sergeant. Perhaps this'll throw a bit of light on proceedings. Get every man we have on stand-by.'

Sergeant Beagles returned the security key, saluted and left. Brigadier Crichton was about to turn back to Cavendish when he noticed Corporal Ishani still hovering in the doorway.

'Sorry, sir, but the courier's still waiting.'

'Tell him I'm on manoeuvres, Corporal.' He picked up the Home Office letter and walked to a filing cabinet. He filed it under I for Interfering Politicians. 'Tell him anything you like, but tell him I'm not here.'

Ishani collided with Corporal White in the door. 'Sir?'

'What is it, Corporal? I'm busy.'

'There's two people to see you, sir.'

'Now what?'

'There's a Miss Smith. Says she spoke to you earlier.'

'Aha. The redoubtable Sarah Jane Smith. And who's the other?'

'It's Desmond Pennington, sir. The Education Secretary.'

'Good God, not together?'

'No, sir.'

Crichton turned to face his desk. It was a moment before he realized that the room was empty. Cavendish had gone, and so had the file on the London Event.

24

The Boat

Somewhere something was chugging gently. The Brigadier seemed to be floating, a cradled drifting motion that was so comfortable and pleasing that he wanted to stay asleep. He opened his eyes and saw Kate bending over him.

'Hello, Dad.' She smiled with an affection that he had forgotten could go with families. He realized that she had been holding his hand. It was another dream. Behind her, a shoal of coloured fish hovered in the air, flashing and flickering.

'Where am I?' he mouthed. He felt woozy. He could see a low ceiling and a window that ran parallel above the side of the bed where he was lying. Lights darted back and forth across the surfaces.

'You're on the boat,' Kate said gently.

'Ah.' That brought everything into focus. He saw that the fish were part of a hanging mobile that was turning in the afternoon sunshine. It was reflecting lozenges of light around the cabin.

Kate squeezed his hand again. 'We had to bring you here. How do you feel now?'

'We?' he asked and tried to sit up. He winced. Something had just hit him on the inside of his head.

She pushed him firmly back into the pillow. 'No, Dad. You stay there. You were mugged by some Chillys. Danny ran after me and fetched me back.'

'Danny who?'

Another figure slid into his field of vision. A young man with gelled hair and glasses. He was holding a mug of tea and had a terribly familiar look to him.

'Daniel Hinton, Brigadier. School House '91.' The boy

had the sort of nervous smile that usually meant he couldn't hand in last night's prep.

Lethbridge-Stewart smiled. 'I remember.' Everywhere today it was memories. He was drowning in them. He hoped it wasn't his life flashing before him.

He took the tea. The mug had a fierce picture of rampant nurses waving banners and was marked 'Save the NHS'. One of Kate's, no doubt. He eyed the boy again. It was difficult to think of him as anything other than a pupil, even if he had forcibly departed Brendon three years before. 'We've met again quite recently. Am I right? On something called the astral plane.'

Danny beamed with satisfaction. 'It wasn't entirely wasted then.'

'Extraordinary,' declared the Brigadier and sipped his tea. The chugging sound altered in pitch and the cabin dipped for a second. The fish mobile swung freely from the drawing-pin that held it up.

'Hello,' the Brigadier said. 'We're moving.'

He ignored Kate's protest and pulled himself off the bed. From the window, he could see the water and a bank of green foliage sliding past. Still uncertain of his legs, he made his way, hand over hand, to the steps that led up on deck.

The little man with wild hair and a huge scruffy coat who was working the tiller came to attention as soon as he saw the Brigadier emerge.

'Sir. Glad to see you're all right, sir.'

Lethbridge-Stewart squinted in the sunlight at their unlikely pilot. Behind him, Kate was saying, 'Harrods saved you from the Chillys, Dad.'

The little man nodded. 'Bunch of hooligans, sir. The lad reckoned we were best off well away from them.'

'Thank you er . . . Harrods?'

'Sir,' he barked.

The Brigadier surveyed the canal banks. They were a mass of overgrown vegetation. The narrow boat was chugging west, away from the city. It occurred to him that after today's fiasco on the roads, this was the most reliable way to travel. It had been a sensible move to get away from trouble, even if he wasn't quite sure exactly where they were going.

The narrow boat looked in good shape, colourfully painted with troughs of daffodils set along the roof. But then that sort of orderliness was just what he would have expected from Kate. He liked to think she took after him in that respect. Gardening was something he had never had time for as a soldier, but he'd kept a spruce patch in his quarters at Brendon, and once he'd retired, he was going to have a place with a large plot to indulge himself in. Above anything, he had always wanted an apple tree.

He glanced at Harrods again. The little tramp was still standing to attention. 'Army, aren't you?' the Brigadier observed. 'On your uppers?'

'RAF, sir. Flight Sergeant Haroldson. Squadron got disbanded, sir.'

That was a familiar enough story. The Brigadier could only sympathize. 'Like losing your family.' He noticed Kate's affectionate smile again and returned it with interest.

'Get called Harrods, sir, 'cos I'm fussy where I kip down.'

He had standards too. The Brigadier would far rather lead one man like Harrods than a hundred of the self-satisfied types that Cavendish represented. 'Thank you, Flight Sergeant. Carry on.'

'Sir.'

With a look of approval, the Brigadier ducked back under the door. 'The company you keep's a real eye-opener, Kate.'

'I thought they were with you,' she said.

Danny snapped shut the lid of a metal trunk, but not before the Brigadier saw a jumble of coloured bricks and train tracks inside.

'We can't stay here, Brigadier,' the boy said urgently. 'The Intelligence is hunting us.'

'Both of us?' The Brigadier sat down on the bed again. Under Danny's coat he glimpsed a green and yellow sweatshirt. 'Aren't you one of these Chilly characters too?'

Danny was in earnest. 'New World's a front to bring the Intelligence back through. It's an evil spirit that got bound to the Earth.'

This was the sort of hokum that the Doctor usually came out with, and he was usually right. Of course, the Doctor had never had to write an official report after the event. Over the years, Lethbridge-Stewart had become a dab hand at glossing down the sometimes unbelievable evidence of his own eyes for the upper echelons to read. This sort of talk took him right back to what *they* now termed 'The Blunder Days'. He had learned to be a lot more open-minded during that era. Frankly, *they* didn't know what *they'd* missed.

Daniel Hinton had certainly been a misguided nuisance when he was at school, but he had never been a liar. There was a distinct possibility that the boy was right. The Brigadier could remember some garbled explanation that the Doctor had given about trying to reverse the power on the Intelligence. The blasted thing was defeated, not destroyed. But he and the Doctor were barely acquainted in those days and he'd never really understood the implications. As it was, he was working on his own now.

'Trust no one. Isn't that right, Danny? Not even my people at UNIT.'

Kate had been watching the two of them with a look of growing perplexedness. 'Just listen to you. Who do I call first? Police, exorcist or psychiatrist?'

Danny ignored her. 'The whole city's fouled up. The computer Internet's virally infested.'

At last, the pieces were forming up together. The Brigadier looked to his pupil for confirmation. 'And that's the Intelligence's new body?'

Danny frowned almost apologetically. 'It won't stop there.'

This was not what the Brigadier wanted to hear. His daughter had been threatened and he refused to believe that some shapeless mass of malevolent thoughts that didn't even feasibly exist was carrying out a personal vendetta against him. No one had so much as seen any Yeti, even he had only imagined one. He was determined to find some other acceptable explanation. If he could, he would put it down to bad dreams after a toasted cheese supper, or too much nutmeg on one of Celia's rice puddings. The rest was just coincidence.

He looked at Danny's Chilly sweatshirt and knew that he was fooling himself. That really annoyed him. Out of sheer perversity, he suddenly snapped, 'Nonsense. The Intelligence was driven out! I was there!'

'No!' exploded Danny. 'It's trapped. It can't break its link until all its old icons of power are destroyed. One icon still remains. The final Locus.'

'How do you know?' said Kate.

Danny shrugged. 'Just do. The link was reversed. The icon that the Intelligence used now binds the Intelligence. The Intelligence has become the pawn.'

Outside, the note of the engine began to grind upwards.

Deep in thought, the Brigadier said, 'Cavendish asked me about keepsakes . . . And when I think, there *was* something.'

Danny turned sharply towards him. 'Yes?'

His tutor shook his head. 'No, I lost that years ago.'

'Like what?' said Kate.

'It was when you said "pawn", I suddenly remembered. A little carving of a Yeti, like a chesspiece. Tibetan, I think.'

'Dad.' Kate stood up, suddenly very afraid.

He watched her open the metal chest and rummage through the toys inside. From the bottom she produced a grubby figure carved in ivory. 'Like this?' she asked and held it out to him.

He took it and studied the object. It was almost comical. A bulbous, ethnic representation of a furry creature bearing little resemblance to the massive horrors that had stalked London so long ago.

'Yes, that's it.'

The boat gave a sudden lurch.

'But I've had that thing since I was a kid,' insisted Kate.

The Brigadier steadied himself as the boat appeared to turn. 'It's infinitely dangerous. We have to get rid of it now.'

25

Taking the Knight's Pawn

Harrods watched a heron that was flying along the canal in the *Mananda*'s wake. It seemed like a good omen, but then he had just polished off a beer and the last of the sandwiches that the young lady had given him. Suddenly everything seemed a lot better. He reckoned they had put trouble behind them for a bit. Perhaps the Brigadier could find him a situation of sorts. He wasn't going back to the New World if he could help it, except maybe to collect his things. Then he might travel a bit for the summer. He could do Ascot, Wimbledon or Henley Regatta. The sorts of place where you got a better class of rubbish.

He'd find a nice new shack too. A holiday shack. Or he'd get a narrow boat. He'd only just discovered boats and they were easy. But they'd never beat flying, never beat wings. Nothing beat the view from the cockpit of a Hercules. That's what he really wanted back. But the bird-boy was his best bit of luck since a delivery lorry had taken a corner too fast and he'd dined out of tins of spaghetti hoops for three weeks. Danny knew what was what. Best stick with Danny and he might get some too. He watched the heron as it followed them on great lazy wings.

The tiller arm jerked and nearly had him over the side. It pulled at him, suddenly getting a life of its own. He guessed something was jammed on the rudder and struggled to work it free.

The tiller jerked again and hit him full in the chest. The narrow boat was starting to turn in towards the bank. Harrods pushed his whole weight at the arm trying to keep the course steady. As he puffed for breath he saw, further along the bank, a group of Chillys staring out across the water.

'Sir, sir,' he muttered to himself.

He could feel the pull of their collective thoughts. The bleeders were pulling the boat towards them just by sheer bloody-minded willpower. They weren't having him. Not old Harrods. Not bloody likely. He put all his weight against the tiller, but he could hear the engine revving up too. They were having a go at that as well.

One of the Chillys, who seemed to be the leader, was holding something towards the boat. It gleamed metallically in his hands.

The *Mananda* was going faster and faster. It hit the bank with a crash of mud and timber. Harrods practically fell into the cabin.

'Sir. We have company, sir!'

The others were still picking themselves up off the floor. Overhead they heard the thump of boots on the roof. The *Mananda* was being boarded. Faces were appearing in the windows. Faces in yellow peaked caps, hanging over from above, staring hungrily in at them.

Kate panicked. 'Get them away! Get them off here!'

'Everyone out now!' shouted the Brigadier. He turned for the door and found Danny blocking his exit. The boy reached for the little chesspiece.

'I'm sorry, Brigadier,' he said. He had a green pallor and looked feverish.

'Out of my way, Hinton.'

The boy was shaking his head apologetically. 'I didn't know. I swear it.' He was staring at the heads in the windows, drawing on their power. The energy in the room was almost tangible. It made Danny look huge.

Harrods grabbed at him. 'What are you on about?'

With one flick of his arm, the boy sent the old tramp tumbling backwards onto the kitchen floor. His eyes never left the Brigadier. His hand was covered in web. It was reaching out like a claw. 'I warned you, didn't I? Don't trust anyone! The Intelligence used me to seek you out. It's taking new forms now. I'm the trap!'

The Brigadier reached into his jacket. 'I'm warning you, Hinton. Stand back!'

'Give me the Locus!' yelled the boy. He lunged for the piece as the Brigadier pulled out his Browning.

'No!' Kate was shouting. 'No guns! Not in here!'

All around the windows, the Chillys turned their heads to stare at the cabin entrance.

The Brigadier heard a sound that filled him with dread. A high-pitched repeating blip. 'Get back!' he shouted as a silver sphere, the size of a croquet ball, rolled into the doorway and stopped at the top of the steps. It rocked a little in its place as if surveying its victims.

Instinctively everyone pulled back. Only Danny remained, pushed frozen against the wall, a look of abject terror on his face. The sphere dropped casually down the steps. It rolled towards him.

It leapt.

Danny's hands closed over the sphere as it plunged into his chest. There was a crack of breaking bones. He stumbled forward choking, a hole torn in the front of his sweatshirt. There was no blood. The sphere had been cleanly absorbed.

No one dared move. They could still hear the bleeping. The cabin was alive with energy. As they watched, the shape of Danny Hinton began to grow. Little storms of electricity played over his expanding, darkening body. He yelled and the yell coarsened into an animal snarl, then a roar revealing massive yellow incisor fangs. His clothes tore and burst out in eruptions of red-brown fur. His head filled out to take in the massive shoulders. His new form reached to the ceiling. Driven by the dark thoughts embodied in the sphere, Daniel Hinton, School House '91, became a Yeti.

The Brigadier raised the gun to shoot, but one swipe from a flailing claw knocked the weapon from his grip.

Harrods, scuttling clear, was knocked flying.

In the crammed mêlée, the Brigadier saw the chess-piece rolling on the bed. He saw Kate make a dive for the object.

She gasped as the pawn leapt out of her fingers and into the Yeti's outstretched claw. The monster bellowed in deafening triumph, turned and forced its way out of the splintering cabin door.

The group of Chillys formed a corridor on the bank as the Yeti strode off the boat clutching its prize.

The Brigadier scrambled up from the cabin and watched from the deck as they marched away. He hefted his gun in his hand. He had been a fool, and an old fool too. No wonder they'd retired him early. And now he had brought all this on the one person he had forgotten that he loved. There was no one to trust, not even himself, it seemed. But he had to put things right and avenge the boy's death.

As he ducked inside the broken door, he heard Kate saying, 'This is my home! What's happening?'

She was sitting on the bed, too shocked to cry, and Harrods was crouching by her, trying to console her. When he saw the senior officer, he stood, but not to attention.

'They've got what they want. Now they're going,' the Brigadier said grimly.

Harrods edged a look out of the window. 'Back to New World, sir. That's where it all comes from.'

Kate stared at the floor. 'What sort of job *do* you do! That boy was . . .' She faltered, unable even to explain what she had seen.

The Brigadier knelt beside her. 'I have to go after them, Kate. I'll explain later.'

'Just go then,' she snapped.

Lethbridge-Stewart looked up at Harrods. 'Flight Sergeant?'

The little man nodded. 'I'll come, sir. For the lad's sake.'

'Good man. Just wait outside for me.'

'Sir.'

The Brigadier waited for Harrods to clear the cabin. Then he turned back to his daughter. He thought this might be the most difficult moment of his life. He sat on the bed beside her. 'Kate,' he said as gently as he could muster.

'What?' She didn't want to look at him.

He paused and then said, 'Just tell me one thing. Why do you have a box of toys down there?'

She sighed. Then she reached for a drawer by the bed. There was a pile of loose photographs inside. She lifted one out and passed it to her father.

'He'll be five next week,' she said flatly.

He laid down his gun and took in the picture slowly. He wasn't sure what he had hoped for or expected. It showed a small boy with sandy hair who grinned cheekily out at him. He looked a little terror.

The Brigadier worked to find the words, but all he could say was, 'I have a grandson? *My* grandson. I never dreamt . . . Good Lord.'

There was so much he wanted to say. He thought his heart would brim over with excitement and pride.

'Gordon,' said Kate. 'After you. Gordon James. He's safe, away from here.' Tears were getting the worse of her. 'I'm sorry, Dad, I couldn't tell you.'

He was squeezing her hand. 'I have a grandson.' Something in his eye and something catching in his throat, yet he was glowing with the joy of it. Poor Kate. She had kept this from him for so long. Was she so angry or was he so terrifying? 'Kate, can I keep this?'

She nodded tightly.

He squeezed her hand again. 'Thank you, Kate. It's getting late. We'll talk later. I'll be back.'

He stood, still clutching the photograph of Gordon James Lethbridge-Stewart, and left the boat, closing the door as best he could.

26

Truth is Relative

Victoria's mind was spinning so that she could not sleep. She dreamed even when she was awake now, unable to cradle herself in her own chosen thoughts. Wakefulness and sleeping vied with each other to be the more nightmarish. The two states melded into an impressionistic haze.

Professor Travers, if indeed it was Travers, sat in her chair, behind her desk. It was what she had wanted, but far from what she expected. Her long-awaited tutor was ancient and unkempt. He was slumped like a puppet tied up with spider strings. This Travers had promised the Light of Truth, but his gift revealed things she did not want to see. She no longer knew light from shade, truth from fantasy. She dreamed horrors – but suppose she was lying to herself?

Was this light also the cold light of day, or the *lux aeterna* of heavenly compassion? Might it not be the *ignis fatuus* that leads travellers from the path?

Which one? she thought. Which light is true?

She had grown up instructed in the virtues of faith and hope and charity. The three tiers on her mother's grave. Such values were antique in this new age of self-aggrandisement. Virtue was a sign written in neon that said, *Use Me*.

No matter now. She was stranded on the sidelines. A watcher, as events she had instigated hurtled past uncontrolled and out of her reach.

In her mind, she stood at the top of a stairway. From below, a lurid green glow seeped like a festering nest of hatred feeding in the dark recesses of her thoughts. A hatred just as real as wisdom or enlightenment.

Hatred is strength.

Now Travers was enthroned. She flanked him on one side, Christopher on the other, eager to grab at something she doubted was there for him to snatch.

Sliding out of her thoughts, she noticed that another person had joined them. A uniformed army officer whom she did not recognize was standing beside Christopher. A handsome, dark-haired man with ice-cold eyes and an arrogant demeanour. Under his arm he carried a battered file embossed with the initials 'MoD'. She wondered what he had been told or what he assumed but had never asked. And what *was* he doing in her office? She had run out of words. She had never felt so achingly, wearisomely alone.

Her nightmare resumed.

She heard the high metronomic pulse of a silver sphere control unit. The door swung open and a massive bear-like creature strode into her office.

'*Dzu-teh, dzu-teh*', she heard the street vendor calling. She could no longer ignore what she already knew.

The Yeti gave a roar of greeting. Its shaggy coat was red-brown and its haunches were caked with mud. It was slightly more compact than the robots she had seen in the London Underground during the London Event; and it was less bulky than the robots she had seen sixty years ago in the Himalayas. Its movements were more instinctive, less mechanical, and its eyes burned like torched rubies. Something flapped around its rear leg above the clawed foot. It was the upper half of a trainer, still tied with blue lace, as if the foot had exploded out tearing the shoe apart.

Travers rose jerkily from the chair and his trembling hand stretched out. The Yeti dropped a little ivory figure into his palm. Victoria recognized the tiny carving as Travers's bony fingers tested its cracks and contours. She had spent years searching for this icon. This was the Locus that she had failed to recover. He had said it contained the power to unlock the future of all mankind.

She knew it could destroy them all.

He wasn't who he said he was.

She, so full of compassion, so blind to evil, had been so easy to take in.

She knew now. She was close to despair. She had opened the way to events, but could only watch helplessly as they unfolded.

'At last,' he growled.

She could see the muscles in his tortured throat contract and expand as if the usurper in his body was still learning how to use them.

'I created this tiny object. I invested it with my power and in turn it bound me in darkness.' He raised the pawn to the level of his cracked spectacles. 'Which of you shall release me?'

Victoria felt a frisson of excitement and fear. She reached instinctively for the object, but Travers's hand moved away out of her reach towards Christopher.

She watched him take the carving with a smile for her benefit. He dropped it onto the carpet and brought down his boot hard.

Thunder rumbled distantly as fragments of the Yeti pawn spun across the floor. The air crackled. Travers was thrown back into the chair, flares of blue light playing under his skin, silhouetting his bones, as if lightning was flickering inside his body. He gasped and croaked, his hands flying up to cover his eyes.

Finally he uncovered his face, squinting slowly about him. The voice in Travers's throat was no longer weak. It was in shock, but it deepened with a growing malevolence.

'Light . . . Symmetry of colours and shapes. No more tomb of darkness. My strength is growing again.'

His hand rose and clawed at the texture of the air.

'I grasp it. Form and substance. Now let my Great Plan take its shape!'

The pyramid of ivory on the desk was flickering with white light. It began to steady, pulsing in time with the bleeping signal of the Yeti.

Victoria felt a pull of fascination in the light. She saw

Christopher and the army officer, their cold eyes filling with the pulsing glow. They were being drawn in.

The officer's file tilted from his grip and spilled a cascade of documents onto the floor. Among them, Victoria saw a photograph of the young Lethbridge-Stewart.

Her thoughts, chilled with shame and remorse, appeared resilient as marble. Decorum, deportment and carriage, just as her mother had taught her. She pulled away and left her office.

A tiny bolt of light cracked from the eyes in Travers's face and arced into the pyramid on the desk.

The old man jolted back in shock. A vice had just released its grip on his thoughts. He croaked from his dried throat and stared about in alarm at the office that he had never seen before.

A woman in a dark green suit was hurrying out of the door. A huge Yeti-like creature, rearing on its hind quarters, stood rocking to and fro on the other side of the desk. *Dzu-teh? Ye-teh?* No. Those species both had grey fur, camouflaged for the rocky terrain they inhabited between the forest and snow lines.

Not a recognized species then. Unless . . .

He listened to that wretched high bleeping in his ears. Damned tinnitus again. They were always playing this tune.

Two figures, one on either side of him, were leaning forward, staring intently into the strobing light from the pyramid.

Either they'd finally put him in a home or a disco. He was sure he'd forgotten to do something important, but was damned if he could remember what. He struggled painfully to his feet and pushed his way out past the tubby fellow with the hideous jumper.

He peered at the Yeti and it growled softly at him, but did not hinder his departure.

Why should it when he was already dead?

* * *

The corridors of New World were not a place to wander in. The walls and fixtures, all inlaid, maintained and serviced by the computer, had become oppressive and threatening. The air did not move and the lighting had dimmed as the output of the university generators was redirected into the computer.

Victoria needed air and space before she could think, so she headed for the upper terraces of the Bryce Gallery. The quickest route was through the computer studies room, but when she reached the entrance she heard the chanting begin.

She edged a glance round the side of the window. In the half-light, she could see the rows of Chillys seated unmoving at their terminals. Their chanting was no longer the gentle litany of their daily meditation. Their voices had deepened into an unearthly unified growl. It turned the Lotus prayer into a repeating ground bass of elemental power over which some new chaconne of horror, some dance of death, would be composed.

She thought of Danny Hinton and suddenly guessed his fate. Doors that had been deliberately slammed shut in her memory were creaking open to let in the cruel light of truth. It was an ominous grey dawn with clouds gathering like storm crows.

Behind her, she heard scuffled movement and the approach of something that wheezed as it breathed. She ran the full length of the corridor away from it and tried the lift. The response was sluggish. It was quicker to use the stairs.

The air outside was too humid for spring. She reached the terraces attached to the gallery building and crunched across the raked gravel. At least she could breathe again, but she could not think. She only saw, she could not react. The huge orange and silver carp in the pool swam to the edge, mouthing at her, expecting to be fed, but she had nothing for them.

The Japanese maples she had planted were showing their first scarlet leaves. Beneath them, there were drifts of white narcissi and the last of the crocuses. But it was still too early for her pride, the blue Himalayan poppies propagated from the stock that Charles Bryce had once sent her. Or was it just too late for her to see them again?

She looked down from the terrace over the New World campus. Chillys were moving everywhere like yellow-headed beetles. The purpose that her students had always displayed, that marked them out from the students at other establishments, was now all too clear. They were all on the business of the computer – or rather, the mass of hateful thoughts that lived in the computer. Compassion and the search for what she most wanted had made her blind to that.

She heard the gravel crunch behind her, but she no longer cared who, or what, was approaching.

The voice of the old man sounded flat and tremulous in the open air. 'I had a daughter once. What happened to her?'

On a sudden impulse, she turned. 'Father?' She was looking up into the watery eyes of the intruder.

Travers peered down at her, studying her through his cracked spectacles. The face was no longer cruel or tortured, just searching and very lost. This was the real Travers again. A broken old man. After a moment, he shook his head angrily. 'No. No, not you. Anne.' He grunted with disapproval and turned his gaze out over the university and the hills beyond.

'*Yeti Traversii*,' he proclaimed in despairing tones. 'Brought *It* back from Tibet. All my fault!'

Victoria grasped the rail of the balcony and looked down into the depths. 'My father died on a cold world, a thousand light years away.'

Acrid smoke from the burning Dalek city and ash like coarse grit blowing in Skaro's wind.

Chillys moving on their business.

Travers rallied a little in response to her words. 'I died fifteen years ago,' he informed her. 'Saw it in *The Times*. "Professor Edward Travers CBE." Silly old fool!' He angrily yanked the white scarf from round his neck and threw it on the gravel. ' "No Flowers By Request." They still sent them though. No one listens!'

Victoria was gazing out into nothing, seeing nothing. 'Sometimes I can't even remember his face.'

She was slightly startled as she felt the old man's hand move gently onto her shoulder. She brought up her hand to touch his.

'And I travelled in time,' she said. 'Where do I belong now?' Anger, simmering for so long behind doors that had been slammed shut in her mind, finally spilled out. She rounded angrily on Travers. 'Don't you see? We've been tricked. It was the Intelligence all the time!'

A rage began to seethe up in him too. He rocked back and forth and spluttered into his beard. 'Unfinished business!' he stammered. Tears were streaming down his wizened cheeks.

A loud boom echoed across the campus. They saw the apex of the pyramid roof of the central computer block stabbing shafts of concentrated light up into the lowering clouds.

27

Special Powers

Sarah had a problem keeping up with the UNIT convoy. Getting past the hundreds of abandoned grid-locked vehicles was less of a problem for them than for her. The UNIT jeeps simply drove full speed on the pavements, but Sarah's Spitfire had to take it more carefully.

Brigadier Crichton had not wanted her to come, but she insisted that she knew the layout of the university and would have followed even if he had warned her off.

The new UNIT helicopters, complete with their computer data feeds, were not deemed safe transport either. In fact, with no radio and most of the latest razor-smart computer weaponry up the Swannee, they were back to basics. Sarah suspected that her own Brigadier would feel very much at home, if only they could find him.

It transpired that Desmond Pennington MP, the Education Secretary, had been concerned about New World University for some time. Although initially enthusiastic for these ground-breaking computerized developments in further education, he had been disturbed by the behaviour of some of New World's luminaries. In particular their Marketing Facilitator, a grasping young man with a penchant for power and pullovers like knitted migraines. Pennington had spent an unnecessary but fascinating amount of time discovering just how far Christopher Rice's ambition extended. He reckoned he was nowhere near the limit, when events, the computer virus and the threat of being beaten to the post by the hot-air-powered Clive Kirkham, decided that action must be taken.

There were also increasing numbers of accusations

about computerized brainwashing cults and the general appearance and behaviour of the Chillys, as the tabloids had dubbed them. Such things were fine restricted to California, but not in the government's own backyard. Pennington, an old Brendonian, had been MoD liaison with UNIT before the last reshuffle but one, and had spent time studying the organization's classified reports. He had been much bemused to discover the part played in UNIT's origins by his former maths master.

He had already revealed most of this when he realized that Sarah, who was sitting in on the conference, was a working journalist. Crichton had to vouch for her security clearance, before the minister was prepared to continue.

Pennington had no chance of consultation with the Defence Secretary, who was on vacation on Mauritius. The PM was on holiday on the Isle of Wight. No one even knew where the Home Secretary was. The UN was incommunicado. Every possible communications channel had been knocked out by the virus. Pennington therefore took it on his own back and promised Crichton the *carte blanche* mauve card for Extraordinary Peacetime Operations. Someone, he said, had to make a move.

Crichton was following laid-down contingencies for socio- and techno-disintegration scenarios. He immediately rounded up the few troops he had to hand and sent his own adjutant to call out support platoons from UNIT's green-field HQ near Guildford. Leading the sortie himself, he and the convoy set off for New World with Sarah in pursuit.

They were travelling along the emergency lane of Westway when the lights in the sky started. Pencils of green and white light were shooting up into the cloud base. They seemed to be coming from somewhere north of Ealing – Alperton or Perivale. The direction of New World University.

Kate Lethbridge-Stewart watched the flashes in the sky from the window of the *Mananda*. She could hear the booms like approaching thunder. Her head couldn't begin to cope with what had happened, let alone believe what she had seen. Her dad had brought chaos into her home. Her emotions were all over the place. The only thing that had helped was the sudden unearthing of the secret she had kept hidden far too long. But now she felt deep remorse for having kept her dad in the dark all this time. Gordy would have to meet his grandfather one day, except that his grandfather was mixed up in something inexplicable that she had to protect her son from.

That made up her mind. For better or worse, she would not see her dad again.

She started to clear up the mess, picking up strewn books and the overturned photo of Grandad, who lived on the shelf. The frame was broken and the glass cracked.

The thunder was getting louder. She sat on the bed and looked out of the window. To the west, the clouds were being churned. The sky was boiling. Fingers of light were shooting upwards from somewhere close, north-west of the canal. Directly above that point, something was forming in the sky – a glaze of grey-silver light hanging in the air that glittered malevolently.

Kate wanted to take the boat home now. She pulled away from the window and knocked a cushion off the bed.

The gun had been under the cushion. It lay on the blanket, black and vicious, an instrument of death. Her father's gun. She knew he would need it. Without hesitating, she lifted up the weapon, surprised by its weight, and slipped it into the inside pocket of her coat.

She locked up as best she could, pulled her tatty bicycle off the boat and set off along the towpath in the direction her father had taken.

The towpath of the canal ran along the south boundary of New World University. From the foot of the hill, the Brigadier and Harrods surveyed the complex. Its array of ziggurats crowned the rise like a maleficent fortress. The place looked deserted. The needles of light from the pyramid that crowned the largest building were still forking up into the sky. Directly overhead, a glittering canker was forming, slowly throwing strands of material outwards to form a canopy in the air. Here and there, tiny shreds of web were floating down through the trees.

Harrods seemed undaunted by the spectacle. He produced some fruit he had 'borrowed' from the boat and offered an apple to the Brigadier. 'Sir? What now, sir? Take the place by storm?'

'If we must,' said Lethbridge-Stewart. He felt in his jacket and faltered. He started to slap his other pockets in growing disbelief. 'Damnation. I'm an old fool.'

'Sir?' queried Harrods.

The Brigadier shook his head. 'My gun. I didn't pick it up.'

He felt so old. His faculties were slipping away. How did he miss his gun? He remembered putting it down on the bed. He reached into his inside pocket again and touched a card. It was the picture of his grandson. No wonder he was losing his marbles after a shock like that.

'Want to go back?' Harrods asked.

The Brigadier touched the card again. No need to look. 'No, too late for that,' he said with grim foreboding. 'Come on.'

He set off up the hill with Harrods marching behind him.

The Intelligence flexed its power. It was spreading outwards through every connection, sending rings around the Earth. Blind darkness no longer confined it. It saw through thousands of eyes, lived in thousands of shapes. Its webs were spreading over the globe's surface and filling the sky above. And once the planet was cocooned, it would all be the Intelligence. One mass of thoughts in one global body.

Since that malicious reversal in its fortunes contrived by the Doctor, it had waited, slowly building its power, feeling its way into the Earth's power systems. Everything leading to this moment of release and rebirth.

It would have happened sooner, but the Intelligence

had been weak and the humans unreliable. It had lodged in Travers, but he was not enough. The monks of Det-sen tried to trap it, but could not wholly withstand its influence. Charles Bryce had been meant to find the Locus, but he died, carried away by some unforeseen Earth virus and the Intelligence had been too weak to save him. So the task fell to Victoria Waterfield and that was better, because it fulfilled a grudging lust for revenge against the Doctor by using one of his servants.

Entranced by the shapes it inhabited, the Intelligence flexed its power again. On a railway line in Kent, an abandoned Eurotrain shuddered and suddenly reared above its tracks like a snake. Hundreds of tons of screeching metal turning this way and that. Eventually the Intelligence got bored and threw the train down an embankment in ruin.

In the Hong Kong Stock Exchange, dozens of deactivated computer terminals logged themselves in again and rose above their work stations as high as their cables would allow. In a demented dance of computer death, they flung themselves back and forth, smashing to pieces against desks, walls and workers.

From Manila to Mexico City, bank cashpoints unexpectedly spewed streams of paper money onto the streets. In Stockholm, the computer-based heating system of the Söderström Corp went into overdrive and the building went up like a torch.

Data was displaced and transferred from one system to another. Cancer research scientists in Brazilia were regaled with theatre ticket availability in Vienna. Monitors in the Kremlin watched in amazement as the contents of the CIA database were transmitted live on Russian television.

The Intelligence launched an array of tomahawk missiles from a cruiser in the Gulf. It played with them like toys in the air over Baghdad, engineering near misses, weaving smoke trails, finally letting them drop useless and unprimed into the desert.

Workers in nuclear power stations across the globe

struggled to maintain their safe systems, as sudden inexplicable interference threatened to drive all their reactors critical. There were explosions in Andhra Pradesh and the Ukraine.

From every connected television receiver in the world, the Intelligence looked out and watched the humans on sofas and floors, eating, sleeping and performing other unrecognizable functions.

From every loudspeaker and tannoy system came the sudden thunderous burst of maniacal alien laughter.

A sudden alarm ran through the web. Instantly several million eyes turned inwards.

Christopher Rice sat in the chair in Victoria Waterfield's office in the New World Administration Block. His slumped head jerked into life and stared into the glare of the computer terminal.

Unauthorized personnel were moving across the quadrant towards the building's entrance.

'Intruders,' whispered the voice in Christopher's throat. 'Go and greet them properly.'

The eyes of the Yeti behind his chair flared angrily and the brute lumbered away on its mission.

Harrods pulled at the skein of web that covered the doorway into New World reception. He followed the Brigadier warily into the dark foyer. It looked as if it had been abandoned for years. An eerie glow came from the blank terminal screen on the reception desk, lighting the web that hung in festoons from the ceiling.

Harrods sniffed. 'Sir, something rotten in here, sir. I can feel it.'

The Brigadier smiled grimly. 'Too quiet.' He marched on past the desk towards a lift door in the back wall.

Harrods was certain they should have gone to his garage first. They were sure to have found something to use as a weapon there – a tin-opener or chair leg or something – if the Chillys hadn't been and cleaned it out by now. But they'd seen neither sight nor sound of a Chilly since they'd arrived. He saw the receptionist's terminal flare for a moment. In the half-light, he was sure it swivelled towards him.

'Let's start at the top,' said Lethbridge-Stewart and pressed for the lift. The door took an age to open.

Rather against his better judgement, they stepped into the clinical interior and he pressed for the doors to close. As the machine began to judder upwards, Harrods looked down at his grubby boots and said, 'Did you ever go to the Variety shows, sir? Loved the Variety, I did.'

The lift appeared to judder to a complete halt and the lights dimmed. The Brigadier jabbed at the control panel but nothing happened. He turned to Harrods and found he was looking at Danny Hinton.

The boy looked decidedly pale.

'Sorry, sir,' he said sheepishly.

'I give up, Hinton,' complained the Brigadier. 'Am I asleep or are you dead?'

Danny shrugged. 'Never did philosophy, sir. You're in the lift. I'm in the computer system. We have interface.'

Nothing had really surprised the Brigadier for years. Not until he'd seen his daughter that very afternoon. He tried to take everything in his stride, but there were times when he was sorely tested. 'So I'm talking to a ghost in a machine, am I?'

The boy nodded. Strangely, he didn't seem to be that distressed about being dead.

'And what's the warning this time?'

Danny edged closer. 'The Intelligence has got into the logic systems of New World's computers. I snuck a ride too. It's a virus. It's already spreading across the Internet . . .'

'Transmitted from this building?' interrupted the Brigadier. 'Well, we'd better put a stop to that.'

The boy seemed in earnest. He nodded towards the control panel. 'I'll take you in, sir. As far as I can.'

'And what do I do when I get there?'

The boy was gone already, but his voice lingered. 'Trust me.'

'That's what you said before,' the Brigadier muttered.
'Sir?' asked Harrods, suddenly back. The lights came up and the lift was moving again.
'Nothing, Flight Sergeant. I just walked over someone's grave.'
The answer seemed to satisfy the tramp, who scratched at his fingers and peered at the floor-indicator.
The lift stopped with a clunk, but the doors stayed resolutely stuck.
After a moment, the Brigadier struck at the door with his fist and complained, 'Come on Hinton!', as if the boy was late for class.

28

Something in the System

Kate chained her bike to the rack outside the administration block. Some of the other bikes had strands of web attached to them.

Overhead, the web canopy caught and reflected the flaring lights back down onto the angular buildings. The deserted campus was like Docklands at weekends. A film set waiting for the action to start.

Kate felt the dead weight of the gun inside her coat. She pushed her way warily into the reception area. The swathes of web inside intensified the gloom. They rippled like living things in the draught she had created. She wanted to run straight out again, but a sudden movement attracted her attention.

A figure was seated behind the reception desk. The pale glow from the terminal screen gave him the eerie appearance of a ghost. He looked up at her and the blank screen appeared as two white squares in his glasses.

Kate was incredulous. 'I thought you were . . .' She couldn't say the word.

'Maybe.' Danny's face was flattened by the glow. 'I need your help, Kate. And so does your dad. You'd better come and sit down.'

She didn't argue, but by the time she had edged round the desk, the apparition had vanished from the chair.

'Go on, sit down,' he said, suddenly emerging from the shadows behind her.

'What do I do?' she asked.

'Sit.'

She did as she was told and faced the blank screen.

He was no more than a face at her shoulder, lit by the glow. 'This whole place is part of the computer. The machines and the buildings too. That's what's causing all this.'

'The virus in the computer. That's what you said before.'

'It's alive inside the computer. It's extending its web outwards. Beyond the buildings here, right across the world. That's why your dad's here. He's in terrible danger inside the building.'

'I've got to reach him. That's why I came.' She started to stand again.

'Not that way. You can help him better here.'

'How?'

'By accessing the database. That way you let him through.'

'But I don't know how. What about you? What was that thing, that monster that you . . .'

There was a pause. 'I got absorbed,' said Danny coldly. 'I'm in here too.'

'*You* are in the computer?'

The head gave a disembodied nod. 'But I'm still me. Kate, please just follow my commands. I can find my way round in here, but I can't control it.'

She sighed. 'I don't know. I'm not even used to this system.'

'But *I* am,' said the boy's ghost. 'Ever heard of automatic writing? Put your fingers on the keys.'

She obeyed and watched, startled, as her fingers started to move independently of her own will.

The screen darkened and started to scroll with a rush of data.

Harrods stood back from the lift doors, his fingers aching from trying to force them apart.

'It's no good, sir. I reckon something's jamming them.'

The indicator above the door was lit only on the number three.

'Typical,' complained the Brigadier. 'Blasted boy always disappears when you want him.'

As if in answer, the lift doors clanked and ground

slowly open. The two passengers stepped out into the hallway relieved to be out of the cage.

The corridor outside was equally unwelcoming. With all the gloom, they might have been in a basement or crypt. The air was muggy. The web-shrouded walls creaked and rumbled like sleepy beasts shifting restlessly in their stalls.

The Brigadier hefted a fire-extinguisher from its place on the wall. 'Better than nothing,' he said and set off slowly along the passage.

A worrying thought had just occurred to him: if Daniel Hinton now existed only in the systems of the New World computer, what would happen to the boy if the computer was switched off?

He wondered if he was going mad.

'Sir?' called Harrods. 'Where are we going, sir?'

'Don't worry, Sergeant. I have someone working on it.' The Brigadier eyed a security camera on the ceiling. 'As long as he doesn't lead us on too long a dance.'

Harrods was having to scuttle to keep up with him. He was grinning to himself.

'Ever see Wilson, Kepple and Betty, sir?'

Lethbridge-Stewart wondered if they were both going mad. 'The variety act? Two funny little men in Egyptian clobber doing sand dances? And a girl doing a sort of exotic belly dance?'

'Oh yes, sir. My favourites, they were.'

'Really,' the Brigadier said, trying to sound interested. They had turned left, left and left and were in severe danger of turning left again and ending up where they had started.

If Hinton was acting as their spirit guide, where was he when they needed him?

'Three times I saw them, sir. And every time the Betty was a different person.'

'Three different, Bettys.' The Brigadier laughed appreciatively. But he doubted that Time Lords toured the universe performing novelty acts on the variety circuit.

On the other hand . . .

'Sir!'

Harrods was crouched by a doorway marked 'NW FM'.

There was a shape inside. The figure of a man dressed in a Hawaiian shirt with headphones draped round his neck. He was slumped against the glass, covered in swathes of web and his dead eyes were staring wide open.

The door was jammed tight.

'Gets worse, doesn't it, sir?'

'It does indeed, Sergeant. Let's keep moving.'

Faced with the opportunity of going left again, the Brigadier opted for right. The way was closed.

Since there was no promised clue from Hinton, he settled on left instead.

A deep chanting noise was emanating from the gloom. Before they reached the lift, they came to another viewing window in the wall. It looked into a large room resembling a language lab. In the dim light they could make out row upon row of computer terminals with a Chilly seated in an attitude of contemplation at each. The same web was draped over the students and the machines. It caught the light of the terminals, glittering malevolently as the Chillys kept up their chanted dirge.

'Like a morgue,' whispered Harrods.

'Like a trap,' corrected the Brigadier. He could see that several of the Chillys held silvered spheres on their laps. Some of them were starting to rise from their places.

Where the hell is Hinton? he thought.

'Come on,' he said. 'Back to the lift!'

It had been a struggle to get the lift as far as Floor Three. Almost as soon as the Brigadier had left the confines of the lift, Danny had felt a new command in the system.

The lift was being summoned to Floor Eight, the top level.

Danny put a countermand option through Kate's fingers, but his momentary lapse in concentration had let things slip.

The doors closed and the lift went up unhindered.

He fed Kate a command to stop the doors opening at the top, but was overruled again.

She was a good medium for his thoughts. She had let her mind loosen, allowing him open access to move her fingers over the keys. No longer confined to his human body, no longer genetically challenged, he found that his thoughts were freed up too. It was the flying he had always wanted. He was able to think so fast now that he was afraid of hurting Kate.

He fed her another instruction: a command to stop the lift in its tracks.

He sensed the doors closing on the eighth floor. He put in an override command to open again.

He felt the doors judder. The logic commands were counteracting each other. He wanted to keep this up for as long as possible, but he heard Kate gasp.

'I can't move my fingers,' she protested. 'What is it?'

'Hold it there!' he snapped. He had to stop whatever was in the lift from descending.

He knew what was in the lift. He still felt the tug of what had once been his body. The Intelligence's powers had widened. It no longer needed to construct robots to serve as its heavy brigade. The university had a whole section devoted to nanotechnology and atomic engineering. The Intelligence could overwhelm and transmute any form into its instrument.

For a moment, Danny was stifled. A shrill repeating beat swamped his thoughts. His chest burned with an inner fire. His man's shape was thick with sinew and fur. He could only move clumsily in the confines of the imposition. Through red eyes, he saw the metal walls of the lift and the doors juddering back and forth in front of him as he struck at them.

With an animal roar, he broke free again. He was back at Kate's shoulder, forcing the claw shapes out of his head.

His concentration had slipped once more. In the computer systems, he felt the doors slam shut and the lift begin its descent.

'I'm sorry, I'm sorry, I'm sorry,' Kate was saying.

By now, the Intelligence would be hunting him too.

The Brigadier and Harrods reached the lift and saw the floor indicator descend from eight to seven. The mechanism was emitting confused electronic grindings.

'Brigadier! Get back!'

He saw a woman standing in the shadows at the far end of the corridor. He didn't know her voice, but her shape and demeanour were familiar. She had an intensity that had been plaguing his dreams.

Behind him, the lift mechanisms were snarling their protest.

The woman was hurrying towards him. 'Please get back from that lift. I was wrong. Now please get away from there!'

He turned to see the floor indicator sink to six.

Danny struggled to countermand the lift signal. Kate's mind was clouding up with stressful thoughts, making it impossible to channel his own will clearly.

'It's fighting back!' she yelled.

Through her fingers, he could feel the pressure of the function keys forcing upwards against him. 'I must hold it down!' The keyboard was starting to get hot.

'People in glass houses . . .' he shouted aloud.

The Intelligence couldn't fight back too violently or it would destroy every delicate circuit in which it wreathed itself.

Through the security camera on Floor Five, Danny could see Lethbridge-Stewart arguing with someone right by the lift doors. It was Victoria Waterfield. Now she was in danger too.

Staying in the system any longer meant deletion for Danny, but he had to save the Brigadier.

Victoria was pulling at the Brigadier's arm.

'Come away please, Brigadier! You shouldn't have come here.'

He wrenched himself free. 'It's a bit late for apologies, madam!'

'Sir!' warned the little tramp and he pointed along the corridor.

A group of Chillys, covered in tatters of web, were advancing on them.

The lift screeched a protest as it finally reached their level. The door mechanism whirred, but failed to open.

Victoria stepped forward to meet the Chillys. 'Go back to your studies,' she commanded. 'There's nothing here you want!'

Boom! Something began to beat repeatedly on the inside of the lift doors.

Nobody moved. Nobody dared.

Boom! Boom! Boom!

'Quickly!' Victoria urged the Brigadier and the tramp along the corridor away from the Chillys. She ushered them through a fire door towards the emergency stairwell. Glancing back, she saw that, instead of pursuing them, the Chillys were setting their hands to the lift doors, trying to claw them apart.

Boom! Boom! Boom!

Victoria fled through the doorway. She found the Brigadier waiting on the stairway.

'This way,' she gasped, but the Brigadier pulled her back.

A tide of Chillys was descending the stairs. More of them blocked the way down. The students ignored Victoria's orders and advanced on the Brigadier. Too late, he raised the fire-extinguisher to defend himself. He vanished under an anemone of grasping hands.

Kate's fingers were burning. She could not take them off the keys. 'Please,' she was begging. 'Please. I can't hold them any longer.'

But the presence at her shoulder was remorseless. 'You must! You must! Think of your dad!'

She was crying. 'Let go! Let go of my mind.'

There was a crack of electricity that threw her back in

her chair. The screen flared white and went dead.

Kate sat in the dark alone, squeezing her scorched fingers. A sudden fresh breeze from the door stirred the cobwebs. The apparition of Danny had blown away.

The lift doors on Floor Five cranked themselves open.

The Chillys fell back.

With a roar of rage, the released Yeti emerged and strode forward in search of its prey.

29

Call in the Cavalry

The Brigadier was drowning on dry land. Waves of hands smothered him, dragged and pinioned him against a stack of dusty chairs in the corner of the stair-well.

A face swam into view. A clean-cut youth with empty eyes like blue ice. Lethbridge-Stewart was sure the Chilly had been one of his pupils. It was revenge at last for all the boring lessons and preps and detentions he had inflicted. The young man impassively raised a pair of headphones. They emitted the relentless bleep of the silver sphere.

'Acolytes!'

A voice echoed down the concrete stairwell. The Chillys faltered. An old man, leaning heavily on a stick, stood on the steps above them.

'You know me. Now stand away!'

Travers, thought the Brigadier.

Surely not. Professor Edward Travers had died years ago.

The old man waved his stick angrily. 'Release him! Let him go free!' He began to edge painfully down the stairs. The woman went to his assistance, taking his arm proudly in hers.

It was Travers, the Brigadier was sure of it. And the old fellow was no zombie either. Today everything that he'd reckoned dead and buried was up and walking as if it was some sort of medieval judgement day.

The Chillys were starting to back slowly off. Harrods pulled free of his captors and was immediately at the Brigadier's side.

The woman, now he could see her properly, wasn't the

apparition he'd dreamed about at all. Her modern executive clothes were at odds with the Victorian ghost that haunted him. Yet at a distance, in the gloom, the likeness had been uncanny.

The fire door all but crashed off its hinges. The Yeti stormed into the area with a massive roar. The stack of chairs collapsed across the floor. The Chillys fell back as the Yeti launched straight at the Brigadier.

'Sir!' Harrods grabbed up the discarded fire-extinguisher and swung it at the monster.

The weapon was torn out of his hands and tossed away. The Yeti seized Harrods' head between its claws. As his body was dragged to the floor, they heard his skull splinter.

The Yeti let the little man's body drop onto the concrete with a smack. It rounded on the others and faced the woman who was nearest. She held its gaze for a moment that almost seemed like a recognition. The Yeti growled softly as it swayed in front of her.

Travers stumbled past, determinedly heading for the door. 'Must shut down the mainframe,' he muttered.

'Professor!' shouted the woman.

The Yeti flung an arm wide and knocked the old man to the floor. It began to advance on the Brigadier.

He grabbed up a chair and, holding it by its back, tried to fend the brute off lion-tamer style.

The Yeti seized the legs and tore the chair apart like matchwood.

'Leave him alone!' the woman yelled.

The Chillys suddenly pincered in from the sides and held the Brigadier, offering him to the monster.

The Yeti loomed over its victim. One claw lunged out and clamped around the back of the Brigadier's neck.

'All right. All right, I was coming anyway,' he choked.

Like a march to the scaffold, he thought, as the monster drove him forward. He saw that the woman was also being held tightly, but there was no sign at all of the ancient Professor Travers.

The Yeti led its prisoner back towards the lift, followed

by its entourage of Chillys.

In the distance, the Brigadier could hear the sound of claxons.

Through the surveillance systems, the Intelligence saw the convoy approaching the campus. This was the threat it had anticipated.

Sixteen silver sphere control units activated and plunged into the chests of the Chillys assigned as hosts. A frenzied chorus of staccato bleeping. Chairs clattered to the floor of the computer room. Figures reeled and tore at the web that blanketed them. Nano-instructions from the control spheres induced immediate atomic restructuring and multiplication. Shapes rose massively in the gloom. Sixteen pairs of burning red eyes. A clamour of roaring as the new Yeti quit the room.

The remaining Chillys sat in passive contemplation of the patterns of web on their terminal screens.

The convoy drew up on the outer perimeter road of the university. Brigadier Crichton, not a happy man, surveyed his meagre squad of twenty as they piled out of the UNIT jeeps. He'd taken every available soldier he could find, leaving UNIT HQ on skeleton staff. They were highly skilled soldiers, trained to deploy cutting edge weaponry – gadgets that the regular forces would pay their eye teeth to be able to afford. Except that computer technology had outsmarted them. It was suddenly too dangerous. UNIT was back to basics, issued with entirely manually operated guns. When they'd broken them out of store, the men had joked about *The Antiques Roadshow* and about not knowing which way round to hold the weapons.

Crichton was taking no chances. He was out on a limb. One time or another they'd all trained with these guns, but it was just training, not put into practice. He positioned his men to cover the front of the main block and tried to call his adjutant on an ancient walkie-talkie.

There was no response from her.

'Captain Bambera? Do you read me? Please respond.'

The radio buzzed with a random electronic jamming pattern. It pulsed in time with the beams of light shooting up from the New World buildings.

The sky overhead was cut off. The web canopy was extending in all directions out towards the horizon, throwing out fingers like frost flowers through the atmosphere. Web strands were drizzling down, catching in the trees like spanish moss. Increasingly frustrated, Crichton decided to take the bull by the horns.

'Sergeant Beagles. Six-man escort now. I'm going up to knock on the front door.'

His entourage set off across the lawns, heading towards the glass-fronted reception area. As he reached the concourse, a door in one of the side buildings opened. A figure in full uniform lurched out.

'Not that way, Brigadier,' rasped Captain Cavendish. His voice was a tortured parody of itself. His face had become a mask behind which his cold-blooded eyes darted like a reptile's.

Not that way, Brigadier . . . Brigadier . . . Brigadier . . . echoed the campus PA system.

Crichton ignored the mockery from all around him. He already had the young man in his sights. 'You are under arrest, Cavendish. Where's that file you stole?'

The PA system roared with cold laughter, throwing its voice from one speaker to another across the campus. Finally the laugh settled in Cavendish's throat. He moved like a puppet, his uncoordinated limbs jerking to the reflexes of an outside force.

The voice said, 'Your Captain is no longer answerable to you.'

'Who are you?' called Brigadier Crichton.

'I am many!'

Many! Many! Many!

Cavendish's arm rose and indicated the door leading into the building. 'Come inside and see for yourself.'

Crichton glanced briefly round at his men. 'No thanks. I prefer to talk out here.'

'Sir,' whispered the corporal next to Crichton. He

nodded with his eyes to the parkland beyond the administration block.

Several objects were moving through the trees – large shapes striding out of the shrubbery about to cut off Crichton's group from the rest of the squad.

'Yeti!' shouted Crichton.

Three more of the bear-like creatures ducked out through the doorway behind Cavendish.

Crichton's practised eye took in their situation. Cavendish, or whatever was controlling Cavendish, had hoped to get them surrounded where they stood. Lawns by their nature afforded little cover. 'Pull back and re-form!' he yelled and brought up the rear as the group withdrew to the 'safe' position of a nearby herbaceous border.

Captain Cavendish stood back as the Yeti started to advance.

Brigadier Crichton crouched in the flowerbed, his boots sinking into the muddy topsoil. The men round him were tense, fingering the triggers of their automatic rifles.

'Call this a rapid-reaction force?' he muttered. 'Where the hell's Bambera with that back-up?'

Sarah had left her Spitfire further along the road, out of sight of the convoy. Its windscreen wipers were clogged with web.

She had watched Crichton's confrontation with the young officer from a safe distance behind a laurel bush.

Twigs cracked. She ducked into the foliage. Two furry shapes as big as grizzly bears lumbered past no more than twelve feet from her. They walked upright with a rolling gait, their forepaws clawing the air.

Yeti, she thought, and tried not to think too much of Charlie Bryce. Somehow these hulking creatures didn't look like the shy, endangered species that the documentaries always made them out to be. Or like fluffy bundles that bit prime ministers. They also emitted a persistent high-pitched bleeping signal.

She saw Crichton's group start to retreat. More of the

huge brutes were emerging from the trees on the far side of the lawns. And still more from the building.

Blue UN berets were visible ranged across the parkland. Battle lines were being drawn up. Sarah ran through the layout of the campus in her mind. She heard the first rapid gunshots as she skirted the bushes and headed for the administration block.

There was web on the inside of the reception windows. She cautiously pushed open the door and went inside. The squeaky-clean place she had visited only yesterday had changed beyond belief. The air was stale and clogged. Something unearthly was in residence here. She had sensed it on her first visit, but it was no longer just an uncomfortable gut feeling. It had erupted into visible form, filling the place with an evil nebulous gossamer. She immediately thought of spiders and parlours and giant versions of things that kept eating her roses in the garden at home.

In the gloom, Sarah was suddenly aware of a figure seated behind the curve of the desk, a young woman with long blonde hair and her head buried in her hands. She slowly looked up, plainly exhausted. Sarah knew her identity immediately.

'It's Kate Lethbridge-Stewart, isn't it?' she said enthusiastically. 'Your father said it might be a family affair.'

She reached across the desk and heartily shook the perplexed woman's hand. 'Sarah Jane Smith. Hello. This place is like a beacon.'

In truth, she also recognized Kate from a photo of a little girl that the Brigadier had always carried in his wallet. The family resemblance was striking.

Sarah flapped her hands in a busy sort of way. 'So show me where to find your dad. I used to work with him sometimes.'

There was a pause. Kate hardly reacted.

'Are you all right?' asked Sarah.

Kate was rubbing her fingers. They looked raw. 'I don't know,' she said. 'I feel used, dirty. A *computergeist*.'

A clanking sound came from further inside the gloomy

building. They heard a high-pitched bleeping signal approaching. Sarah darted through the open side of the reception desk beside Kate. They ducked below the counter as a Yeti emerged through the veils of hanging web.

It passed the desk and stopped in the centre of the foyer, facing the main doors. It seemed to be waiting.

The signal died. The massive shape did not move.

Sarah and Kate crouched close to the floor, too terrified to breathe.

Above them, there was a slight burr as the computer terminal on the desk activated. The screen started to glow with an empty pallor. It began to turn slowly back and forth like a cyclopean eye searching for them.

Sarah pulled Kate down tight under the desktop until they were practically chewing carpet. The screen continued to cast to and fro, searching in frustration.

Finally the glow died.

Silence – apart from the distant gunfire.

Signalling Kate to stay still, Sarah rose slowly to peer over the top of the desk.

The Yeti had not moved a shaggy muscle. It still faced away from them towards the door.

Sarah waited an age. She wondered if Yeti slept standing up. Any minute the gunfire, which was getting nearer, would wake it. Finally she signalled to Kate to crawl out through the back way as slowly and silently as she could.

Kate did as she was told, inching her way out, a look of forced concentration almost certainly stifling a yell of terror.

Sarah, unable to take her eyes from the statuesque monster, willing the brute not to wake up, began to follow. She collided with the chair and lost concentration for one moment.

The bleeping signal started up.

The Yeti's head suddenly swivelled, owl-like through a half-circle, facing to its back. Two burning eyes like red torches caught Sarah in their glare.

It roared and started to turn fully for an attack.

Sarah looked for a weapon. She grabbed up the phone base-tablet.

The Yeti lashed a set of claws across the desk at her. She hit at it with the phone. It lunged again. She threw the phone at its head. She grabbed up some files and threw them as well.

The Yeti raised an arm and brought it down hard, smashing the end of the fitted desk away. The counter splintered sideways, blocking Sarah's escape. The monster started to crunch across the broken plywood.

With a yell, Kate barrelled in behind the monster, hammering at it with a metal vase. The Yeti gave one backward punch with its arm and sent Kate tumbling backwards clutching her ribs.

Sarah, trapped in the corner of the desk, laid hold of the only thing left to throw. She struggled to heave the computer monitor off its station. The Yeti loomed. She saw its fangs as it bellowed. She hefted the monitor up to throw. She thought her arms would break. The screen activated. Its piercing glare blazed directly into her face. Her eyes burning, she reeled backwards under its weight and hit the desk.

Half the windows in the foyer blew in with a tremendous boom. The battle had arrived right outside. The Yeti stumbled back under the blast. The monitor flickered out.

Sarah felt Kate's arms pulling her up over the desk. They scrambled through into the back of the building and up the stairs.

On the second landing, they stopped. Sarah was still holding her throbbing ears, afraid of losing them if she let go.

From a broken window on the stairs, they saw the Yeti lumber out of the foyer below, not using the door. Apparently the battle outside was more important than they were.

They could see that the other Yeti were engaged in hand-to-hand combat with the UNIT troops.

Kate mouthed something at Sarah and pointed into the distance.

'I can't hear you,' shouted Sarah. She could hardly even hear herself.

Kate banged her own ears with her fingers. She mouthed, 'Can't hear you. I've gone deaf!' and shrugged. She pointed at the sky again.

Through the trees, under the web canopy, there was a bulky old-fashioned helicopter coming in to land.

30

Under Siege

UNIT's grenades had reduced the lawn to a churned battlefield. Crichton was losing too many men already. The Yeti were reputed to be robots, but these were sustaining flesh wounds. Surely nothing alive could take that many hits and still keep moving.

In answer to the sweeping onslaught of bullets, the Yeti simply stretched out an arm and shot streamers of smoking plasma over their opponents. The stuff hit the targets and fanned out over them as web. Crichton had seen his men writhing and choking under the mesh. They collapsed and suffocated almost immediately.

He saw Private Rooks, who was assigned to record the raid on video for future reference, stepping out of cover to get a better shot of the battle.

Crichton shouted a warning as a Yeti burst out of the undergrowth behind the soldier. Rooks turned and swung at the monster with the camera. The Brigadier ran at the hostile, unleashing a salvo from his pistol.

The Yeti, determined to deal with one task at a time, floored Rooks and stamped on his chest. It turned towards Crichton and shot a flood of plasma from its claw.

Crichton dodged away between the trees, but the blast caught his shoulder leaving flecks of the web clinging to his battle gear.

In the frenzied moment, Crichton saw Sergeant Beagles run past him yelling, like a fast bowler with a grenade. Beagles launched it at the Yeti. The explosion blew the creature off its hind legs, but as the smoke cleared, the bulky mass of fur and sinew twitched, rolled over and scrambled to its feet. Enraged, it seemed to have twice the strength.

'Regroup at the road!' shouted Crichton, pulling Beagles away with him.

As he had hoped, the Yeti stood their ground, forming into a line of strategic sentries along the perimeter. As far as he could ascertain, none of them had been destroyed or even disabled.

Only seven UNIT soldiers straggled back to the jeeps.

Crichton, determined not to lose momentum, barked, 'Sergeant, break out the Bonze ATR. Yes, I know it's got a smart-map homer, but I'm not risking any more men.'

He waited for a second, but Sergeant Beagles was staring at him.

'Sergeant. The ATR launcher!'

'Sir, your shoulder,' exclaimed Beagles.

Crichton angled his head. The web caught on his jacket was moving. Its mycelium was throwing tiny filaments out over the camouflage material.

The Brigadier slid out of the jacket and threw it into the gutter. Shreds of sky web were still drifting around them. He surveyed the enemy line. He knew it had been too quiet lately. His battles had been with the lobby to cut back the British Forces contribution to UNIT – to make the organization less militaristic, more civil-service-based. The government, of all people, complained about too much secrecy. Crichton's promotion was at risk. His wife kept mentioning separation.

The sound of an incoming helicopter turned their heads. There was no immediate reaction from the Yeti. The helicopter was a Hind 63 troop-carrier, rescued from a museum from the look of her. She settled in the field across the road swirling up clouds of dead web.

Captain Bambera jumped down and ran towards Crichton. Behind her, a line of troops began to disembark and fall into line. Bambera saluted. 'Zen Platoon Three reporting, sir. Where do we start?'

Viewed through the observation window, Modem Nucleus Room One was empty.

Travers shambled through the door, slicing at the web

with his stick. He stopped at the first modem terminal and began to run his trembling fingers over the keyboard.

He faltered, trying to recall the log-in codes.

All the monitors in the room turned towards him. Their screens began to glow.

A voice in the audio system hissed out at him. 'Travers? What happened to your faith, old man?'

The Professor guffawed. 'Huh. Saw your Light of Truth, that's what. Brought it back here from Tibet. But I'll put a stop to it.' He started trying to force open the maintenance panel on the terminal.

There was a burst of laughter from the loudspeaker system. Travers turned and saw a group of Chillys staring coldly in through the observation window.

A distant claxon was sounding.

'More intruders as anticipated,' announced the Intelligence.

Travers watched the Chillys file into the room. They approached a web-covered metal coffer. Its lid slid open for them. In turn they each extracted a silver sphere.

The Chillys stood in a circle. The spheres bleeped and leapt, vanishing, absorbed into the human bodies.

As the shapes burst into their new monstrous imagos, Travers gave a wail of anger and started to strike at the nest of computers he had designed and created.

The voice mocked his rage. 'Travers, Travers! You are still my closest instrument of all!'

The screens flared.

Travers was caught in a globe of light. The radiant envelope slowly faded, leaving only a cold gleam that froze over the old man's watery eyes. He stumbled and reached helplessly for the desk. His trembling fingers suddenly gripped it hard, feeling the shape and contours. A power indivisible from hatred and need gripped the shape and contours of his thoughts again.

The new Yeti ignored him, striding off to reinforce the university's defences.

The Brigadier reckoned he'd had some close calls in his

time, but this call came closer than anything he could remember. Obviously his arrival was not a moment too late.

So they called his days Blood and Thunder, did they? Well, he didn't feel like Attila the Hun. As much as the battles, he remembered the men who died. He had always undertaken to break the news of a death in action to a soldier's family himself. He had done it many times. And every time it was painful.

That made his own family, for what it was, so much more precious. Now Kate was threatened, he saw it all from the other side. He wanted there still to be a world for his grandson to inherit. People had died today who were not even under his command, yet their deaths felt like sacrifices enabling him to go on. He was supported by people that society had rejected. He coped with that burden the only way he knew how: the fight he undertook was for them.

Hinton et Harrods requiescat in pace.

Their loss must not be in vain.

As he was marched along the endless corridors, a monster's claw on his throat like a vice, his thoughts turned inevitably to the Doctor. Facing the Great Intelligence was, after all, where it had all started.

What would the Doctor do?

Why wasn't the Doctor here?

Inevitably, the Doctor would do the one thing that was least expected. Frequently aggravating, but generally splendid stuff.

The Brigadier had infinite respect and admiration for the Doctor, but the man could be impossible. The Brigadier always had to fight not to play second fiddle to the Doctor's whims and Machiavellian leaps of imagination. He was rarely even granted the status of magician's assistant – a position usually already taken. He generally felt more like the unsuspecting volunteer from the audience. It could have been worse – he could have been the rabbit.

But when he got something right, why did the Doctor

always look surprised?

Well, this old buffer wasn't going to be outdone by an alien who changed his face as often as normal people changed their socks.

'My dear Brigadier, there are no *normal* people here.' He heard the Doctor's irritated response.

Faced with his imminent retirement, the *second* time he had retired, he decided that if necessary, he would go out in a blaze of heroic glory. Anything rather than dwindle away organizing fêtes and flower shows.

He watched the woman who was being escorted by Chillys in front of him. There was something vaguely familiar about her, but he was damned if he could think what. Perhaps he had seen her at one of those interminable parents' evenings, where he repeated the same deadly joke to every mother and father about leading a platoon being no different from getting his maths class through their GCSEs.

As the party emerged into the open air, they heard a not-so-distant explosion and the clatter of gunfire. The Brigadier guessed that it should be dark by now, but the web canopy in the sky was casting a sickly phosphorescent glow over the buildings. The web crackled overhead. The beams directed up from the roof pyramid played over its surface like spotlights.

They were on a square bordered by steps on three sides like an amphitheatre. Row upon row of Chillys sat transfixed there, awaiting the start of some unspecified spectacle in the arena.

The Brigadier expected gladiators or lions to arrive at any moment. Only recently Celia had related some first-former's joke to him.

Monsieur, Monsieur. I want to see Madame Guillotine.

You can't. She's out chopping!

At the centre of the square stood a plinth on which was set a pyramid of silver globes. Two figures waited there. A heavily built man in a frantic pullover and a Captain in full uniform. The Brigadier recognized Cavendish immediately and despised him.

With another boom, a fresh bolt of gold light shot up from the roof pyramid and punched *through* the canopy.

The party stopped abruptly as they all stared upwards.

Turning her head slightly, the woman whispered, 'Distract them, Brigadier. This is my fault. If I can shut down the mainframe . . .'

'I'm sure we've met before,' he murmured.

She paused for a moment and then said quickly, 'I doubt it.'

The new bolt of light shot up from the curve of the Earth. Reaching an altitude of 67.08 miles, it struck the UNIT NAVSAT 61 in geo-stationary orbit over north-west Europe.

The beam refracted in a dozen new directions across the globe. A dozen new canopies of web began to branch out like giant snowflakes in the upper atmosphere.

The line of Yeti seemed unbreachable, but Crichton's determination had been renewed when Captain Bambera arrived with another platoon. She always kept him on his toes anyway. Given the choice, he thought, he would rather face a herd of stampeding education secretaries than the African officer with battle light in her eyes.

His hopes sank again as he saw fresh Yeti reinforcements striding out of the university buildings.

'Stand by!' he barked at the positioned men.

'I'm not sure about that ATR launcher, sir,' said Bambera. 'You know it has a smart-map facility.'

Crichton glanced across at the open-backed jeep where a corporal had set up the anti-tank rocket-launcher. The squat barrel was embossed with the Bonze steel chrysanthemum logo. A private was standing by, ready to load.

'It also has a manual override,' scowled Crichton. 'Ready when you are, Captain.'

'I'm ready, sir.' Bambera, not long returned from plenty of action on a peacekeeping term in Bosnia, had not lost her appetite for a fight.

'Carry on, Bambera. But not too many heroics, or

you're liable to get yourself promoted.'

He thought he heard her say 'Shame' as she ran back to the helicopter. It rose above the field whipping up a storm of dead web strands and circled away from the campus. Across the road, the jacket he had discarded had become a mass of pulsing web.

From behind him, he heard shouting. The Yeti were advancing again.

'All right. Chaps with fur. Fire at will!'

The soldiers waited.

The ATR operative lined up the barrel. The weapon fired with a massive *KCRRWMPP*. The rocket zipped the air apart. The two front Yeti went down with the first huge explosion.

Glass cascaded from the university windows beyond.

A cannonade of shots erupted from the platoon.

The two floored Yeti did not get up.

31

World Wide Web

'What are we waiting for?' complained the Brigadier loudly.

No one on the square had moved, but the atmosphere of expectancy was tangible.

'Are we going to stand here all evening?'

The Yeti had not relaxed its grip on his neck. In front of him, the woman slowly shook her head and sighed deeply.

Something was shuffling behind them: Travers walking with a directness and certainty that belied the years of his old body.

'Bring my gaoler here,' commanded the icy voice as he passed.

The Brigadier felt a rough push as the Yeti released him. Two more Chillys stepped in beside him and began to march him forward. He deliberately took his time, pausing like a contemptuous inspecting officer in front of Cavendish, who stared coldly ahead. The Chillys tried to pull him forward, but he resisted for a moment. The students guarding the woman moved forward to assist their confederates.

Instantly she grabbed her chance and darted away across the square, back into the building.

'Victoria!' commanded Travers.

The Brigadier stared sharply after her.

'Stop her!' bellowed Travers. 'This time, destroy her!'

The man in the pullover smiled to himself and moved after her. Behind him lumbered the Yeti.

The Brigadier, bored with other people's agendas, wrenched himself free of the Chillys and approached Travers.

The old man, eyes staring and white hair tangled, gazed up at the crackling canopy a mile over their heads. 'My strength is growing, gaoler. All your defences are powerless to stop me.'

Lethbridge-Stewart smiled urbanely. It was usually the Doctor who got to play these confrontation scenes. 'I'm amazed at your ingenuity . . . Travers.'

The cold eyes swivelled towards him. 'The *late* Professor Travers,' corrected the voice in Travers's body. 'This is my world now.'

'Of course,' the Brigadier assured him. 'Doubtless you'll make a better job of it than we humans have.'

The power inside Travers's body began to chuckle.

A strand of web drifted against the Brigadier's face. He snatched it away. 'We humans are basically a gregarious race . . . Great One,' he continued. 'Despite exceptions, like Daniel Hinton.'

'Deleted from my system,' snapped the voice.

The Brigadier nodded grimly. 'I see.' He gave a smile of supplication. 'Resistance is obviously . . . what's the word?'

'Useless!' exclaimed the Intelligence in Travers eagerly.

Typical unimaginative response, thought the Brigadier. What about 'resistance is to be expected', or 'resistance will be crushed'?

Travers's head had turned to watch the progress of a helicopter that was swooping in over the campus.

Captain Bambera watched from the cockpit of the Hind. A smell of tension. Behind her, in the belly of the helicopter, sat a dozen hand-picked soldiers, ready to storm the centre of the university.

The Swedish pilot, a veteran flier from Gothenburg, circled the helicopter round and approached the campus from the south. 'Don't think the blades will take much more of this web,' he said.

Winifred Bambera chewed at her lip, the way she'd done since she was a kid in Zambia playing tag with a lost leopard cub in Musi-O-Tunya National Park. When the cub's mother turned up, Winifred's older brother tried to rescue her with their father's rifle. He was so slow, he got badly mauled. Winifred, aged eight, had to use the gun to rescue them both.

Her father thrashed her. Her brother called her Professor Chicken, because she had no business still being alive.

Ahead, Bambera saw the first explosion designed to draw all the Yeti defences to one point. Stoney-faced as ever, she snapped out her order to the pilot: 'No time to waste, Londqvist. Take us in.'

Londqvist's own glare was suddenly fixed and icy. The helicopter began to swoop down towards the campus.

Sarah pulled Kate back into hiding as someone came running along the walkway. Victoria Waterfield, New World's Vice Chancellor, was heading towards the university's maintenance service area. She looked desperately unhappy. The sound of guns echoed across the campus.

'Where's she off to?' hissed Sarah. She was about to go after Victoria, when Kate pulled a gun out of her jacket. She held it out between her fingers as if she couldn't bear to touch the thing.

'Sarah, take this. It's for my father.'

'You could have used that on the Yeti. You should have said.'

Kate cringed and stuttered. 'Sorry, but please just take it.'

Sarah folded Kate's fingers round the weapon and half grinned. 'No, you hang onto it. I'm a rotten shot.'

'I don't want a fight,' snapped Kate. 'I want my dad back!' She gasped as Sarah pulled her back out of sight.

Christopher Rice, the Marketing Facilitator, was hurrying up the walkway. He had a gun in his hand too. Not far behind him lumbered a Yeti.

'Where's the back-up got to?' Sarah complained.

They heard the drone of engines. A helicopter was coming in low over the canal. As it flew, it angled wildly in the air.

* * *

'Londqvist, I said put us down over there!' yelled Bambera.

The pilot gave a growl of determination. He was squeezing the controls so hard that one of the hand grips cracked across. The helicopter held its speed. Its course did not alter.

'Londqvist!' Bambera grabbed at his arm, but he thrust her away with his fist. Suddenly he was no longer the sober, bookish Swede whose twin passions for rollmop herrings and yak butter tea were legendary. His mouth had pulled into a rictus grin.

The Hind swerved in towards one of the university blocks.

'My Great Plan at last,' snarled the mouth.

The helicopter buzzed the pyramid tower and headed on over the complex. Bambera pulled her gun.

'Back on course now.'

Londqvist ignored her. Strands of web glistened on his jacket.

'I said, now!'

As they cleared the complex, Bambera saw smoke and explosions. The line of Yeti was sweeping Crichton's troops before it. They were pulling back to the convoy.

The Hind bore straight down on the jeeps.

Collision course.

Bambera grabbed at the steering-column with a yell.

Londqvist's hand went in her face, but she pulled at the controls as three hulking squaddies locked onto the pilot.

The helicopter tilted sideways and up. The convoy vanished under them.

She fell into Londqvist's seat as he was hoisted out. His boot hit the side of her head.

She swerved the Hind wildly, angling between two trees, clipping the top of a third.

Londqvist gave a cry of fury behind her.

The sky opened up in front. Bambera, her head ringing, steadied the helicopter into a broad turn, which would bring them back round again.

Londqvist was suddenly silent. Bambera angled a glance

behind her and saw five squaddies sitting on him.

Ridiculously, she started to laugh.

The helicopter had come so close that Crichton could see the struggle in the cockpit.

It shot over the convoy with only feet to spare.

Crichton turned back to view the rout and tripped over Corporal Ishani lying face down in a shroud of web. He had given the order to pull back and forgotten to do it himself.

A Yeti loomed over him. He emptied his pistol into the brute point-blank. One blood-red eye spluttered dead. The creature reeled back momentarily. Crichton rolled out of its shadow and careered for cover.

As he ran, he decided to tell his wife everything. UNIT, Yeti, bug alerts, everything. Then he could plead insanity to whatever grounds for divorce she filed against him.

He reached the shelter of the convoy and ducked behind a jeep. The Yeti were still advancing. In the distance, the helicopter, apparently back under control, was turning over the west campus.

'What's happened to that rocket launcher?' he bellowed.

There were shouts from the next jeep, where the ATR was mounted. Then a cry of pain.

One operative fell backwards from the jeep, knocked off his balance by a blow from the launcher barrel, which was swinging wilfully on its mounting.

'It's loaded! Get down!' yelled the other squaddie as he wrestled with the weapon. The machine swung again and batted him away like a tennis ball.

For a moment, Crichton was looking into the muzzle – a judgemental finger singling out the blame and about to carry out execution. Then it swung away and trained itself on the distant helicopter.

Brigadier Crichton threw himself up onto the back of the jeep. He stabbed repeatedly at the ATR's manual abort button.

The LCD announced that the computer sights had mapped out their target. FIRE SEQUENCE INITIATED.

Crichton slammed a fist down on the control board. No response. He saw the barrel adjust slightly. The launcher fired itself. The recoil slammed him off his feet.

A stem of smoke cut the sky and flowered in gold and vermilion on the belly of the helicopter fuselage.

The Hind tilted and lost height rapidly, vanishing behind the far side of the university.

Before they heard the boom, the Yeti were attacking the convoy.

The explosion thundered back and forth between the buildings. From the square, Lethbridge-Stewart watched a tower of oily smoke rise from behind the refectory block. The helicopter had come down near the canal. The alarm of the battle was fading.

Travers's head turned to watch the prisoner. Travers, but not Travers. Every movement of the old man's puppet body was awkward, overblown. Invisible hands were angling and adjusting the head and limbs. The face contorted in a grimace of triumph.

'Tell me, Brigadier,' it confided jovially, 'which part of my Great Plan do you think most strategically successful?'

'None of it,' said Lethbridge-Stewart.

'What?'

'For a so-called Intelligence, it's pretty damn stupid. You're still trapped.'

Travers's hand extended. Travers's head studied it. 'No!' The whole frame shuddered. The stick stomped angrily against the ground.

'That's not a body,' scoffed the Brigadier. 'You've trapped yourself in a web of cable and silicon. All of it stolen. And you can't venture beyond it.'

Travers's shape drew itself up to its full height – scarcely enough to contain the energy focused through it. The brittle bones cracked in protest. The crown of the head bulged. A tear opened up on the left side of the temple. It ran down the cheek, stopping at the base of the ear. Green light seeped out. The old body bag was coming apart at the seams.

'I slammed the door on the darkness. I shall perpetuate myself in every machine and being in *my* world.'

'Balderdash!' The Brigadier surveyed the audience of Chillys. Rows of torpid young faces, all infuriatingly impassive to the fate of their world.

A movement caught his eye. A face was staring down from a sharp concrete angle on one of the walkways. He recognized Sarah immediately. She nodded slightly.

He flung his arm wide and played to the gallery. 'Your real power goes no further than the mainframe on this campus, Great One.' He pushed the performance up a couple of notches. 'All anyone has to do is pull the plug!'

He glimpsed Sarah mouthing 'Right' to herself, before she vanished.

And for heaven's sake hurry, woman, he thought. Even an ego the size of the Intelligence must have a limit on how long it's prepared to gloat.

The steely eyes in Travers's head were watching him closely. 'Protect the generators,' ordered the voice.

Several Chillys rose from their places and headed out of the arena.

Kate crouched back into a crevice as she heard footsteps approach. A figure rounded the corner and jumped to see her.

'For a minute I thought you'd gone,' gasped Sarah.

'Not yet.' The truth was that Kate was too confused to move. She'd walked into a war zone and had already compiled a list of questions to which she needed answers.

'Stay out of sight until I'm back,' said Sarah.

'But . . .'

But Sarah had already gone.

Kate felt nauseous. She didn't want to be involved and she didn't want to be left out. She wanted Gordy now. Her hands had clamped into fists clammy with the frustration of inactivity.

Her fingers were still stinging. She had been possessed

by something – something that she thought was in her head. But that thing had also been in her home. She had seen it for the monster it was.

She always took care of herself. No one gave her orders.

But she had lost control. She *never* lost control.

The gun was heavy inside her jacket. She stared up at the play of light on the inside of the sky canopy. The world was being closed in. The air had an acrid, burnt taste. Strands of web were catching in her hair. It was no good. She had to do something. Her dad was around her somewhere.

She slid from her hiding-place and started to dodge across the concrete, out along the walkway overlooking the university's central square.

She reached the stairs and glanced down. She was face to face with several Chillys on the way up.

32

Access Denied

The generator plant was built under the maintenance road. The air inside hummed.

Victoria clattered down three flights of metal steps to reach the control centre. She counted three security cameras on the way. Each of them had swivelled in its housing to follow her progress.

The cavernous generator chamber was like a small cathedral in size. It was deserted. A row of huge grey cylindrical turbines crouched along one side of the chamber. Like everything else at New World, the turbines had been designed by the Chancellor, or what Victoria had believed was the Chancellor. She had tried to persuade him to invest in solar-powered generators. Now she had seen the canopy blotting out the sky, she knew why he had resisted so vehemently.

She had one chance. She was certain that her own password into the computer system would be deleted by now, but she still knew the Chancellor's personal access codes. She had secretly made a mental note of them long ago – an act of kindness in case the old man, who never seemed to write anything down, ever forgot them. If the system still accepted the codes, she would override and shut down every function on the mainframe and see the bulldozers in on the following morning.

There was an access terminal set up beside an output guidance console at the far side of the chamber. She set to work at the keyboard, concentrating, using the disciplines she had learned from *him* to stay calm and think clearly.

The log-in code took a full minute to be accepted. Victoria proceeded through a maze of menus that led her eventually to select the Generator Output System.

As she waited she heard the clatter of feet on the metal stairs. The screen flickered and scrolled with checks for viruses and trojan variants.

It finally cleared and displayed its text:

ACCESS DENIED

She began to try other codes. Any codes.

ACCESS DENIED

ACCESS DENIED

'Access denied, Victoria . . . my dear.'

She spun round and saw Christopher Rice watching her from the centre of the chamber. His usual cold smile had an odd warmth to it. He was levelling a gun at her. Behind him, a Yeti loomed, rocking slowly on its hind claws.

'I have to stop it,' Victoria protested.

Christopher began to advance. 'Way, way out of time.' Plainly he was back to his normal self, turning on his oily charm at the most inappropriate moment. 'Let's see what the New World has to offer.'

Victoria knew that her ruin was the objective he had set himself. He didn't seem to have noticed that something else was now setting the agenda.

'The Intelligence doesn't care about you,' she insisted.

'I look after myself.'

The Yeti was growling softly behind him. Victoria caught a look in its eye that pierced her. She saw through the cold vice of alien hatred that gripped and drove the huge creature, glimpsed something that struggled deep inside. Another tormented will that strove just to comprehend its own existence. The Yeti seemed to have a soul.

Christopher was moving closer.

'Get away from her!'

A woman was running towards them. It was Sarah

Jane Smith, unarmed and apparently unconcerned by the danger to her herself.

Christopher stepped backwards with a grin, swinging the gun back and forth to cover both women. 'Well, the press never miss a trick, do they?'

Sarah looked beyond him with a gasp. 'Mr Pennington! Look out!'

Christopher turned, startled, momentarily fooled.

Sarah ran at him, twisting his gun hand. He struggled against her. The Yeti bellowed. In the midst of the mêlée, the fun fired.

Christopher yelped with pain and fell back clutching his arm. There was blood on it.

'Sorry,' exclaimed Sarah. She was toting his gun in her hand now.

Victoria saw the Yeti raise its claws and stalk towards Sarah. 'Behind you!'

'Bloody little Miss Gutterati!' choked Christopher from the floor.

Sarah was dodging away from the Yeti. 'Turn off the power!' she called.

Victoria was back at the keyboard. 'That's what I'm trying to do!'

The screen flared and came up white, staring like an eye.

The shape of Professor Edward Travers stood at the centre of the university square. It turned slowly, its stick raised. The Intelligence was apparently taking in the breadth of its achievements.

To the Brigadier, even the air seemed to have been charged and activated with an oppressive energy. The pyramid of silver spheres was starting to give off a pale aura. The halo seemed to flicker around Travers too. The rupture on the side of the old man's face was widening.

His eyes settled back on Lethbridge-Stewart and he grinned. 'I shall impose an organizing order on your chaotic world. One thought to burrow deep into the Earth's roots and reach high into its skies. The humans shall provide me with new machines and new bodies.'

There was no sound of fighting now. And no sign of Sarah either. Only the crackling of the canopy overhead. The Brigadier determined to play for as much time as he could muster. He longed desperately to see his grandson, if it was only for his one last moment.

Travers's head jerkily turned to look at the steps. Two Chillys were leading a figure down into the square. A young woman with long yellow hair.

'Dad,' she called out.

The Brigadier was suddenly wearier than he had ever known. All those years when he had struggled to keep his two lives apart were swept away. He had medals for bravery and distinguished service. He had been made a CBE shortly before he left UNIT.

As a family man he had no honours.

Perhaps the two worlds he kept so separate had been colliding all that time.

His daughter walked with a dignity that he was infinitely proud of. He was scarcely proud of himself at all.

'Dad,' said Kate again as she reached him. It was rare that they ever looked at each other so directly.

'As bad as your mother,' he said awkwardly, hardly managing to disguise the deep tenderness he rarely admitted.

There was a sickly gurgle of laughter beside them. Travers was watching in fascination. 'You have blood ties, gaoler.' He mouthed the words eagerly as if they were something excitingly forbidden. 'Very well. I need more Yeti workers. *She* can be the next.'

Captain Douglas Cavendish was suddenly animated. He moved towards the pyramid of silver spheres and lifted the topmost from the stack. It started to bleep.

'For all the torment that you gave me, gaoler,' hissed the Intelligence in Travers.

Cavendish set the globe on the ground. It moved immediately, homing in on Kate. The Brigadier dared not move for fear that the Chillys would restrain him too. The sphere stopped directly in front of Kate. It paused, rocking back and forth, preparing to leap.

The Brigadier threw himself across in front of his daughter as the sphere flipped into the air.

He caught it in both hands. He saw his face in it. It pummelled at his wrists, spinning and struggling in the cage of his fingers until it burned him.

The two Chillys holding Kate pushed her roughly aside and moved forward to assist the sphere. Kate stumbled and felt the weight in her coat pocket.

Her father lurched backwards under the globe's attack. He swung his clenched arms like a mace, forcing the Chillys back.

The machine's nerve-jangling bleep had become a shriek as it forced towards his chest.

The army officer stood impassively over him.

The wild-haired old man, eyes gaping, tottered forward, eager to see the tournament. Willing it on.

Kate was blocked out. The gun metal was cold in her hands.

The old man was a monster. He was causing this. He was the driving force. When she was little, he lived under the stairs. Now he lived under the bunk and kept Gordy awake at night. He wouldn't have her father too.

Two gunshots cracked out.

The old man staggered and fell. He turned to gasp in amazement at his assailant.

Rage froze Kate. The pistol levelled in her outstretched hands. Her face was tight, locking in the scream.

You are Transgression. I am Retribution.

'Kate!' called the Brigadier as he dropped to his knees.

The sphere was unrelenting.

She gulped air and woke out of the trance. Her fingers loosened and dropped the pistol in disgust.

The emotionless audience of Chillys round the arena were coldly scrutinizing her.

She saw her father fighting for his life. She was running to his aid.

The broken shape of Travers, wounded, bleeding, punctured by darts of light, lurched into her path.

Victoria shielded her eyes as she fell away from the staring screen.

Gunshots splintered the air of the generator chamber as Sarah Jane Smith fired the gun again and again. The Yeti was bleeding, but it never faltered – a shaggy hill driving Sarah into a corner.

The gun ran out of rounds. She flung it uselessly at the brute. The monster bellowed in triumph and raised its clawed hand to strike.

'Daniel!' called Victoria.

The claws faltered, dipped slightly, then rose again.

'Daniel! I know you're still clinging there.'

Again the monster faltered. It angled slowly towards Victoria, its clawed hand still raised.

She crossed the floor, walking straight up to the huge creature. 'Daniel. Remember your disciplines.'

The Yeti turned completely, towering over her. She faced up to its gaze. Its hand came down in a strange human gesture of contemplation, tapping at teeth it did not have in its colossal head.

From the floor close by came Christopher's burst of mocking laughter.

The Yeti started to growl.

'Daniel,' Victoria repeated quietly. 'What do you seek?'

The creature stirred uneasily, but its attention was held.

Victoria thought back to Tibet. An ancient lama had once asked her that question. Whatever else had happened since, the answer she had given had been undeniable.

'Daniel. Remember the disciplines you have learned. Remember your inner strength. We all have it. You among all of us are strong. Above all things, remember the Truth.'

She felt the stirrings of his mind trapped inside the thing he had become. It was all confusion. There was guilt and sorrow and terrible pain. More than anything, she recognized a will to survive, not to give in. There was a single thought that she heard repeatedly. It said, I want to fly away.

'Remember what we are taught, Daniel,' she said. 'Fight the evil. Remember the sword that cuts through the thorns of deceit. Be the Sword of Truth, Daniel. Cut yourself free. Remember.'

The Yeti stirred again. Its claws started to rise.

'Daniel!' scolded Victoria.

A face slid in from the side. 'You're dead, Danny boy!' sneered Christopher.

A rage erupted in the Yeti. It roared its fury. Victoria ducked clear as the monster went berserk, flailing and thrashing in the air. Fighting an invisible force. Fighting inside itself.

Christopher did not move fast enough. The Yeti snatched at him, catching him in a monstrous bear hug.

'No, Daniel!' pleaded Victoria. 'Not him! Destroy the generators!'

The Yeti tossed Christopher's broken corpse aside. Still enraged, it was casting wildly about for anything on which to vent its confusion.

'Here!' Victoria called, pointing to the control consoles.

The Yeti bore down on her instead.

'Daniel!' she shouted. 'The Truth!'

The creature reeled in despair.

Sarah suddenly charged out of nowhere, cannoning into the Yeti with all her might. Caught off balance, the huge creature toppled sideways onto the console.

There was an eruption of smoke and sparks. In the heart of it Victoria could see the Yeti striking repeatedly at the disintegrating machinery.

The whine of the generators began to pitch down.

No longer. He couldn't hold the shrieking sphere off any longer.

The Brigadier saw the cadaver that had once been

Professor Edward Travers lunge wildly at Kate. Smoke was seeping out of its clothes. The corpse swung at her with its stick, blocking her path to him.

'Access denied!' declaimed its tortured voice. 'Access denied!'

The pyramid on the stone plinth suddenly fell apart in an eruption of sparks. The globes scattered across the square around him like a break on a snooker table.

The beams from the roof pyramid flickered and died.

The UNIT Captain slumped to the ground like a discarded puppet. Two Yeti at the top of the steps swayed and tumbled forward, reeking of smoke.

The attacking sphere lost all of its will. Lethbridge-Stewart tossed it contemptuously aside and struggled to his feet.

The Travers body was casting about in the detritus of its perdition. 'I am not defeated!' it croaked.

The Brigadier marched towards it, ready to show it the door. 'Leave our world alone.'

'*My* world!' Travers's arm rose up to strike like a Yeti. The Brigadier caught it by the skinny wrist. It was hot as a fever – burning up.

Eye to smoking eye.

'You're not wanted here. Go back to Hell. Back where you came from!'

The Intelligence in Travers darted its eyes around the arena.

Everywhere the Chillys were standing, pulling off their headphones. The Children of the New World, Children of the Old Earth, eyes ablaze with the power it had unlocked in them.

The power turned back on the Intelligence. Systems failure. Malfunction at Server. Its computer body shut itself down.

Confined to Travers's broken shape, it pitched over onto the ground.

Faces of hatred. Chanting of the Earth mantra.

It writhed under their onslaught.

'Nowhere to go! Nowhere!' It had slammed the door on its escape route.

It sank back. The ghost of a wind blew strands of web against its body.

A figure stood on a balcony above.

Travers's head lifted towards her. 'Victoria,' it whispered.

She returned its cold glare, dismissing it from her life and her world.

The head slumped down on the ground. Its eyes watched a single ant making its way across the concrete. The Intelligence tried to put out its will, to take a new shape, but it had no strength. It was exhausted. It was time to let go.

The Brigadier opened his arms wide to embrace Kate. As she clung to him, they heard a thunderous roar from above.

The sky funnelled in on the body of Travers – an inverted pyramid of energy and web that boiled downwards, emptying into a smoking mummified cocoon where he lay.

Finally the energy blazed down into a single locus and collapsed into nothing.

'Dad,' whispered Kate, still holding on tightly.

There was a cloudless night sky overhead. The air seemed cleansed. Without the glare of city streetlamps, the stars were clear as an infinite number of crystals.

The Brigadier took a long breath of the rich night air as he hugged his daughter. 'It's all right. It's gone. This time it's gone for good.'

There was a clatter of footsteps on the square.

'Brigadier?' called Sarah in the dark. She embraced him like a long-lost uncle.

'Miss Smith,' he said, both embarrassed and delighted. 'I knew there was someone I could rely on. Have you met my daughter?'

Around the square, the dazed students of New World University were picking themselves up and staring at the spectacular sky.

Lights were moving on the walkway above the square. A group of blue-bereted soldiers carrying torches was descending to the concourse. At their head was an officer in combat fatigues.

'It's Brigadier Crichton,' Sarah murmured.

Lethbridge-Stewart nodded, waiting until his replacement reached ground level before letting go of Kate and going to meet him.

'Brigadier Lethbridge-Stewart. Thank God. Are you all right, sir?' Crichton saluted like a junior officer. He was plainly exhausted.

'I'm surviving, Crichton. Against all odds.'

Crichton nodded wearily at Sarah. 'There's still a lot of things to clear up. It's been a mess.'

Lethbridge-Stewart edged one of the dead silver spheres with his foot. 'How many?' he asked quietly.

'Too many.' Crichton looked at the smoking body of Cavendish, lying face down on the concrete. 'I'll need you for the enquiry.'

'Of course, old chap.' Lethbridge-Stewart glanced over to where Kate was talking to Sarah. 'Family,' he confided.

Crichton looked surprised. After a moment he said, 'I'll deal with this end. Do you need transport?'

Lethbridge-Stewart smiled. 'No, no. I think I have somewhere to stay.' Quite unnecessarily he added, 'Carry on, Crichton.'

He walked slowly back to his daughter.

There was a moment's silence.

'Well, just like old times, eh?' exclaimed Sarah. She punched the Brigadier affectionately. 'And I still don't know what's going on!'

A wave of euphoria swept over them all. What losses there had been could not overshadow the things that had been saved.

The Brigadier wanted to think about that later. He picked up his gun from the ground and pocketed it. But not in the same pocket as the photograph of his grandson.

He took Sarah on one arm and his daughter on the

other. 'Someone else can clear up tomorrow. Let's just go home.'

From the balcony above, Victoria watched them leave together.

She shivered. Lights swung to and fro on the dark campus below. Torches and headlights. There were several fires burning in little pockets of red glow.

It was all gone, all smashed. She had nowhere to go now. No one to talk to. Her emotions had run dry.

In the aftermath of occasions like this, the Doctor had always slipped away in the TARDIS, leaving more questions than answers. But what could she do? Would that take away the hurt?

'Victoria,' her father said disapprovingly, 'to take no responsibility for our actions is both malodorous and impious.'

Sometimes her father could be priggishly self-righteous.

She walked away from the balcony and across the dark terrace.

She heard the carp swishing their fins in the pool. They needed feeding. The garden needed tending.

Let someone else do it.

She could already make out the shapes of the ziggurat buildings. There was a pale light in the eastern sky.

A new dawn.

An old world renewed.

33

Old Worlds For New

The helicopter rose out of the brown water. It swung in the air, hoisted on chains. Water cascaded from the flooded fuselage. The Brigadier could hear the crane creaking.

In a feat of virtuoso flying, the pilot had managed to ditch the damaged machine in the Great Coker Canal. The only official injury had been to one corporal who had sustained what was claimed to be a broken arm.

'Well, I saw it,' Sarah told the Brigadier, 'and it looked more like bite marks to me.'

Lethbridge-Stewart had written enough press statements in his time to know not to trust them. He was delighted, however, to find that Sarah had lost none of her charming ebullience and could still worry at a problem like a ferret after a rabbit. To be honest, he was glad of her company today, even if she did twitter just as much as he remembered.

'And there was another body on board, you know. One of the frogmen told me. Not a victim of the crash, either. He said it was burned out from the inside. Sounds like what happened to Cavendish, doesn't it?'

'You must get very bored with D-notices,' the Brigadier said. 'You never got to report on any of your involvement in UNIT activities.'

She shrugged wistfully. 'I signed the Official Secrets Act. Anyway, you always paid well to keep me quiet.'

'Rather better, I recall, than we paid our Scientific Advisor. But don't tell him that.'

'Did he have a bank account?' she asked. 'I bet he never used it. He's owed me a tenner for about twenty years.'

Her mobile phone trilled. He heard her talking to

someone rather acerbically. She seemed to have trouble getting a word in edgeways. 'Yes, I'm fine . . . Yes, of course . . . K9, can I say something, please? Look, I'm sure you have . . . Yes, well done . . . But do we have to go through this every time . . .? K9, I'm warning you! K9 . . .! *Pets Win Prizes!*'

A pause.

'That's better. Actually, I do need some information . . .'

The Brigadier, bemused, watched a group of squaddies pounding across the far side of the campus. The pyramid on top of the main university building was broken like a dead volcano.

There was no sign of any Chillys. He reckoned that Social Services would have their work cut out dealing with the poor saps.

He thought for the first time in two days about the school. Someone would have to pay for the damage to the cloisters. He would have a word with Crichton.

He supposed the affair had ended positively, but only by the skin of their teeth, he felt. The sacrifice of Harrods and Danny would prey on his conscience for ever.

Sarah had put away her mobile and was watching him. 'Penny for them, Brigadier,' she said gently.

'I have an appointment. Let's walk,' he said and set off along the towpath.

She took his proffered arm. 'We've just been trying to trace your car for you.'

'Oh? Probably towed away, I shouldn't wonder.'

'Well, there's no record at the moment; apparently the police computer is still down. Maybe it's still where you left it.'

He frowned. 'Where *do* you get your information from, Miss Smith? This friend of yours? Is he some sort of hacker?'

'More of a retriever really,' she grinned. 'It's an old joke. It keeps him amused.'

Still perplexed, he looked out over the canal. Sunlight dazzled on the water.

'I retire from Brendon soon. I've been teaching there for twenty odd years – some of them very odd. Readying people for the world. I'm just not certain it's the world I know any more.'

'Of course it is, Brigadier. Last night, it felt as if we claimed it back.'

'Perhaps,' he said and walked quietly. There were things that they both knew and that could go unsaid.

In the distance, he saw a boat moored to the bank in an unlikely spot as if it had just washed up there.

He stopped for a moment. 'That Vice Chancellor woman.'

'Victoria Waterfield?'

'Still no trace her of her, I take it.'

'I've been meaning to ask you about her. Both she and you were involved in something called "The London Event".'

'Good Lord. You got that from your retriever friend again, I suppose.' He sighed. 'I knew I'd come across her somewhere before.'

'I don't think you need tell me how,' said Sarah. 'She dropped quite a few hints, unintentional or otherwise.'

'She must have been in her late teens when I met her.'

Sarah looked a little wistful. 'And she travelled with the Doctor?'

'So it would appear.'

She squeezed his arm. 'You know, I remember once going through the TARDIS wardrobe and I found this dress, long and white and old-fashioned, and he said it had belonged to Victoria. And I said, "Well, as long as Albert didn't wear it." '

'And you think it could have been her.'

'I don't know,' said Sarah. 'Nor does the retriever. She just vanished into thin air. They're still looking.'

He shook his head. It was the old story. '*Certain* people make a habit of that. It applies just as much to families.'

Sarah was almost giggling, although he found it hard to know why. 'You know, *Companions* used to be something only dowager aunts had.'

'Who knows, Sarah?'

She nodded along the path. 'And talking of families . . .'

He saw the approaching figures and braced himself. He adjusted his sleeves and straightened his cap. This was as nerve-wracking and splendid as any battle he had faced.

Kate was leading a young man aged about five towards them. The youngster seemed to be holding back too.

'Dad, this is Gordy,' said Kate with the broadest smile she had ever given him. 'Gordy, this is Grandad. Say hello.'

The Brigadier, unsure of the right way to address so important a person, crouched slowly down and said, 'Hello, Gordy. You're not shy, are you?'

Young Gordon James Lethbridge-Stewart angled his head timidly and whispered, 'I've got another friend too.' He was still clinging onto his mum.

'Have you?' smiled the Brigadier. 'What's his name?'

Gordy slipped his hand from his mother's. He looked along the canal bank and pointed. 'Danny. But only I can see him.'

In the dazzle of sunlight there might have been a figure – a young man in a heavy coat, shoulders slightly hunched. He might have given a wave.

It might just have been the sunlight.

'Oho. You'd better tell me all about him,' the Brigadier confided. He stood up slightly creakily and let his grandson lead him away along the towpath.

Just another happy story that'll never get into print, thought Sarah. She deliberately did not notice as Kate dabbed a finger at her eye. The Brigadier's daughter looked as if the world's burdens had been lifted from her shoulders.

'You've made his day,' said Sarah.

'Which him?' grinned Kate.

There was a pause as they watched the Brigadier's and Gordy's progress.

'Do you look after him alone?' Sarah asked.

'Yes.'

'Sorry. Being nosey's my job.'

'It's all right. Jonathan, Gordy's dad, wanted us to get married. I didn't. It's silly.'

'No,' said Sarah. 'Not if you're independent.'

'It wasn't that. I just didn't want Gordy to lose the family name.'

Sarah, who had never been able to fathom her own family out, heard herself saying, 'Of course. I understand.' The Lethbridge-Stewart clan were plainly a force to be reckoned with. She held Kate's arm gently. 'How about you? How are you feeling?'

Kate started to rub her fingers. 'I'm not sure. I'm a private person. If it was Danny, *really* Danny . . . well, I had to help him. It was only using the computer, that's all. But someone else in my head . . . I felt soiled, you know?'

Sarah nodded with a deep sigh.

Kate seemed to rally a little. She was looking along the canal bank at her father and her son. 'This is more important. I've wanted this so much for years.'

'I won't say a word. Don't worry.'

'Thanks, Sarah.'

'That's all right. Just another D-notice.' She could always tell her dog about it, just as she told him all her other secrets. As long as no one stole his database. She tried to think of more pressing matters. 'I'm ravenous! Fancy sending out for a pizza?'

Kate grinned. 'Or a curry? But I think I'd rather have a pint.'

Compromise time, thought Sarah. She took Kate's arm and they headed for the boat. 'Make it a cup of tea and you're on!'

34

Golden Afternoon Revisited

'Lewis Carroll. Extraordinary chap, old Dodgson. Had an answer for just about everything.'

Victoria smiled indulgently at the tall white-haired gentleman in the flamboyant cape. She was wearing sunglasses and a light summery dress of a decent length. Her hair was loose down to her shoulders. She decided that the gentleman was rather overdressed for the hot June weather.

The playing of a string quartet, by turns spiky and lyrical like a chain of unfettered thoughts, wafted in from the Oxford garden outside. The exhibition of Mr Do-do-dodgson's photographs, many of them newly discovered, was attracting good business. Not that business mattered – the costs had been covered by a hefty donation from an *anonymous benefactor.*

'And he was a brilliant mathematician,' the gentleman continued. 'Served rather good lemonade as well. And muffins.'

Victoria had been miles away. Years away. Floating above the trees of an old Oxford garden, where a rather petulant little girl was having her photograph taken. The little girl's father fussed round the photographer, generally holding things up.

Enough to try the patience of an oyster.

It was one hundred and fifty years ago and nearly teatime. The sunlight was slightly yellowed.

The past was always in sepia.

On the gallery wall opposite Victoria, amid the posed studies of children and Carroll's own drawings of dancing Gryphons and Mock Turtles, there was a photograph of a little girl on a stone seat under a tree. She was clutching a doll and looked like someone else. The photograph was labelled 'Sitter Unknown'.

'Don't cry, Victoria Waterfield,' said the gentleman in the cape.

She could not conceal a sudden look of fear. 'Harris,' she said. 'Victoria Harris.'

'Of course, m'dear. I won't give away your secret.' He had sat down beside her. His eyes twinkled with reassuring kindness.

She tried a half-hearted smile. 'Someone said just that to me last week as well. An eccentric man with an incredible scarf. He said he was a Doctor.'

He looked a little taken aback. 'Eccentric?' He peered round the gallery to see who else was there.

'I think he was teasing. He said he would appear but three times. He told me to see if I could spot him.'

'Did he indeed? And have you?'

She glanced round the gallery as well. 'I don't think I could miss him.'

'Well, I'm the Doctor too.' He grinned and shook her by the hand. 'How do you do? Confusing, isn't it?'

Victoria didn't find it in the least bit confusing. '*The* Doctor sent you, didn't he?'

Another look of bemusement. 'Well, yes. I suppose he did. In a manner of speaking.'

'He was always very kind. Is he well?'

'Infuriatingly so.'

'I do wish he was here. And dear Jamie too.'

'I thought . . . *He* thought someone should call by – just to see how you were settling in.'

It seemed to be about twenty years too late for that sort of visit. 'Tell him I'm fine,' she said quietly.

'Good,' said the gentleman and studied her for a moment before returning his attention to the exhibition.

She wondered how much the Doctor knew. Or how much he had told this gentleman, this doctor.

She had slipped away as quietly as possible after what was probably now referred to as the 'New World Event'. It had been too much to take in. The hurt of delusion was too deep. Instead, she returned to old haunts.

Mrs Cywynski's garden was filled with a mix of the blue poppies, gentians and figworts from the parcel that Charles Bryce had sent Victoria years ago.

Victoria had never seen him again, although she met his wife briefly at the opening of the Memorial Gallery. A cool, polite meeting. The 'Tibet Event' was never mentioned.

'The garden's just like the Himalayas, dear,' said Roxana. 'But murder to keep the cats off.'

There were fourteen cats at the moment. A baker's coven. She seemed to have completely forgotten the other lodger in her husband's room.

'The police came looking for you. But I told them you had gone abroad and I never heard from you.' The old lady was as redoubtable as ever. 'You could always come back. I'll clear the coven from upstairs.'

Victoria hugged her and declined courteously. She accepted a jar of rhubarb chutney – 'Ten years old, so just about ready, dear' – and left promising to stay in touch.

She had also found her mother's grave.

She dreamed it first. Three-tiered, overgrown by wheels of weeds, in a place she had passed a dozen times.

In the dream, Daniel Hinton was there, pushing aside the undergrowth to lay a small bunch of bluebells on top of the slab.

She visited Highgate and found the grave where she had seen it in the dream.

Sacred to the Memory
– of –
My Dear Wife
EDITH ROSE WATERFIELD
Mother of Victoria Maud
Who Fell Asleep On The
23rd day of November 1863
Aged 37 years

Kind, Gentle, Loving And Beloved

There was a space on the headstone for Victoria's father.

The music from the string quartet in the garden swelled into a passionate rhapsody.

'Leoš Janáček,' declared the white-haired Doctor. 'Extraordinary chap. Didn't even get into his stride as a composer until he was in his eighties. I said to him, Leoš, old chap . . .'

'I'm sorry,' interrupted Victoria. 'It's no use running away, is it?'

'I think you had a lot to run away from,' sympathized the Doctor.

'Yes. I gather I'm on Interpol's Most Wanted list.'

He raised a surprised eyebrow and took her hand gently in his. 'You can always come away with me, you know.'

She smiled and shook her head. 'Thank you, Doctor, but I have things to face up to here. I must make amends. That's why I've finally written to Brigadier Crichton at UNIT.'

'Crichton?' The Doctor looked at his watch. 'Good Lord, has Lethbridge-Stewart retired or something?'

She couldn't tell if he was teasing or not. 'Your offer's very kind, Doctor. Perhaps one day, when all this is sorted out. Besides which, I can travel on my own now. Anywhere I like.'

He studied her again for a long time. 'I'm sure UNIT will be entirely sympathetic over . . . erm . . .' He coughed non-commitally.

She nodded sadly. 'I hope so.'

'And you're sure you won't come with me?'

It was what the other Doctor had said to her as well. The Doctor with the long, long scarf.

'Thank you. Perhaps one day.'

He smiled an amazing smile for her. 'One moment.' He produced a notepad from his pocket and began to scribble. He tore out the sheet and folded it into an envelope.

'A short letter of reference,' he said and handed it to

her. 'Give it to Brigadier whateverhisnameis. It may help.'

She was amazed. 'Thank you, Doctor.'

'A pleasure, my dear. Well, goodbye.'

He turned and marched across the gallery.

'Doctor?' she called.

He stopped in the doorway.

'If you see the Doctor, please tell him I've found what he was looking for. It's safe now.'

'I remember,' he said without turning to look.

'And give him my love.'

He nodded and walked out into the sunny garden.

Available in the *Doctor Who – New Adventures* series:

TIMEWYRM: GENESYS by John Peel
TIMEWYRM: EXODUS by Terrance Dicks
TIMEWYRM: APOCALYPSE by Nigel Robinson
TIMEWYRM: REVELATION by Paul Cornell
CAT'S CRADLE: TIME'S CRUCIBLE by Marc Platt
CAT'S CRADLE: WARHEAD by Andrew Cartmel
CAT'S CRADLE: WITCH MARK by Andrew Hunt
NIGHTSHADE by Mark Gatiss
LOVE AND WAR by Paul Cornell
TRANSIT by Ben Aaronovitch
THE HIGHEST SCIENCE by Gareth Roberts
THE PIT by Neil Penswick
DECEIT by Peter Darvill-Evans
LUCIFER RISING by Jim Mortimore and Andy Lane
WHITE DARKNESS by David A. McIntee
SHADOWMIND by Christopher Bulis
BIRTHRIGHT by Nigel Robinson
ICEBERG by David Banks
BLOOD HEAT by Jim Mortimore
THE DIMENSION RIDERS by Daniel Blythe
THE LEFT-HANDED HUMMINGBIRD by Kate Orman
CONUNDRUM by Steve Lyons
NO FUTURE by Paul Cornell
TRAGEDY DAY by Gareth Roberts
LEGACY by Gary Russell
THEATRE OF WAR by Justin Richards
ALL-CONSUMING FIRE by Andy Lane
BLOOD HARVEST by Terrance Dicks
STRANGE ENGLAND by Simon Messingham
FIRST FRONTIER by David A. McIntee
ST ANTHONY'S FIRE by Mark Gatiss
FALLS THE SHADOW by Daniel O'Mahony
PARASITE by Jim Mortimore
WARLOCK by Andrew Cartmel
SET PIECE by Kate Orman
INFINITE REQUIEM by Daniel Blythe
SANCTUARY by David A. McIntee
HUMAN NATURE by Paul Cornell
ORIGINAL SIN by Andy Lane
SKY PIRATES! by Dave Stone
ZAMPER by Gareth Roberts
TOY SOLDIERS by Paul Leonard
HEAD GAMES by Steve Lyons
THE ALSO PEOPLE by Ben Aaronovitch
SHAKEDOWN by Terrance Dicks

The next Missing Adventure is *The Man in the Velvet Mask* by Daniel O'Mahony, featuring the first Doctor and Dodo.